SLOW BURN

**Leo Waterman Mysteries by G. M. Ford
from Avon Books**

WHO IN HELL IS WANDA FUCA?
CAST IN STONE
THE BUM'S RUSH

SLOW BURN

A Leo Waterman Mystery

G.M. FORD

AVON BOOKS NEW YORK

This is a work of fiction. Names, characters, places and incidents either are the product of the author's imagination or are used fictitiously. Any resemblance to actual events, locales, organizations, or persons, living or dead, is entirely coincidental and beyond the intent of either the author or the publisher.

AVON BOOKS
A division of
The Hearst Corporation
1350 Avenue of the Americas
New York, New York 10019

Copyright © 1998 by G. M. Ford
Interior design by Kellan Peck
Visit our website at http://www.AvonBooks.com
ISBN: 0-380-97556-4

Library of Congress Cataloging in Publication Data:
Ford, G. M. (Gerald M.)
    Slow burn : a Leo Waterman mystery / G. M. Ford.—1st ed.
        p.   cm.
    I. Title.
PS3556.06978S58   1998   97-28604
813'.54—dc21   CIP

First Avon Books Printing: March 1998

AVON TRADEMARK REG. U.S. PAT. OFF. AND IN OTHER COUNTRIES, MARCA REGISTRADA, HECHO EN U.S.A.

Printed in the U.S.A.

FIRST EDITION

QPM   10   9   8   7   6   5   4   3   2   1

To **Rex Stout** and his enduring creations: Nero Wolfe,
Archie Goodwin, Fritz Brenner, Theodore Horstmann,
Saul Panzer, Fred Durkin, Orrie Cather, Johnny Keems,
Bill Gore, Inspector Cramer, Purley Stebbins,
Lily Rowan, Marko Vukcic, Lon Cohen, Nathaniel Parker,
Doctor Edwin A. Vollmer, Lieutenant Rowcliff,
Arnold Zeck, Lewis Hewitt, Ben Dykes, Dol Bonner,
Ethelbert Hitchcock, Del Bascom, Sally Colt,
Ruth Brady, Sol Feder, Herb Aronson, Bill Pratt,
Harry Foster, Lieutenant Con Noonan, Avery Ballou
and Carla Lovchen.

I never meant to break his thumb. All I wanted was a ride in the elevator. The burnished brass doors were no more than ten feet away when I was gently nudged toward the right.

"Pardon me . . ." I began.

He was a big beefy kid with a flattop, smelling of scented soap and Aramis. He kept pushing, his blue blazer now locked on my elbow, his big chest bending my path steadily toward the right, toward the stairs, away from the elevators.

I planted my right foot and swung back, only to find myself nose to nose with another one. African-American, this time; otherwise, same blazer, same size, same grimace.

"What's the problem, fellas?"

"No problem," said Flattop. "You just come along with us."

I stood my ground. "What for?" I said with a smile.

He reached out and locked a big hand onto my upper arm, squeezing like a vise, sending a dull ache all the way to my fingertips. His hard little eyes searched my face for pain. "Listen, Mr. Private Dick . . ." he sneered. "You just . . ."

I took a slide step to the right, putting Flattop between me and his partner, jerked my arm free, grabbed his thumb with one hand, his wrist with the other, and commenced introductions. Something snapped like a Popsicle stick. His mouth formed a silent circle. When I let go, he reeled backward, stumbling hard into his buddy as he danced in circles, gasping for air and staring at his hand.

"Whoa, whoa," his partner chanted.

"You want some, too?"

He reached for the inside pocket of his blazer. I froze. He flipped open a black leather case. His picture over the name Lincoln Aimes.

"Hotel security," he said quickly.

Flattop was still turning in small circles, eyes screwed shut, cradling his damaged hand, whistling "The Battle Hymn of the Republic" through his nose.

I shrugged. "All you had to do was say so, fellas."

He rolled his eyes in the direction of his partner. "Lance wanted to," he said with a sigh. "You know, he—"

His explanation was interrupted by a familiar voice rising from behind me.

"And what's this?"

Marty Conlan had put in his twenty-five years with SPD and then gotten himself a steady job. He'd been the security chief for The Olympic Star Hotel for the better part of ten years now. Other than having an ass that was cinched up tighter than a frog's, he wasn't a half-bad guy. "These belong to you, Marty?"

He ignored me, glowering instead at the twirling Lance. "Did he attack you?"

I don't think Lance heard the question. He was otherwise occupied, making noises like a suckling pig and hopping about like a weevil.

Conlan turned his attention to Lincoln Aimes. "Well? Did he?"

Aimes thought it over. "Not exactly," he said.

"Did you identify yourselves?"

"Not exactly," Aimes repeated.

"I thought I told you two—"

This time, Aimes interrupted. "Lance wanted to . . ." he began.

Conlan waved him off, checking the lobby, whispering now. "Jesus Christ. Take him down to the staff room. Call him a doctor. I'll be down as soon as I can."

We stood in silence as the pair made their way around us, heading down the hall in the opposite direction from which they'd been trying to move me. "All they had to do was identify themselves," I said.

"Yeah, Leo. I know. You're famous for being the kind of guy who comes along quietly." He heaved a sigh. "Come on up to the office for a few minutes, will ya? We need to talk."

I checked my watch. Five minutes to ten. "I've got a meeting at ten."

"I know," he said, turning away. "That's why we need to talk."

I followed him up the carpeted stairs to the mezzanine and then around to the security office. Security consisted of two rooms. The first was filled with a U-shaped bank of TV monitors which nearly covered the room from floor to ceiling. Maybe a dozen in all. The cameras covering the entrances were left on all the time. The others, which monitored selective areas of the hotel, could be used on demand.

Another kid in a blue blazer stared at the screens as we entered the room. He had a wide mouth, large liquid eyes and absolutely no neck. His blue-and-red-striped tie seemed to be pulled tight, just beneath his ears. He looked like Stimpy. He started to open his mouth, but closed it with a click when he saw me.

Marty paused to speak. "Call Frank Cooney," he said. "Tell him we need him down here for the week."

"Frank's off this week, Mr. Conlan. He and the missus are gonna—"

Marty cut him off. "Tell him it's an emergency." He threw me a glance. "Tell him Lance had an accident and is going to be laid up for a while." Stimpy still hadn't moved. A mouth breather. I pictured him red with a blue nose and inwardly smiled.

"Call him," Conlan bellowed.

As the kid dove for the phone, Conlan pushed his hands deep into his pockets and kicked open the door at the back of the room. I followed him through, into his office.

Marty made his way around to the back side of the polished oak table that served as his desk and wearily plopped himself down into his black leather chair. "Have a seat," he said.

I stood in the center of the room and checked my watch. Two minutes to. "I have an appointment upstairs," I said. "Room sixteen hundred."

"If you say so."

The smile evaporated. "What is it with you, Leo? Always the hard guy. Always making a pain in the ass of yourself."

"Color me with a crabby crayon, Marty, but I don't like being strong-armed by amateurs. You know what I mean? It's not good for my image. So either get to the point, or I'll be on my way."

He quickly stood and pointed a manicured finger at me. "Listen, Leo, I don't have to let you in here at all. You know that, don't you? This is private property. I can have you removed."

"You'll need a lot better help."

A film fell over his eyes. "The corporation won't pay for it," he blurted. "By the time I get 'em house-trained, they're outta here. The suits just don't get it. You can make as much in a frigging Burger King as they pay these kids. All they do is bust my ass about the high turnover."

I gestured at the well-appointed office, with its plush carpet, gilded mirror, real wood paneling and awesome collection of framed photographs and certificates.

"Beats the hell out of a squad room," I offered.

"Some days," he said. "Other days . . ."

I seemed to have found a sore spot.

"They're bouncers with Brylcreem," he lamented.

I was tempted to point out that it was more likely mousse and that the Brylcreem reference seriously dated him, but this didn't seem like the best time. I settled for: "I guess that's how come you're making the big bucks, Marty," an utterance which earned me only a short porcine snort.

He rolled his eyes toward the ceiling and pointed at the wall behind me. I knew what it was, but I craned my neck anyway.

There, lovingly framed and mounted on the wall, was the infamous UPI photograph of the ten lousy seconds which, much to my chagrin, seemed destined to serve as my solitary contribution to local popular culture. Marty was rolling.

"And here I am, spilling my guts to the bozo whose actions constitute the single most embarrassing moment in the history of this chain of forty-nine hotels. How's that?" he demanded of the ceiling.

In the photo, I stood, up to my knees, in the fountain at the hotel's main entrance, my hair flopped down over my right eye and plastered to my head, my pants seriously sagging. That was bad enough. It was, however, the two nearly naked hookers to whom all eyes were inevitably drawn.

"They use that frigging picture at training seminars. It's been in all the industry journals. We're a laughingstock. You know that?"

I reckoned how I might have heard such a rumor.

The irony was that I hadn't even been in the hotel that evening. I'd been on my way to meet Rebecca for a couple of quick drinks and an even quicker appearance at a mayoral fund-raiser, when my progress across the driveway was blocked by a white stretch limo which jerked to a halt inches in front of my toes. I heaved a sigh and started the four-mile hike around the rear of the car.

At first I thought somebody had popped a flashbulb inside the limo, as the interior was suddenly filled with a bright blue-green light. The violent rocking of the car and the four-part choral screaming suggested otherwise, however.

Without thinking, I grabbed for the nearest door and pulled. The blonde came out first, wearing a pair of crotchless panties, a red feather boa and a pained expression. Both the boa and her hair were on fire. I used her own momentum to hustle her past me into the fountain pool, where she landed facedown with an audible hiss.

The little Chinese woman was another matter. Screaming in agony, she burst out through the limo door like a cannonball, butting me hard in the solar plexus, leaving me hiccuping for breath as she flailed wildly at herself and began tottering down the drive.

She was wearing a pale lavender corset-type thing that left her small breasts bare, a tiny matching garter belt and white shoes and stockings. All of which were on fire as she hotfooted it down the drive, her blind terror pushing her in exactly the wrong direction.

I sucked in one long breath and ran her down, lifting her from the ground with one hand and tearing at her burning clothes with the other. In the time it took to turn back and take the two steps into the pool, her flames claimed my eyebrows, and the heat of the small metal corset hooks blistered my fingers. Ten measly seconds.

A nameless UPI photographer, sent down to cover the fund-raiser, had caught the action at just the moment when I lifted the two women from the pool, one arm around each, all of us grinning for all we were worth. One big happy family.

Turned out they'd been freebasing cocaine and balling a pimp who called himself Eightball when the red velour interior of the limo, having finally reached its chemical saturation point, spontaneously burst into flame. Despite his best efforts, the driver, one Norris Payne of Tacoma, had been unable to extricate himself from his seat belt. In his thrashing about, Norris had inhaled a couple of lungfuls of the brightly colored flame and died under heavy sedation a couple of days later up at Harborview.

Eightball had eventually managed to roll himself out the far side and, with the help of several bystanders and a handy fire extinguisher, had successfully saved ninety-nine percent of his considerable epidermis. As irony would have it, however, the remaining one percent consisted of none other than his wanger, which, in a travesty of bad timing, had been experiencing liftoff at the very moment of ignition and thus took heavy lateral damage. He still calls himself Eightball. Behind his back though, they call him Brother Beef Jerky.

Marty Conlan peered over my shoulder at the photo. "Maybe if you hadn't all just seemed to be having such a hell of a good time," he mused.

"People who find themselves suddenly on fire tend to be somewhat elated when the fire goes out," I countered.

"Or if *you* hadn't been the one holding the dildo."

"I don't know where it came from, either, man. It was just floating there in the water. I thought it was an arm or something. I just instinctively picked it up. It must have been part of the ensemble."

Resigned, he flopped back into his chair. After a moment he asked, "You know who's in sixteen hundred? That's the Edwardian Suite, you know."

I decided to give him a break. "As a matter of fact, I don't, Marty." I told him how the message on my machine had merely requested my presence at ten A.M. on Sunday morning. It had assured me of a day's pay, no matter what. Said I'd have to check in at the desk, because there was no elevator button for the private floors. A special security key was required.

"Sir Geoffrey Miles," he said.

"A sir, you say? You mean like nobility?"

"I do."

"Where do I know that name from?" I asked.

"Food. He's famous in food."

Yeah, that was right, food. Sir Geoffrey Miles. The world's foremost authority on food. The Guru of Gourmands. The Bagwan of Bouillabaisse. The Ayatollah of Gorgonzola. Dude.

"In town for the big food convention?" I asked.

"Nice to see you still read the papers."

"An informed citizenry is the backbone of a free society," I said.

His nostrils suddenly flared in a manner usually reserved for sniffing long-forgotten Tupperware containers.

"They're all here," he said. "At least all the muckety-mucks. We palmed a few lesser luminaries off on the Sorrento, and the hired help is camped out down at the Sheraton, but everybody who's anybody is here."

According to the *Times*, for the next five days the best and brightest of the world food community would be holding their annual confab in beautiful downtown Seattle. The article had gone on to note that it was only following prolonged political wrangling at the highest levels that Le Cuisine Internationale had ever so reluctantly consented to the Seattle venue. Never before had the event been held outside Europe. A number of aquiline noses were seriously bent.

Marty wasn't through. "I figured, you know, these were classy people. Robin Leach. *Lifestyles of the Rich and Famous* and all that, and, you know, it's a holiday weekend, so I figured we could get by with a skeleton crew . . ." He shook his head sadly.

"No, huh?" I prodded.

"Biggest bunch of assholes I've ever encountered," he said. "Bar none. No lo contendo," he enunciated carefully.

"How come?"

"Everybody hates everybody else. These people got grudges going back thirty years. I don't watch my ass, I'm gonna have an ethnic cleansing right here on the premises. The service staff is pulling its hair out. These people complain about everything. Nothing is good enough for any of them. They fax room service ten-page instructions on how they want their lunch prepared and then send the sucker back, anyway. I've got royalty on sixteen. I've got armed camps hunkered down on fourteen. I've got—"

I interrupted his litany. "Wadda you want from me, Marty?"

He was ready. "You know, your old man and I—"

"Stop the bus," I said quickly. "Don't take me there. Just tell me what you want. I've gotta go."

My father had parlayed an early career as a labor organizer into eleven terms on the Seattle City Council. Four times he narrowly missed being elected mayor. The good people of Seattle had instinctively known that Wild Bill Waterman was not the kind of guy to be left running the store. It was bad enough that nearly every city department was headed by somebody named Waterman. As several opponents had suggested, both Wild Bill's sense of humor and his inclination for nepotism were simply too advanced for any office with wide discretionary powers. From what I hear, he knew everyone, and everyone knew him.

Everyone but me. I was left with an uncomfortable composite of myth and remembrance upon which, at times like this, nearly anyone who had so much as passed him on the street could be expected to attempt to trade.

Marty Conlan nodded his head at me and laced his fingers together. "Yeah . . . I suppose you must get sick of that shit, huh?"

"I've gotta go," I said, turning. Ten-oh-seven.

"So, Leo . . . you'll keep me informed, huh? I've got enough troubles already without trust-fund private eyes roamin' about the hallowed halls, stirring up trouble."

"What's that supposed to mean?"

"Don't get me wrong, Leo. You've always been straight with me. Far as I know, you've always been straight with everybody. I'm not saying you're not a stand-up guy. I'm just saying that if I had my drothers, I'd rather be dealing with somebody who needed the money. That's something I can relate to. You understand what I'm saying?"

What he was saying was that he, like nearly everybody else in town, was aware that my old man had left the family fortune in trust. Whatever his other failings, the old boy was a hell of a judge of character. He'd always sensed in me something less than a firm commitment to the Puritan work ethic and had wisely arranged to protect me from my own worst urges. The result was a trust fund of truly draconian complexity. For over twenty years, the trust had repelled all attempts to break it. A succession of greedy relatives, annoyed creditors and one remarkably resolute ex-wife had squandered bales of cash, only to be left on the outside looking in.

"What the fuck does that have to do with anything?"

"Hey, hey," Marty said. "Don't get upset. I didn't mean anything. It's just that you tend to act unilaterally."

"Unilaterally? I act unilaterally?"

"You're just not a good team player, Leo."

"Exactly what team would that be, Marty?"

Conlon ignored the question. "Just keep me informed. Okay, Leo? No surprises. I've got all I can handle. Okay?"

"I'll do the best I can," I lied.

He stood, placing his hands flat on the desk in front of him.

"I best get downstairs and see about Lance."

2

He was a mound. A kimono-clad Kilimanjaro rising rotundly from the surrounding plains of burgundy silk. Across his middle, a silver serving tray lent a flat working surface to what otherwise was all slippery slope.

He worked his massive jaws slowly, his eyes closed, his brow knit as he chewed and finally swallowed the last morsel of sausage from the silver plate before him. With a sigh, he opened his eyes, looking around the room as if returning from a dream state. Satisfied as to his surroundings, he made a flicking motion with his fingers, seemingly shooing imaginary flies from the piled plates.

From the far side of the bed, his manservant stepped forward and removed this morning's repast, lifting it carefully over the mountainous middle and setting it on the rolling cart along the far wall.

Finished, he turned back to his employer. "Well, sir?"

Sir Geoffrey Miles pursed his small lips and wagged his head.

"A reasonable effort at saucisse minuit, I suppose. Ambitious and agreeable, but lacking . . ." He wiggled his fingers again as he searched for a word. Unable to locate the proper reproach, he suddenly turned his attention to me instead.

"Of course, I apologize for the delay, Mr. Waterman," he began. "I had planned on your joining me for breakfast."

Propped up in the bed by a platoon of pillows, he now folded his well-manicured hands over his stomach and ran his clear blue eyes over the length of me.

"My fault," I offered. "I was late."

He wiggled his three lower chins in agreement.

"I take great pride in the regularity of my indulgences. Breakfast at ten, lunch at two, dinner precisely at eight. Precision lends a certain substance to that which might otherwise be mundane."

When I didn't disagree, he went on. "The playwright Luigi Pirandello once noted that while a man with consistent habits can be said to *have* character, a man with ever-shifting habits can merely be said to *be* a character. Do you agree, sir?"

I reckoned how I did and waited for him to get to the point. His stock rose with me when he got right to it.

"I have a delicate and demanding matter with which I believe you can be of service, Mr. Waterman."

"What matter is that?" I asked.

"The matter of various people staying in this hotel, whose very lives I believe to be in mortal danger."

"I don't do bodyguard work."

He pursed his rosebud lips. "Really? And, pray tell, why not?"

"Because when you take on a bodyguard job, you're saying you're willing to get hurt in the client's place. Which I'm not. I mean, I'll take on physical risk as an occupational hazard, that's part of the business, but not as an assignment."

"Indeed?"

"It's like saying the client's life and well-being are somehow more important than my own. Could be I'm provincial, but I just don't see it that way. The way I figure it, my life is every bit as valuable as anybody else's."

"What a wonderfully American notion."

"Besides that," I went on, "anybody who wants to kill anybody else bad enough can't be stopped."

"You will be pleased, then, to know that guarding a body is not what I had in mind for you."

I waited. Before he could open his mouth again, someone knocked twice on the hall door. The manservant twitched an eyebrow at Sir Geoffrey, whose attention remained fastened on me. "Rowcliffe," Miles intoned, "I believe that will be Mr. Alomar. If you would be so kind."

As Rowcliffe left the room, Sir Geoffrey said, "I had hoped to have our business concluded before his arrival but . . ."

I got the impression that I was again supposed to apologize for being late. I hate a repeater, so I shut up.

Alomar was a tall, distinguished gentleman of sixty or so, in a splendid cream-colored suit and a brown silk tie. Very smooth. His regal bearing and thick, layered hair reminded me of Ricardo Montalban. I had the urge to call, *al castrado,* "Hey, boss! De plane! De plane!" His sparkling presence also gave me the urge to check and see if my fingernails were clean. I resisted both urges.

If Alomar was in the least surprised that our host was receiving us from bed, he certainly didn't let on. Miles began introductions even before Alomar had eased across the room. "Señor Alomar," he began. "Please allow me to introduce Mr. Leo Waterman, a local private investigator of considerable renown."

No way around it, the guy did have a knack for introductions.

"Mr. Waterman . . . Señor Caesar Gustavus Alomar, president of Le Cuisine Internationale."

Alomar held out his hand; I took it. Rich Corinthian leather. He clapped his other mitt on top of mine and began stroking my hand like a pet ferret. I hate a two-handed shaker.

"My pleasure," I said.

"So gooood to make your acquaintance," he said, suddenly releasing his grip. He had an accent the ethnic derivation of which I couldn't begin to guess. Not Hispanic, something Central European maybe. His courtly manner and exaggerated charm seemed to suggest that meeting me was the highlight of his otherwise tawdry day. I had some serious doubts.

As Rowcliffe appeared in the doorway of the adjoining room, a padded wing chair held before him, Sir Geoffrey began to speak.

"Mr. Alomar, if you will permit me, I was just about to acquaint Mr. Waterman with the nature of our problem and to solicit his assistance."

"Perhaps I can be of some help," Alomar suggested.

Without so much as a glance over his shoulder, Alomar pinched the front seams of his trousers and sat precisely in the center of the chair, which at that moment had just been thrust into position. The movement seemed to confirm that here was a person for whom a chair would always be readily available.

Rowcliffe was heading back toward the other room.

"I'll stand," I said.

He stopped and gazed quizzically back at his employer. Sir Geoffrey wagged an eyebrow and focused once more on me. Rowcliffe closed the door behind him.

"As you wish, Mr. Waterman," Sir Geoffrey said. "As I was saying, this is not a bodyguard job per se. I must, of course, concur with your assessment that anyone who is prepared to ignore any and all consequences of his act is capable of killing anyone else at any time. That much is certainly manifest."

Alomar was checking to see that his cuff links weren't smudged.

"As I am sure you are aware, Le Cuisine Internationale is having its annual convention here in Seattle. But what you may not be aware of, however, Mr. Waterman, is the degree of wrangling required for this event to be held outside of Europe."

"The paper said this is the first time," I offered.

A small sigh escaped from Señor Alomar. "And, quite possibly, the last," he said quietly. Miles ignored him and continued.

"Certain elements within the food community staunchly resist the notion that anything of consequence can take place outside the confines of the continent. These are the type of myopic souls who, under the cloak of quality, actually stand in opposition to any and all but themselves. These people need only the slightest breach of etiquette to press their image of America as a wasteland of mediocrity and poor taste. They consider themselves to be here under duress."

"What kind of duress?" I asked.

"The threat of having their rating diminished."

"What rating?"

Miles and Alomar shared a "poor soul" moment on my behalf.

"You may be aware," said Sir Geoffrey, "that I sponsor a publication which—"

"*The Register,*" I interrupted.

They seemed relieved. "Ah, yes," Alomar said. "You have heard of *The Register.*"

As I understood it, *The Register* was the final, worldwide authority on food. The publication rated restaurants on a scale of one to five stars. One star indicated that livestock would be joining you for dinner. Five stars was a ticket to legend. A paltry one hundred five-star designations were assigned each year and the competition was intense. Fortunes and careers hinged upon the annual publication of *The Register Hundred.*

"You threatened to give them less stars if they boycotted?"

Sir Geoffrey's upper lip twitched. "Suppose we say I intimated that to be a possibility."

I opened my mouth to speak, but he beat me to it.

"These rogues would, after all, be voluntarily distancing themselves from the very heart of the industry which has nurtured them. That type of unprofessional estrangement would most certainly be noted by a publication such as *The Register*. I do not believe it could be cogently argued that matters such as this were not well within the ken of such a publication."

"Certainly not," I agreed.

"I'm sure you understand, Mr. Waterman, *The Register* is nearly two hundred years in its existence. I am merely its present steward. Its founder, the Marquis de la Maine, fought three duels in defense of his ratings; surely I can be expected to do my small part."

"How'd he do?"

"Who?"

"The Marquis."

Miles pursed his lips and tilted his head. "A regrettable two out of three. His last opponent . . ." He searched his memory banks. "A Romanian saucier whose name escapes me at the moment put a musket ball through the Marquis's right cheek. The poor sot survived but completely lost his sense of taste as a result of the scarring."

Alomar and Miles shared a moment of sensory lamentation.

"So some of these people were coerced into coming to Seattle."

"No, no, no," Alomar corrected quickly. "Coerced?" He wagged a stiff palm. "Certainly not! Persuaded, perhaps. "Induced," indeed, might also be more accurate. I would prefer to think that they had been enlightened as to the importance of maintaining a global-village type of perspective."

"Sort of like, it takes a village to raise a soufflé."

Alomar eyed me. "Perhaps," he reluctantly agreed.

Sir Geoffrey retrieved the thread. "So, Mr. Waterman, it is within this quite contentious atmosphere that we begin this year's conference. Señor Alomar and I believe we have put together an outstanding conference program. Superior to its predecessors in every way. I myself will be giving the keynote address on Friday evening and supervising the awards banquet," he crowed.

Alomar broke in. "Such an honor, Sir Geoffrey." He turned to me. "Sir Geoffrey has never consented to our repeated pleas. This is a groundbreaking moment. This is—"

He would have blubbered on, but Miles cut him short.

"We are out on the proverbial limb here, Mr. Waterman. The last thing we can afford is any sort of embarrassing spectacle to lend any credence whatsoever to our detractors. Unfortunately . . ." He let it hang.

At last we were at my area of expertise. Embarrassing Spectacles Are Us. "What is it I can do for you, Sir Geoffrey?" I prodded.

He took a full breath. "Here it is, then. You have here in this country two rival chains of steak houses. One is called Del Fuego's FeedLot."

"Sure," I said. I knew Del Fuego's. Less than a month ago, while visiting Portland, I'd wandered into one and put away a two-pound T-bone and a baked potato the size of an NFL football.

"The operation is run by a pitiable creature who calls himself Jack Del Fuego."

"I've seen him on television."

"With that hat and the . . . what do you call it?"

"A cattle prod."

He threw up his hands. "What else can possibly be said?"

I was fairly certain I was about to find out. He went on. "His archrival is a woman named Abigail Meyerson."

"Abby's Angus," I said. "They're all over the country."

"Forty-one locations," Alomar added.

"And Del Fuego?" Sir Geoffrey asked Alomar.

"He's down to six, if you count the new one."

"Down to?" I repeated.

Alomar explained. "Mr. Del Fuego has, over the past two years, experienced a series of catastrophic setbacks and losses. A number of his establishments have ceased operations and had their equipment auctioned off. Several have actually been taken over by Ms. Meyerson and her corporation."

"Really," I said. "I thought the FeedLot was a nation-wide thing."

"At one time it was," Alomar said.

"Mr. Del Fuego is in ruins. He blamed early losses on his staff and subsequently sacked the lot of them, since which time his business decisions have become increasingly more bizarre."

"And . . ." Alomar let the word hang. "Worst of all . . . Mr. Del Fuego finds himself in direct competition with The Meyerson Corporation."

"Why's that so bad?"

He drew a long finger across his throat. "Assassins," he hissed. "Other than your local Microsoft company, The Meyerson Corporation is perhaps the most avaricious company in the United States."

"These two . . ." Sir Geoffrey again searched for a word. ". . . individuals," he declared charitably, "have a long-standing enmity which goes far beyond the realm of commercial competition."

"Haven't they been suing one another over something?" I asked.

"Ad nauseum," Miles said, holding up a finger. "Which is precisely where you come into it, Mr. Waterman."

I waited as he gathered his thoughts. "Their initial bone of contention was something called The Golden Fork Club." He cocked his head at me.

"Never heard of it," I said.

He wobbled the raised finger from side to side. "But perhaps, just perhaps, you have, Mr. Waterman," he said. I tried to look open-minded.

"The Golden Fork Club has only one function," he continued, "which, purportedly, is to rate the quality of America's steak houses."

"Okay." I tried.

"A simple enough proposition, I suppose, considering the complete lack of artistry required to burn meat."

Miles and Alomar shared another Maalox moment.

"Absolutely aboriginal." Alomar sighed.

"This seemingly innocuous calling is, however, greatly exacerbated by the simple fact that the monthly Golden Fork Ratings appears in every airline magazine on every flight of every airline throughout the world, and, as such, can be statistically demonstrated to have raised the gross sales of its appointees by as much as forty-five percent in any given rating period."

"That much?"

"Indeed. To be counted among the Ten Best Steak Houses in America is to have one's short-term future virtually assured."

"You're right," I said. "I have seen that ad. The list is inside this ornate little black border, right? Looks like wrought iron."

"The same," said Alomar.

"Mr. Del Fuego's establishments have appeared, ranked in the top three, in every list every month since its inception in 1991," Sir Geoffrey said.

Alomar jumped back in. "Ms. Meyerson has never made the list."

"I take it she's miffed," I said.

Sir Geoffrey made a dismissive sound with his lips. "She's taken it all the way to your Supreme Court, is where she's taken it, from whence a decision is expected sometime late next year."

"Just because she hasn't made the list?"

"Because, apparently, Mr. Del Fuego *owns* the list," he said.

"How's that possible?"

"Independent investigation has shown The Golden Fork Club to be a one-man operation, run by a gentleman named Mason Reese. Not coincidentally, Ms. Meyerson alleges, the very same Mason Reese who, prior to the inception of The

Golden Fork Club, served as public relations manager for the FeedLot chain for nearly twenty-five years."

"How convenient."

"Ms. Meyerson contends that the list constitutes fraud, false advertising and an unfair commercial advantage."

"What does Del Fuego say?" I asked.

"Mr. Del Fuego at first denied any involvement whatsoever in the list. He acknowledged that Mr. Reese used to work for him and thanked Mr. Reese for including him on his list."

"You said, 'at first.' "

"Yes. Del Fuego later recanted, saying that he had used his relationship with Mr. Reese to further his ends and had indeed provided the seed money for the project. He then took credit for what he claimed as a stroke of marketing genius."

I started to speak, but Sir Geoffrey raised his voice. "Oh, no," he boomed. "That's by no means the end of it, Mr. Waterman. No. No. That would be far too tidy for our Mr. Del Fuego. He then flip-flopped again. Claiming that his assumption of responsibility for The Golden Fork Club had merely been a self-sacrificing attempt to alleviate some of the pressure from his old friend Mr. Reese."

"And Reese, what does Reese say?"

"Mr. Reese has, until now, remained completely mute on the subject."

"Until now?"

"Mr. Reese has scheduled a press conference for ten o'clock Monday morning, at which he promises, for the first time, to address the issue to conclusion."

"You said that was their first conflict. I take it there've been others?"

"A list far too voluminous for repetition," Miles replied. "Ms. Meyerson has recently accused Mr. Del Fuego of vandalizing her restaurant signs. Mr. Del Fuego, for his part, is presently suing Ms. Meyerson on charges of industrial espionage. He claims that Ms. Meyerson has spies inside his organization who relay his expansion plans directly to The Meyerson Corporation. This infiltration, according to Mr. Del Fuego, is the sole reason for his recent spate of bad fortune."

Alomar sensed my next question. "They're here."

"Who?"

"All of them. Del Fuego, Meyerson, Reese."

"Why?"

"Because," Sir Geoffrey snapped, "they intend to use this golden opportunity to air their linen in full view of the world food community. They intend to use the glare of our culinary spotlight to continue their war of invective. They both have arranged to be opening restaurants here in Seattle this weekend. The timing is by no means coincidental, I assure you. These people have no shame."

"You said this Reese guy is here, too?"

"On the eighth floor. And for precisely the same reason. He seeks to lend an air of credibility to himself and his pathetic publication by making his pronouncement in the shadow of our organization."

"Any idea what Reese is going to say at his news conference? "

"None."

"I know what I'd be doing," I said.

"What would that be?"

"I'd be cutting myself a deal with one of them, long before the news conference. With that much at stake, it's a good bet that either or both of them are willing to throw money at him."

"I had much the same thought myself," Miles said.

I made my words a statement. "And you want me to find out what they're up to."

"Quite unfortunately," said Alomar, "we know all too well what Mr. Del Fuego is up to."

Sir Geoffrey showed me his palm. "Please permit me one further digression, Mr. Waterman. I merely want to be certain you understand the depths of depravity to which these people have sunk."

Miles looked smug as he leaned to the left and plucked a photograph from the nightstand. After studying it, he again made that dismissive sound with his lips and stiff-armed the photo in my direction. I walked over to the side of the bed and took it from his fingers.

I looked it over. "You don't usually see that many cattle on a downtown city street," I said finally.

"Four hundred head," said Señor Alomar.

"I didn't think there were that many long-horned cattle left."

"Some fool in Alabama was raising them as pets."

Among the glass-sheathed high-rises, Jack Del Fuego, wearing a straw hat the size of a hot-dog-stand umbrella, marched along in front of the herd, grinning wildly at the crowd from above the curved forest of horns, high-stepping it, brandishing his trademark cattle prod like a majorette's baton.

"Atlanta. Five months ago," said Alomar.

"You see that tall double garage door which is visible at the extreme left edge of the photograph?" Miles asked.

"Yep."

"Engine company number three of the Atlanta Fire Department." I waited. "At precisely the point where the herd was midway past the firehouse, an incoming fire alarm automatically threw open those massive doors." I knew what was coming. "The attendant lights and sirens . . ." He massaged the bridge of his nose.

"Stampede?" I asked.

"Made Pamplona look like a petting zoo," said Señor Alomar.

"There were, of course, rumors."

"What rumors?"

Alomar looked pained. "Regarding Ms. Meyerson's son, Spaulding. Initially, the investigation turned up two citizens

who said they had observed Spaulding Meyerson pull the
fire alarm directly across the street from the engine house."

Miles took over. "They later retracted their stories,
however."

"And moved into better homes," Alomar finished.

"And now this," Miles lamented.

I did a Bud Abbott impression. "This what?"

Alomar started to speak, but Miles shook him off. "A couple of facts. Ms. Meyerson has a daughter Brie."

"Like the cheese?"

"All too much, I fear, but that is neither here nor there.
Ms. Meyerson also has considerable land holdings in rural
Virginia, where she raises the bulk of the nearly fat-free
Black Angus cattle which she so proudly trumpets in her
TV advertisements. She is, I understand, considered to be
one of the foremost experts in the husbandry of this new
strain of Angus cattle."

I kept reminding myself that I'd been guaranteed a full
day's pay.

Sir Geoffrey went on. "Young Miss Meyerson, whom I
believe to be about eighteen years of age, in what is called
a Four-H project, raised a grand-champion Angus bull of
both prodigious size and superior lineage. The animal's pet
name was Bunky."

"Bunky, you say," was the best I could manage.

"At the propitious moment," Miles continued, "Miss Meyerson sent the beast for Four-H auction, which I understand
is the custom in that organization. In this case it was purely
charity, of course. Miss Meyerson hardly needed the money.
She was merely seeking to benefit the organization and the
breed. She assumed, quite correctly, that, considering the
incredible size of the animal and the perfection of his lineage, Bunky's future would hold little more than a lifetime
at stud. The beast was irreplaceable."

"Why didn't she keep it, then?"

"A matter of genetics, I'm afraid. Her bull was too closely
inbred within Ms. Meyerson's bloodline. As such, he could

not be used for breeding and thus would have required alterations."

I've always hated that particular euphemism. The image somehow always seems just a tad cavalier to me. You can alter your plans. You can have alterations made on your trousers. But when it comes to gonads, as far as I'm concerned anyway, the only animal that ought to be subjected to a little snip here and there is a Chia Pet.

Miles continued. "Young Miss Meyerson opted for what most certainly seemed to be best for her beloved Bunky."

I did Bud Abbott again. "But?"

"Bunky was eventually purchased by a Mr. Hyram Henessey for the princely sum of three hundred sixty thousand American dollars. Mr. Henessey purported to be a cattle rancher from Juno, Texas; his stated intention was to further propagate Ms. Meyerson's low-fat strain for the betterment of mankind."

"Purported?"

"Mr. Henessey, it turned out, was actually a headwaiter in the employ of Mr. Del Fuego."

"Noooo . . ." I began.

"Yesss," Miles finished. "Which brings us to the unfortunate affair in Cleveland eight months ago."

Miles took a deep breath, while Alomar hid behind his hand. Sir Geoffrey continued. "Mr. Del Fuego's first attempt to gain retribution took place in Cleveland eight months ago. The Cleveland operation, long one of the company's most profitable outlets, had fallen upon hard times and was on the verge of receivership. In a mad attempt to save the operation, Mr. Del Fuego proposed to stage a free barbecue for the homeless. The city was, of course, only too willing to do its part."

"What politician could resist?" muttered Alomar.

"Bunky?" I asked tentatively.

"Indeed," Miles said. "Mr. Del Fuego hit upon what he considered to be a novel manner in which he could gain both publicity and vengeance at a single throw. He engaged a meat-cutting firm whose dubious claim to fame was the possession of a mobile slaughtering unit of such facility as to allow the beast to be led live into one end of the unit and to then appear as packaged goods—ready for the grill, as it were—a mere ten minutes later at the other end of the lorry."

"The miracles of modern science," I said. "What stopped him?"

"Ms. Meyerson," Alomar said quickly.

"Yes," said Sir Geoffrey. "In a particularly canny move, the Meyerson woman rallied the forces of animal rights to her banner. I am told they came from the width and breadth of the Midwestern section of your country to support her cause."

"Four thousand Four-H members alone," Alomar added.

"As I understand it, the truck driver refused to jeopardize either the truck or his own well-being by forcing his way through the crowd and summarily attempted to leave."

"Attempted?"

"Yes," said Sir Geoffrey. "In a most unfortunate move, Mr. Del Fuego then tore the driver from his seat and attempted to flatten the crowd himself."

"The police intervened," Alomar explained.

"Mr. Del Fuego's actions provoked a veritable riot among the demonstrators. Several businesses were set afire."

I was agape. "And he's going to try it again here in Seattle."

Alomar was hiding behind his hand again.

Sir Geoffrey took the lead.

"Mr. Del Fuego has since changed his tactics somewhat. He has now sworn to roast the beast whole at the opening of his Seattle operation, five days hence. At nine o'clock this Friday evening."

"Whole?"

"On a spit. In a pit," he said.

I stiffened my chin and stifled a grin. He went on.

"We have been led to believe that you enjoy a rather close relationship with city government."

"I'm related to a whole bunch of people who work for the city, if that's what you mean."

"We want you to use your contacts to ascertain whether or not Mr. Del Fuego has obtained the proper permits and such necessary for his planned debacle. Perhaps we can crimp his plans in that manner."

"That's easy enough," I said.

Alomar and Miles now shared another glance. "We have also been given to understand that you are able to muster a fair number of field operatives to assist you," Miles said.

"You seem to have done your homework."

"We think it best that all parties be kept under surveillance."

"You want them followed?"

"Yes, we do. We hope that by doing so we may garner some advance warning as to their plans."

"That's going to get real expensive. I'm going to need somewhere between ten and a dozen people to work it. At a hundred bucks a day, plus expenses, it adds up in a big hurry."

"Money is no object," offered Alomar.

I liked these guys better already. I decided to level with them.

"I should also tell you that following people around a city of this size is not an exact science. It's not as easy as it looks on TV. If any of these people want to make sure they're not being followed, it's not rocket science to lose a tail."

Alomar took the lead. "Perhaps we can facilitate your task somewhat," he said, reaching into his jacket. He came out with a short stack of laminated cards. I leaned over and took them in my hand. According to these documents, I, Leo P. Waterman, was the official security coordinator for Le Cuisine Internationale. Dude.

"Not a very good picture of me," I commented.

Alomar gave me a small bow. "We were forced to act in haste. But I believe they will suffice for our purposes."

"Which are?"

"We supposed that, in your capacity as security liaison, you would be likely to consult with Ms. Meyerson, Mr. Del Fuego and Mr. Reese regarding any special security needs they might have. In the process you would be likely to be privy to their schedules, et cetera, thus making the business of keeping them under surveillance considerably easier. I hope we were not mistaken."

"Oh, no," I said. "This will make it a whole lot easier."

"Not only that," said Sir Geoffrey, "but we are prepared to offer a substantial bounty for certain other services. Clearly, the debacle cannot take place without the beast. Ergo, it then stands to reason that the animal must be stored somewhere locally."

"When you say stored, do you mean stored dead or alive?"

"We have no idea. And, quite frankly, it matters little to us whether the beast is a-hoof or a-hook. What matters is that the animal be found and at least temporarily liberated."

"We are prepared to offer an additional five-thousand-dollar bonus for the rescue of the beast," said Alomar.

"A bovine bounty, eh?"

"Quite," Sir Geoffrey agreed.

Alomar fished in the other side of his jacket and came out with a gray envelope. I took it and peeked in. Hundreds. A bunch of them.

Sir Geoffrey Miles spoke. "We assumed that ten thousand American dollars would suffice to get the operation off the ground."

"It will," I said, trying to appear calm.

"Is there anything else we can do to facilitate your work?"

"Yes, sir," I said. "I can think of a bunch of things."

He folded his arms across his chest as I spoke. When I'd finished with my list, he uttered a single word. "Done," he said.

Sir Geoffrey was dialing the reception desk as Alomar saw me to the door, locking my elbow like an undertaker, stepping halfway out into the hall with me. "When you meet with Ms. Meyerson, Mr. Waterman . . ." he whispered in the doorway.

"Yeah?"

"If she shows you a videotape . . ." He checked the hall.

"Uh-huh?"

"Whatever you do . . . do not laugh."

3

As the young woman in the red blazer whispered into the phone and smiled at me, I leaned back against the reception desk and surveyed the palatial lobby. A dozen separate conversation areas were scattered over the enormous Chinese carpet covering the center of the room. Around the perimeter, a wide mezzanine split the distance between the floor and the ceiling, its elegant marble rail lending an almost classical air to the room.

"Mr. Waterman," she said to my back. I turned. "Sorry about the delay. It turns out you were correct," she cooed. "We have a lovely room for you on the ninth floor. Nine-ten."

The gold name tag read Marie. She was about thirty, short and about a size smaller than the jacket she was wearing. Her brown hair was cut severely high at the nape of her neck, giving her head the appearance of moving forward through space. Despite the deep green contact lenses, her eyes showed the strain of one who had always struggled to see. She slid a pair of electronic keys across the desk at me.

"Are those both room keys?"

She said they were.

"I'll need about three more, please."

She gave me that smile again. "Certainly, sir." From the drawer in front of her, she pulled out a half-dozen blank keys. Using an electronic keypad on the desk, she keyed in a code and ran three keys through the slot. Neat as can be, we make a new key.

As she slid the keys across to me, a door behind the counter opened and a woman stepped into the registration area. She wore a deep blue silk suit and matching shoes. About five-five or so and very solidly put together like a gymnast, she crossed the area behind the desk and made her way to Marie's side. "Mr. Waterman," she said.

The sound of the voice startled Marie. Her narrow eyes stretched wide at the sight of the woman. "Oh, Ms. Ricci," she blurted.

"Thank you, Marie," the woman said.

Marie, who'd instinctively begun looking around for something useful to do, quickly translated the silence, realized that she'd missed her cue and exited stage left in a flurry of paperwork.

The woman extended her hand. "I'm Gloria Ricci."

Her hand was smooth and dry. The kind you wanted to hang on to. Up close, she was about my age. Somewhere between forty and fifty, with the wide oval face of a farm girl hiding the observant eyes of a red-tailed hawk. "Pleased to meet you," I said.

"Marie has taken care of your needs, I trust?"

"Perfectly."

"Good. I wanted to assure you that the resources of this hotel are completely at your disposal. Should you require anything further, please don't hesitate to ask." She stuck two fingers into her side pocket and pulled out a business card and a small gold key. Ms. Gloria Ricci, General Manager, Olympic Star Hotel. "I've added my home number to the back," she said. "The key allows access to all floors. Regardless of the time of day, please don't hesitate—Ah, here he is," she finished.

Marty Conlan nearly tripped over his jaw when I turned to greet him. "Long time no see, Marty."

"Ah," Ricci said from behind me. "I somehow expected that you two would already be acquainted."

Since Marty seemed disinclined, I jumped right in. "Yeah," I said, "Marty and I go way back. You don't know how lucky you are to have a guy like Marty on board." What the hell. One good turn.

As Ricci directed her attention his way, Marty held his face together pretty well. Other than the arrhythmic tic in the corner of his right eye, he seemed almost placid. "Mr. Waterman will be acting as security liaison for the convention. I trust you will provide him with whatever resources he might require."

"Depends on what he requires," Conlan said.

She fixed him with her gaze. "Should Mr. Waterman require any assistance whatsoever, I'm sure that you will be more than happy to assist in any way possible. Isn't that correct, Mr. Conlan?" Her voice held an edge of authority. Apparently Marty thought so, too.

"Anything at all," he said with a smile so tight it threatened his dentures. "Anything at all."

"Funny, Ms. Ricci," I piped up, "but Marty and I were just discussing being a team player. Weren't we, Marty?"

The veins on Marty's head looked like a relief map of Tibet. He nodded slightly and checked his watch.

Gloria Ricci said, "I'll leave you gentlemen to work out the details." She turned on her heel and exited in a rustle, as Sir Geoffrey would say, from whence she came. Marty's expression changed to that of a kid who's been sent to his room without dessert.

I started across the lobby toward the escalator. Marty yapped at my heels like a terrier. "You broke his goddamn thumb, you know that, don't you, you big dumb jackass. You broke that kid's thumb."

"He needs to learn some manners."

"What am I gonna tell the brass? Huh? What?"

"Tell them he hurt it pulling it out of his ass."

"The son of a bitch will be claiming he's permanently disabled. You know that, don't ya?"

"From a broken thumb?"

"These kids are like that, man. They get a blood blister, they're looking for workman's comp."

Halfway across the wide expanse of lobby, I stopped and pointed back toward the elevators. "Are those the only way down?"

"Except for the stairs and freight elevator in the back."

"Is the freight elevator keyed?"

"Yeah. Why?"

I again started toward the escalator.

"I'm going to need to put a couple of guys here in the lobby."

"Not those friggin' bums, you're not. You may think you've got big-time juice with the suits, but you start hanging that crew of yours around here in the lobby, I don't care if it's old Sir Larry Olivier watching out for you, you're all gonna find your asses back out in the street where they belong."

He had a point. The Olympic was the sort of place which considered matching shoes and a full set of teeth to be pretty much de rigueur. My crew was great for the streets. Out there, they were virtually invisible. We've trained our eyes not to see the poor and the homeless. We tell ourselves that these people had their chance. That the rewards of the free society were once theirs for the taking, and they blew it. That they were either unwilling or unable to carpe the diem when opportunity knocked . . . so screw 'em.

"I'll clean a couple of them up," I promised.

"This I gotta see."

Me, too, I thought. I tried something else.

"Why in God's name did you put Meyerson and Del Fuego on the same floor? Wasn't that just asking for trouble?"

"They insisted, goddammit. So worried that one was

going to have something the other one didn't have. One more room. One more chair. Christ. The fourteenth floor has the only two identical suites."

I changed the subject. "Have you got cameras on all the floors?"

"That's proprietarial information."

"Well, in the event that you do, turn on fourteen and eight."

"They're only on the private floors. Fourteen through eighteen."

"Why only the private floors?"

"Same reason as everything else—the suits won't pay for it."

"Well, fire up fourteen, then."

"What I'd like to be able to fire up is nine, so I could keep an eye on you. I hear you're going to be our guest."

As we walked, I reached over and tapped him on the chest. "That's right, and remember, Marty, a guest is a jewel that rests upon a pillow of hospitality."

"My ass."

"There's an idea I hadn't thought of."

"What?"

"You could tell the brass he broke his thumb pulling it out of *your* ass."

"Har, har," he hacked at my back.

I stepped onto the escalator and started down. Marty stood at the top and watched my descent. He looked sad, like a hound dog caught with its nose in the kitchen garbage. From my lowered perspective, the bags under his eyes seemed to nearly reach his ears. I waved bye-bye.

Five minutes and fifteen dollars later, the Fiat magically reappeared in the circular drive. The front of the little car scraped slightly as I bounced out onto University Avenue and gunned it up the hill toward the freeway.

I don't care what the poet said; around here, September is the cruelest month. Just about the time the kiddies are headed back to school, when the resorts are closing up for the season and those of us still propelled by the agrarian calendar feel a need to buckle down in preparation for a long, rainy winter, the weather has this annoying propensity to get nice and to stay that way.

The digital readout on the Safeco Building alternated between eleven-fifteen A.M. and seventy-nine degrees as I pushed the Fiat north toward home, getting off at Forty-fifth, winding my way down under the bridge, heading west toward Fremont.

Fremont is a neighborhood for people who don't have to commute. One of those bohemian pockets of urbanity to which there is, quite literally, no quick or easy route. On a bad day, covering the few miles from the freeway to Fremont can take thirty minutes. Today was a bad day. Still, I was going to miss the place.

You want Guatemalan Expressionist art, we got it. You want a giant concrete sculpture of a troll eating a VW, we got that, too. What about an intact Cold War rocket, repainted and mounted atop a building?

Say no more. And that's not the best of it. Lenin is the best of it. Directly across North Thirty-fifth Street stands a sixteen-foot, seven-ton, bronze statue of Vladimir Lenin, striding out with his greatcoat open to the breeze and his thick boots threatening to shatter the pavement beneath his feet.

A local entrepreneur named Lew Carpenter found the statue in the newly liberated Poprad, Slovakia, where it lay as a toppled symbol of Communism's fall. The rest is, as they say, history. Lenin now stands with his back to The Fremont Hemp Company, striding directly toward The Rocket. Two defanged symbols of the Cold War, forever reaching out, but like Keats's lovers, never quite making contact. Art, once again, outlives politics. Dude.

It was eleven-forty when I kicked the paper through the open front door. I stood in the doorway, watching it slide across the hardwood floor and bump into the nearest cardboard box. One of about forty such boxes into which my gross lifetime product was presently stored.

Moving is an experience that becomes increasingly difficult with age. When I was younger, moving wasn't a problem, because I didn't actually live anywhere, I crashed wherever it was convenient. Friends used to keep entire pages of their address books blank, knowing that the constant changes in my address and phone number would require all that space and more.

Today, the sight of my bare walls gave me the willies. I had to force myself over the threshold, over toward the phone and the Rolodex, which rested on the big wardrobe box. I checked the number and dialed my aunt Karen in Building Permits.

I figured my stock was high with Karen. Just a couple of months ago, I'd managed to show up at the wedding of her youngest daughter, Mary Alice, in a suit, with a present. What a guy.

She answered the phone before it rang. "Building Permits."

"Karen, it's Leo."

"Hey, good-lookin'."

"I need a small favor."

"Of course you do."

Before I could tell her what I wanted, she jumped in. "You know Jean's boy Harvey is getting married again."

I could see it coming. "What's with these people? They get married like other people change their socks."

She ignored me. "Two weeks from next Sunday. That's the thirtieth."

Five minutes later, we'd exchanged my ass at the wedding for a complete rundown of Jack Del Fuego's permit situation. I thought I had it made. No way. "By the way, Leo. About the gift."

"Yeah?"

"No more bun warmers."

"I never know what to buy," I protested.

"Get Rebecca to help you. Now that you two . . ."

"We two what?"

"You know."

"Who told you?" I asked.

"Everybody knows."

"Everybody who?"

"Maureen told me."

If my cousin Maureen knew Rebecca and I were moving in together, then it was a good bet the news had spread as far as mainland China. I gritted my teeth, renewed my promise to show up at the wedding and broke the connection.

The grating of a key in the lock pulled my head around. Hector and I stood open-mouthed, staring at each other.

"Oh . . . Leo . . . I taught jew was . . ." he began.

"I was just . . ."

Hector Gutierrez was both the superintendent of my apartment building and a much valued friend. He managed a small smile. We stood among the dust and boxes, silenced by the mutual recognition of what would surely come next. I'm not good with silence. It makes me nervous, like there's something going on all around me and yet I'm not a part of it. Silence is to be filled.

As I opened my mouth to speak, Hector lost his grip on the great wad of keys in his hand. With a rush, the cable snapped them up to the little spring-loaded gizmo on his belt, taking whatever it was I thought I had to say with them. The quiet was broken only by the muted electronic wheezing of my ancient clock-radio on the table.

After a certain age, the realities of lives diverging can no longer be softened by even the best intentions. Our memories are filled with the hundreds of people who have walked through our lives, touched us in some way and then seemingly disappeared from the face of the earth. Time erodes our willingness to promise once again to keep in touch, and, without willing it so, the Kleenex promises of youth give way to the carefully chosen holiday cards of adulthood.

Hector got his shit together first.

"Jew look like somebody shot your focking dog."

I looked around the place. It looked like a cautionary advertisement in favor of using professional movers.

"I've been here a long time," my voice said.

Hector strode over and stood directly in front of me. His thick mustache was beginning to gray. He'd missed a spot on the left side of his chin when he'd shaved this morning. Most of the remaining bristles were white. He poked me in the chest.

"Jew movin' into a palacio dat you don't got to pay for, wid a beautiful woooman who love you. What jew got to be sad about?"

It sounded good when he said it, but somehow it failed to warm the cold spot at my center.

"I've been alone a long time," I said.

"Oh yeah." He spread his arms and looked around. "Must be tough to gibe up all dis."

Hector was right. The end of my noble isolation was no great loss. What had once been a statement had quietly become a question. What had begun, after my divorce, as an exercise in self-reliance had eroded into little more than a holding action against the inevitable, a pathetic rear guard massacre of years, whose graves were marked by only the profusion of chips in the dishes and the build-up of paint on the familiar walls. He brought his hands down onto my shoulders and then we embraced. When holding one another became too embarrassing, we stepped apart and put ourselves back together.

"I guess maybe I'm not sure I deserve her," I said.

He grinned. "Dat's easy, Leo. Jew shoulda tol me. I can help jew wid dat. Jew ready?"

I nodded. He was still smiling.

"Okay den, here eet is. Eet's seemple. Jew right. Jew don't deserve her. No focking way. Not even close. Mees Duvall eees a great lady, Leo. I doan gotta tell jew dat." He tapped his temple. "Smart. A doktor." He looked at me sadly and shrugged. "Jew ... a private deek ..." Thinking about my career seemed to rob him of words. "She way too good for jew ees what she ees. Jew just count your blessings ees what jew do."

"Gee, I feel better now."

He clapped me on the back and headed for the door.

"Oh, doan worry, jew not de only one. Nobody really feel like dey deserve what dey got. Dey spend their whole focking lives waiting for somebody to come and take eet all back, like eet was all a beeg mistake."

He stopped at the door and turned back my way.

"Jew come round. We have a beer down at the Red Door."

"We'll keep in touch," I said.

"Jew bet."

After he closed the door, I stood for a moment, listening to my own breath, as if expecting my door to open again. It didn't.

I snatched the phone from the table and punched in Rebecca's number at the medical examiner's office. No go. She'd left for the day.

Both pager and cell phone set to voice mail. I left her the basics of where I was going to be and headed for the bedroom. With most of my clothes packed away, I was already living out of a suitcase and a shaving kit. All I had to do was zip them up.

4

Much like salmon, professional drunks follow predictable evolutionary and migratory patterns. Early on, they stay close to the familiar gravel of their home waters. They limit themselves to cozy fern bars near the office. Some place they can hit right after work for a bit of shop talk and some serious stress relief, among cohorts who can be trusted to impound their car keys, call their wives and stuff them into cabs. Nice places like that.

Later, when both wives and car keys are things of the past; when the last of their loved ones has finally had enough and even the occasional truth is met with stony silence; when the next step involves sharing an apartment with a telephone pole and imagining a steady drizzle to be an integral part of any fine dining experience, then . . . then they're ready for The Zoo.

I stood in the doorway and waited for my eyes to adjust to the near darkness. An ornately carved stand-up bar, complete with brass foot rail, ran the full length of the room and down around the corner, where the only four stools in the joint looked back at the door.

Stand-up bars keep a guy on his toes. It's no trick for

anybody to drink himself into a stupor with one cheek perched on a padded stool. Standing up was a whole other matter. A guy had to maintain some shred of dignity or risk falling among the cigar butts, the peanut shells and the slick bronchial emissions composting underfoot.

Bonnie, one of the owners, was behind the bar. I pointed at her and made a face. She pointed at her lower back and made her own face. Terry's back was out again. Bonnie was stuck tending bar. I gave her a two-fingered salute and moved down the left-hand wall, past the six brown leatherette booths, toward the familiar noise at the back of the room. Three beer glasses and three empty shot glasses rested on the far end of the bar. The tops of the stools were covered with an array of coats, sweaters, vests, ponchos and plastic bags. The Boys were playing snooker. As I stood at the corner of the bar and watched, it occurred to me that these old guys were, at this point in my life, my only tangible bequest from my father. Funny that they were the only ones who'd actually known him, and yet they were the only ones who never tried to trade on his name.

George Paris saw me first. Sometime back in the early seventies, George's banking career had fallen victim to both merger mania and his own unquenchable thirst for single malt scotch. His finely chiseled features and slicked-back white hair made him look like a ring announcer. If you didn't look into his filigreed eyes or down at his mismatched shoes, you could easily mistake George for a functioning member of the global village.

"The prodigal returns," he said.

I waved three fingers at Bonnie. "Wine for my friends."

The wine was, of course, purely metaphorical. I mean, they'd sure as hell drink wine if that's all there was. Hell, they'd drink cleaning products if that's all there was, but not if somebody else was buying. No, no. I checked my watch: eleven-fifteen. By now they were well into the shank of their drinking day.

"Leo," shouted Ralph Batista. He stumbled over my way,

the butt of his pool cue clattering across the boards, threw an arm around my shoulder and planted a wet kiss on my cheek. He smelled of diesel fuel and dry vomit. Ralph used to be a well-known port official. In his younger days, he mustered the longshoremen's vote for the old man. The extra folds of skin on his face, combined with a paucity of functioning brain cells, gave him the benign countenance of a cabbage. Inner peace by default.

"Hey, Harry, old boy. Look who's here," he shouted.

Harold Green had sold men's shoes at The Bon and been active in the Retailers Union. He used to be taller. He was one of those drunks who just keeps getting skinnier and skinnier, each lost ounce further emphasizing his baseball-sized Adam's apple and cab-door ears.

Harold was up on one foot, leaning over the table, sizing up a tricky three-rail shot. When he heard the unmistakable sound of boilermakers hitting the bar, he left the cue rolling on the table and hustled over.

"Howdy, kid," he said as he squeezed by me.

Other than an unquenchable thirst, these three had one other thing in common. Each had managed to hang in there long enough to have garnered a meager monthly stipend from his respective employer. Not a full pension, not enough to make it alone, but, with careful management, enough to collectively keep them in liquor and even, sometimes, out of the rain. Simplify. Simplify. That was their motto.

With the precision of a drill team, the twisted trio downed their shots, slapped the glasses back on the bar and chased it with the beer.

"Ah," said Ralph. "The pause that refreshes."

"Ambrosia," confirmed Harold.

George agreed. "Nectar of the gods," he said, wiping his mouth with his sleeve.

"Could you guys use a little work?" I asked.

"You got something for us?" Ralph asked.

"No, you idiot, he's taking a survey," snarled George.

"One hundred bucks a day. Each," I added.

"No shit," said Ralph.

"We're going to need a bunch more people, too."

"How many?" George asked.

"I figure nine more, plus you three."

"Well," George said, "there's Norman, for one."

"Where is Norman, anyway?"

"He's sleeping in."

Harold explained. "He got overserved last night at the Six-Eleven. Barkeep's got no sense at all. Oughta call the city on him."

"Okay," I said. "Norman for four. Big Frank, Judy, Mary and Earlene, Billy Bob Fung, and Flounder for ten. Who else? I need two more. What about Waldo?"

"In the can," George said. "Got some twenty days left."

"Red Lopez?"

"I can find Red," said Ralph.

"One more."

George started to open his mouth. I beat him to it.

"Not the Speaker and not Slalom, so don't even say it. When I tell you what we're gonna be doing, you'll understand why."

He took me at my word.

"What about Dickie or Don?" I asked.

"Donny's doing the long limbo," said Harold.

"Trollin' for topsoil trout," George added.

Ralph sensed my confusion. "He fell off the viaduct, Leo. Busted his neck. Dickie took it real hard. Ain't nobody seen him since."

We finally settled on Hot Shot Scott.

"What's the job?" George asked.

As I began to speak, George found a small spiral-bound notebook in the pocket of one of his coats and started to take notes. When I'd finished, he asked, "What about inside? What are we gonna do about that?"

"I was thinking I'd fix up Frank and Judy."

"Gonna take a lot of fixin'."

"You let me worry about that. That way we've got Harold, Ralph and Norman to run the crews and you to keep the whole thing working. "Any questions?"

"Who's gonna look for the cow?"

"It's a bull, and I am."

"When do we start?"

"Tomorrow morning. But I want to see everybody at four this afternoon."

"Where?"

"Third Avenue. In front of the Rainier Club."

George wrote it down and looked up.

I headed to the far end of the bar and had a few words with Bonnie. Bonnie wasn't real enthused, but she said okay.

5

He had the James Dean slouching-in-a-doorway thing down. He wore a tight pair of jeans, a belt with a rodeo buckle and a white cowboy shirt with pearl buttons and the sleeves cut off. If I had arms like that, I'd cut my shirtsleeves off, too. Hell, if I had arms like that, I'd cut the sleeves off my sport coats.

"Why don't ya just take a minute and have you a good look," he said. "That way we won't be spendin' our quality time together with you sneakin' peaks at me, okay, podna?" I thought his finishing grimace might have been a smile. It was hard to tell.

The face looked like it had been assembled from mismatched parts and, as such, gave conflicting impressions. A vertical scar ran the length, coming out from under his sandy pompadour and eventually disappearing beneath his chin. The scar had puckered an area of skin beneath his left eye, forming a pink teardrop of flesh that seemed to be forever rolling down his ruined cheek. A second, angrier scar ran from the corner of his mouth back under his ear, pulling his lips into an insincere grin. His right ear was fully an inch higher than his left. The patches of skin through which the scars did not pass seemed to have small pieces of gravel sewn beneath the surface.

He gave me a lopsided grin. "Always wear your seat belt, podna."

"I'll remember that," I promised.

It was as if, somewhere inside, a switch was flipped.

"Show's over," he said suddenly. "Whacchu want?"

"I want to see Mr. Del Fuego."

"Lots of folks wanna see ol' Jackeroo."

"I'm Leo Waterman," I said. "I'm here about security for the convention." I handed him my handy new credentials. He took only the briefest glance before handing it back.

He stuck out his hand. "Rickey Ray Tolliver," he said. His hand was callused to something more akin to weathered bone than to flesh, but his grip was light. "They called about you sometime earlier, podna. Come on in, the Jackster wants to have a word with ya."

He swung the door aside and stepped back.

I walked through an ornate vestibule into a large central room. Maybe thirty-five by forty-five. Furniture out away from the walls. Three separate seating areas, one with its own little library corner, a full bar, beige wool carpet up to my ankles that ran down the wide hall, off the back of the room that must lead to the five bedrooms.

He was about sixty, wearing a fire-engine-red suit over a ruffled tuxedo shirt that he wore unbuttoned nearly to his navel. I'd never seen a grown man in a red suit before, but somehow, on him, it seemed to work. Probably because it matched his eyes and his face. His thick head of white hair was welded in place, except for a single shock up near the front that he allowed to fall partially over one eye, lending, he probably imagined, a certain boyish charm to his otherwise dissolute appearance.

He was on the phone.

"I'll tell you what, then, Myron. You just tell them to run what they been paid for. We're paid up through Wednesday. They don't wanna renew the ad, then fuck 'em. Be too damn late by that time anyway. Heh, heh, heh. By the time those damn fools get their shit together, we'll have his big brisket broiled." He pushed the off button and snapped the cell phone shut. He saw me and scowled.

"Rickey Ray . . ." he began.

Tolliver stepped out from behind me. "Name's Leo Waterman, Jack. He's the guy from convention security."

A grin split his face. "Well, hell's bells, why didn't you say so, Rickey Ray." He started across the room toward me. "Get Mr. Waterman here a drink, boy," he said.

Tolliver headed for the bar. I caught his eye. "Mineral water," I said. "Something like that." He winked his injured eye.

Jack Del Fuego threw an arm around my shoulder and began hustling me toward the center of the room. "Yer not a teetotaler, now, are ya, Waterman?"

"Nope," I said. "Just getting older and got a long day in front of me, is all. I start drinking this time of day, I'll have to grab a nap."

He clapped me on the back. "Glad to hear it," he said. "Can't trust a teetotaler. They're damn near as bad as them vegetarians and animal rights assholes. Enough to puke a buzzard, if ya ask me."

When I seemed to agree, he gave me the canned spiel, in the third person, referring to himself as "ol' Jack." How ol' Jack started out with a little joint in Austin, Texas, and built it into a thirty-three-store chain. How ol' Jackeroo had been betrayed from within. How the world would soon tire of what he called Abby's "Styrofoam steaks." How his betrayers had grossly underestimated the ol' Jackalope's legendary resiliency and would now face the wrath of the Jackster.

Rickey Ray produced a lemon-lime water over ice and handed it to me. Jack waited until I had swallowed half of it and then leaned close.

"You been over to see the Meyerson midget yet?" he asked.

"No, sir, I haven't," I said.

"Don't be listenin' to her bullshit, now, boy. That little shit got more stories than the naked city. She starts runnin' me down, tellin' stories, all that, you just ask her about the bone."

"The bone?"

"The pork chop bone her husband, Lutz, choked to death on."

"What about it?"

"She had it gold-plated. Used it for a key chain."

I held his gaze. "Come on. Really?"

"Used to give out little bronze replicas to her employees, you know, like for promotions and employee of the month and that stuff."

"Sounds like one of those stories to me," I said.

He took the arm that wasn't around my shoulder and held it up.

"As God is my witness," he said. "I will, of course, allow you to draw your own conclusions as to how that big old bone got stuck that far down that man's skinny little throat."

"Of course," I said.

"She starts runnin' me down on my parentin' skills, snivelin' about how I didn't do right by my stepkids and all that other crap of hers, you just ask her about that daughter of hers that she don't talk to no more. Nice girl, name of Penny. Married some kind of tradesman. The Meyerson hag dropped her like a hot potato. Couldn't stand to have no blue-collar trash in the family. No, sir. You ask her about that."

I swore to wedge it in at the first conversational break.

"Now, I don't know what you know about my present situation . . ." he said. "I got me some real security problems." He shot a quick glance at Rickey Ray. "Not the personal kind, ya know. Ol' Rickey Ray here's more'n capable of watchin' out for my big ass. Three-time Ultimate Fighting Challenge champeen. Nobody else ever won it twice. Got him every kinda belt in every goddamn gook martial arts discipline known to man. The problem I got is—"

Before he could continue, the lock in the hall door snapped and a tall blond woman bustled through the door, followed by a moving pile of bags and packages. Nordstrom, The Bon Marché, Barney's, Helen's, of course. Downtown Retail grazing at its finest.

"Rickey Ray," she wailed. "Help Bart here for a sec, will ya, honey?" Tolliver didn't move a muscle.

Even without the platform shoes and the hair, she must have been the better part of six-one or -two. Long in the leg and narrow in the hip, she wore a blue spandex jumpsuit so tight that when she turned back toward her packages, I could tell that her brassiere was a two-snap model and that she was wearing a pair of those user-friendly thong underpants. She had a feathered-back pile of bleached hair and a set of those butterfly eyelashes so favored by the wives of TV preachers. Farrah Fawcett meets Tammy Faye Bakker.

She swiveled forward. "Rickey Ray," she insisted.

"I tole you before, darlin'," Jack said. "Rickey Ray is my driver and my bodyguard, not your cock of the month. Ol' Bart here needs help, get him a boyfriend of his own."

She turned in an instant, dipping into the tote bag that swung from her elbow and coming out with a single sheet of paper. She waved the paper in front of her as she crossed the room.

"Need I remind you?" she said. "Need I remind you? You forget what the judge told you the last time? You that dim or what?" She didn't wait for an answer. " 'Course you are. Why in hell am I asking myself that? You'd think I'd know by now. You wasn't that damn dumb, you wouldn't have run the business into the ground, now, would you?"

Jack and Rickey Ray exchanged tired glances. She kept at it. "Rickey Ray is paid by the company. I am one half of that company. He works as much for me as he does for you, and right now I want him to . . ."

It appeared to be some sort of court document she was waving. It was laminated and made a wooga-wooga sound as she flapped it around.

She noticed me for the first time. "And who in hell is this?"

"He's with convention security," Jack said.

"Security, you say? Well, hell, you could sure use all the help you can get there, Sparky."

She stepped my way. "Dixie Donner," she said.

"Leo Waterman."

We shook hands.

"I had the great misfortune to be married to this idiot a while back. Quite a while," she added. "Old Jack here likes his honeys just barely growed up and haired over. The fresher outta high school, the better the old boy likes 'em. Ain't that right, Jackeroo?"

The lack of a reaction did not slow her down.

"Technically speaking, half the restaurants are mine. Community property, ya know? 'Ceptin' if I leave birdbrain here alone, there won't be no damn restaurants to be half of. Be like his poor first wife, poor soul. He may have snookered her, but he sure as hell ain't gonna snooker me. I figured if I didn't take the bull by the horns, so to speak, and make damn sure he don't screw up the rest of it, I'd be out on the street."

"Where, as I recall, you'd feel right at home," Jack sneered.

"Got a court order." She waved it again. "No company business can be conducted unless I'm there."

"Laminated?" I asked.

"Shit for brains kept tearing it up," she explained. "Like that'd make it go away or somethin'. Had it done in clear Kevlar. Not even Jo Jo the Dogfaced Boy over there can tear it up now."

I made it a point not to look over at Rickey Ray.

She hollered over my shoulder. "Bart! Don't just stand there like a bump on a log; take that stuff down to the room."

The pile of bags and packages began to move across the carpet. From what I could see, Bart was an attractive young fellow of about twenty-five, six feet or so, with a slicked-back head of black hair and a pair of thin, hairless forearms.

Dixie Donner focused on me again. "He tell you how we can't take a crap over here without the Meyerson camp knowing whether it was one lump or two? He tell you that? He tell you those people are kicking our asses in damn near every market because they always know ahead of time what we're gonna do? He tell you he's got us in hock up to our asses and if this Seattle store ain't a great big hit, we may all end up wearin' paper hats? Security, my ass."

Without another word, she brushed past me and started after Bart, who had bumped his way around the corner and moved down the hall.

"You so much as break wind without me being there, Jack, and I'm going to haul your big ass back to jail," she said over her shoulder.

Jack opened his mouth, remembered I was there and, instead, went trotting down the hall in her wake. I could hear his plea.

"I can't operate this way, Dixie. It's all gonna go sour. You're just gonna have to take a smaller part here."

"Trust me, Jack," she said. "You got a small enough part for the both of us."

I missed whatever was said next. As I stood still and tried to catch the receding voices, a head popped up over on my left. Visible above the carved wood border on the Victorian sofa was a lustrous mane of sandy-brown hair, connected to a rather lustrous young woman. She must have been lying down. "Poor Jack," she said, rising.

I thought I heard Rickey Ray chuckle as she came around the edge of the sofa. "Sorry if I startled you," she said.

"No problem," I said.

"I'm Candace Atherton."

She was maybe thirty and a beautiful girl. A lithe five-ten, in a white silk blouse, a blue cashmere cardigan and a pair of loose-fitting chinos. She eased herself across the room in my direction, her movements far too graceful to be considered common locomotion.

"I'm afraid I'm what Miss Donner so prosaically referred to as Jack's latest high school honey."

"It's been a while," I said, "but I don't remember anything even vaguely like you in my high school."

"I suppose I'll take that as a compliment, Mr. . . ."

"Waterman," I said. "Leo Waterman, and please do."

From the far end of the hall, a garbled mix of raised voices filtered our way. "How long has this been going on?" I asked.

"She got the court order six weeks ago in Dallas," Rickey Ray said. "Been dogging us ever since."

"Poor Jack," the woman said again.

"You ought to be around when she follows him into the toilet," said Rickey Ray.

"Noooo . . ."

"There's a phone in the toilet," Candace Atherton said.

" 'Cause she knows ol' Jackeroo does most of his business on the can. Says he thinks best in there."

"Oh, now, Rickey Ray," she chided.

"He had me throw 'em out of the suite in Dallas. Two hours later, they come and hauled his ass to the pokey on contempt charges. Took us two days to get him out. The ol' boy was not a happy camper."

She looked at me. "I hope you won't judge Jack by this, Mr. Waterman. He's really a warm, loving human being. Kind and generous to a fault and very self-actualized."

"I'm not in the judging business, Miss Atherton, I'm in the security business. I'm just trying to make his visit to Seattle as pleasant as I can. My employers were concerned that, you know, with Mr. Del Fuego and Ms. Meyerson and Mr. Reese all here under the same roof—"

Candace interrupted, her eyes wide. "Mason Reese is here?"

"Room eight-fourteen," I said.

"We ain't even goin' to the show till Tuesday," Rickey

Ray said quickly. "I don't figure we're gonna have no problems at the show."

I pulled my notebook from my pocket. "What's your schedule for tomorrow?" I asked.

"Oh, Jack'll be clearin' his sinuses till noon, then we'll head down to the new restaurant, and he'll gum up the works down there till dinnertime, and then we'll head back here. After that, it's anybody's guess. Just depends on what comes into his head."

"Anything I can do for you?" I asked.

Rickey Ray moved out from behind the bar, standing between Candace Atherton and me, wiping a glass with a small towel. The knuckles of his hands were buried beneath a half-inch ridge of brown calluses.

"Things ain't gonna get dicey till Friday. That's the night of the barbecue. You know . . . the . . ."

"Hasn't anybody tried to talk him out of it?"

Rickey Ray shook his head. "Hell, everybody's tried."

"Jack's a very determined man," Candace added.

"Got a head like a rock."

Candace Atherton leaned in close. "He was originally going to stage the barbecue in Cleveland, but there were some problems."

"The stampede?" I ventured.

"No, that was Atlanta," Candace said.

"Yeah, in Cleveland it was every goddamn animal rights activist in the world," Rickey Ray reported. "All out in the streets with signs and shit. Hell, we had to get outta Dodge, three days before the opening. City charged Jack thirty-five grand for the mess."

"You think he can pull it off this time?"

"Oh, yeah," he said. "You can pretty much count on it. This time he's the man with the plan. And the closer we get to that, the more downright interesting things're gonna get."

The distant voices rose an entire octave, dueling tenors.

"I better go," Candace said, hurrying off toward the din.

I watched her go. Candace in motion was balm to the eye.

"Jack's a lucky man," I said.

"Luck got nothin' to do with it," Rickey Ray said. "Bought her a new Mercedes convertible for her last birthday and a little cabin on Lake of the Ozarks the year before that."

"How long has she been with Jack?"

"We both been 'round a couple of years. Me, a little longer."

"How'd you—" I started.

Rickey Ray looked over my shoulder, "Hey, Bartster."

When he wasn't buried beneath a pile of bags and boxes, Bart was a real good-looking kid. Six-two or so, black hair, blue eyes. He looked like one of the models in a Sears catalog.

"Don't they ever get tired of that?" he asked Rickey Ray.

"Near as I can tell, no."

He stuck out his hand. "Bart Yonquist."

I took it. "Leo Waterman."

The sound of broken glass sent Rickey Ray into motion.

"Ah, sheeeet. I best break it up."

The voices soared again as he crossed the room. I turned back to Bart. "What's a nice kid like you doing in a place like this?"

He told me. He was in his second year of medical school when he got a notice in the mail. It said the next check he got from his parents' trust fund was also going to be the last. At that point he was twenty-five and had never held a job. Talk about rude awakenings.

Anyone who's ever had to look for work knows how he felt by Friday afternoon, after a solid week of pounding the bricks. The Fates provided Dixie, who, it just so happened, was between escorts at the time and thought Bart was, as she put it, "just as cute as a bug's ear."

Bart, while being both desperate and young, but neither blind nor stupid, respectfully declined. She told him it paid two thousand a week, cash, no taxes. Bart did a little mental math. He figured six months would get him through school and a year might get him an office.

"And you'd be surprised how much better it sounded to me."

It was crude; I admit it. I'd just met the guy, but I had to know.

"Do you, like . . . you know . . ." I was prepared to go on indefinitely without ever using a verb, but Bart got the idea.

"No, man. It's not like that. She had all of that she could stand by the time she was thirty. Just ask her. She'll tell you. She wants a full-time gofer and somebody to be seen with. It's the being seen that really gets her off."

"At two grand a week," I said, "a guy could be seen quite a lot."

"That's what I thought. Beside, Dixie's got a good head, she really does. She's a bit off the wall, but she's good people."

I liked the kid. He still hadn't gotten a steady job at twenty-six. You had to admire a guy who could cheat the system for that long.

"Gotta go," he said. "Take care."

I stood alone for a few moments. The suite had suddenly gone quiet. As I pulled open the door and walked out into the hall, I kept repeating Señor Alomar's words; *Money is no object, money is no object . . .*

6

I rode the soundless elevator down to the ninth floor. In the twenty minutes I'd been upstairs, my bag had been unpacked, my clothes hung neatly in the closet, my unmentionables stowed in the dresser and my toiletries geometrically arranged on the bathroom counter. Dude. The red light on the phone by the bed was blinking. Two messages. Call Rebecca about when to meet at new house. Call Karen at work.

The new house was actually the old house. My parents' house on the east side of Queen Ann Hill. The trust allowed me either to live there rent-free or to lease it out and keep the proceeds. I'd always opted for the latter, feeling that I somehow didn't belong there without them. As if, even as a child, I had simply wandered into the middle of a scene that began before my time and that surely would outlive us all.

Rebecca Duvall and I had known each other since grammar school. If you discounted the three years I'd been married, we'd been dating for nineteen years. Rebecca was the only child of a shore-leave shimmy between her mom, Letha, and an alcoholic merchant marine whose identity had been systematically reduced to the pronoun "him."

My earliest memories of Duvall are of the tall girl with the blue barrettes who sat up front in the third grade and knew the answers to just about everything. According to the oft-told legend, Letha had worked three finger-to-the-bone jobs to get Rebecca through medical school. As if in penance, Rebecca had pledged to see her mother through old age. We had an unspoken understanding that whenever Letha turned in her lunch pail, we would sit down and decide what to do next about our relationship. We counted on her dying, not on her wanting a roommate.

Letha's stormy relationship with her only sister, Rhetta, an equally ancient crone from Lincoln City, Oregon, had mellowed significantly in recent years. What had once consisted of minimal contact followed by months of heated recrimination had weathered into a cozy little ménage of mutual deterrence. The old women now wanted to live out their days in sibling synergy. Time doth make cowards of us all.

All bets were suddenly off. No matter that the Duvall digs up in Ravenna technically belonged to Rebecca. No way Letha was moving to Bumfuck, Oregon. So that meant Rhetta was coming to Seattle. Duvall's choices were thin. Live in the house with the two of them and go shopping for orthopedic shoes, or make other arrangements. It was simple enough. Rebecca kept paying the mortgage; the old ladies got the house and it was time for me to putt or get off the green.

Just so happened that the family manse was between tenants. When the Levines moved to Tennessee, the trust took the opportunity to have the place inspected. As might be expected in a sixty-year-old house, which had been leased out for the better part of twenty-five years, major renovations were needed. They'd sent me the standard courtesy letter detailing what they proposed to do, which was damn near everything, and what it was going to cost me, which was about a hundred eighty thousand bucks. And that wasn't the bad part. The bad part was that I'd made the mistake of complaining about it to Duvall.

All attempts to convince her that it might be best to start this new phase of our relationship on neutral ground had been met with deaf ears. For reasons I'll never understand, the lure of a rent-free, completely renovated, twelve-room house overlooking Lake Union was more than Rebecca could withstand. We were moving in this weekend.

She answered on the first ring. I could tell from the static that she was in her car. "Yes," she said.

"You get my other message?"

"You're sleeping at the hotel?"

"My place is all packed up. It's a godsend."

A short but meaningful silence ensued. Then she said, "I'm going to run some errands before we go up to the house."

The work crews were finished. The house was supposedly ready to go. We had agreed to take a look at it together, this afternoon.

"I'm gonna be late."

"Leo," she said, "you're not cheesing out on me, are you? I mean, I don't want to feel like—"

I cut her off. "I'm doing exactly what I want to do, with exactly who I want to do it with. Period. That's it."

"Okay," she said, without much enthusiasm.

"I've just got a lot of stuff to do."

"Like what?"

I told her. Beneath the clatter of the static, I could hear her rich laughter. "This I've got to see," she said when I'd finished.

"I'm meeting them in front of the Rainier Club at four. I could use some help."

"Like what?"

I told her what I wanted.

"Do you have any idea how hard it was for me to find someone to cut my hair?"

"It's right in the neighborhood. We can all walk."

"He'll shit."

"I'll pay the going rate and tip twenty-five percent."

I heard her chuckle again. "I'll give him a call."

"See you at four."

"All right."

"We'll go up to see the house when we're done."

"Mmmm," she said and hung up.

I dialed Karen and sat through a lovely Lennon Sisters a cappella rendition of "Let Me Call You Sweetheart" before she finally hit the line.

"You always did know how to pick 'em, Leo."

"How's that?"

"Have you seen today's *Post Intelligencer*?"

"No."

"Well, when you get a chance, treat yourself to page three of Section D. It's a full-page ad. Your friend Jack Del Fuego."

"Oh, no."

"You have no idea what's been going on around here."

"Tell me."

"Less than an hour after I spoke to you, in walks the mayor's monkey."

"Harlan the Hatchet was in your office?"

"I've still got the windows open."

"What'd he want?"

"Harlan tells me to find something, anything, to stop Mr. Del Fuego's cookout on Friday night. He doesn't care how I do it, just do it, he says. Not a 'howdy' or a 'please.' Just do it, and he's gone."

"Harlan was the first successful recipient of the charisma-bypass procedure."

"You ain't just whistling Dixie," she said. "So I'm still stomping around the office an hour later when he comes strolling back in, with that stupid grin of his plastered all over his face."

"The one where he looks like a sheep?"

"The very same."

"Lucky you."

"Oh, yeah. And guess what?"

"What?"

"A complete reversal. The barbecue is to go off on schedule. The mayor and his wife will be in attendance, as will
be Mr. and Mrs. Chief of Police and so on down the line.
SPD will provide any extra needed security. I am to resist
any and all pressure. Bingo. He's gone."

"What pressure would you need to resist?"

"Ah, Leo. You think like a true Waterman. I wondered
the same thing, so I called Mary Beth Erdman."

"Remind me, who's that?"

"Your uncle Pat's second wife. She's in Finance."

"And?"

"Seems the mayor got a call this morning from an animal
rights group demanding he put a stop to the cookout."

"Did he faint and wet himself?" That's just the sort of PC
pressure that usually gets old Norm to soiling his briefs.

"No. Quite the contrary."

God, how this woman treasured a good secret. I waited.

"So guess who heads this particular group?"

"I'll bite. Who?"

"Clarissa Hedgpeth."

"That weepy woman with the white poodle? Meat Is Murder and all that crap?" As far as I was concerned, the only
people entitled to complain about animal rights were barefoot, vegetarian nudists. The rest of us were guilty. Such is
life in the food chain.

"That's the one," Karen said.

"Isn't she the one who—"

"Yep, the same one who threw a quart of blood on the
mayor's wife during one of those anti-fur demonstrations.
Outside The Opera House a couple of years ago, when he
was just a councilman."

"Mink, as I remember."

"Blond mink and uninsured, I'm told."

"And you know how cheap that man is, too," I said.

We shared an "Ooooh."

"So His Honor has decided that the shindig is going to go on, no matter what," she said.

"I'm not going to get any help from you, am I?"

"No can do, kiddo."

"Thanks anyway, Karen."

"So . . . you're moving into the old house," she said before I could break the connection.

"Let me guess. Maureen again."

"No, Ruthie told me," she said, naming a cousin so distant I was unable to bring any image of her whatsoever to mind.

I may have growled before I hung up; I can't be sure. Either way, I carefully replaced the receiver and went out to meet the Meyersons.

7

"**S**paulding," she said in a low drawl, "fetch the videotape."

"Aw, come on. This guy doesn't want to . . ."

He was moving toward the hall even as he whined. The fact that I'd known the boy for only about ten minutes had not prevented me from forming an intense desire to kick his pimply ass. Spaulding Meyerson was maybe nineteen. An oily-faced little sack of shit, with a voice like fingernails on a blackboard and a thinning head of black hair that was never going to see forty. He'd inherited the family teeth from his mother.

She'd opened the door herself, but she wasn't alone. On her right, leaning back against the peach-colored drapes, was a guy in a gray silk suit and a narrow black tie. Then there was the matter of the shadow behind the door being way too wide for this tiny woman.

She was no more than five feet tall in heels. Her perfectly arranged hair was the reddish color of a calico cat. She had a shrewd pair of brown eyes, set in close to a turned-up nose. The rest of her face was mouth. If she were a foot taller, she could have been one of those Kennedy women.

The ones who don't even have to crack a smile to show a full square yard of carefully tended dental work.

"Ms. Meyerson, I presume," I said with my best rugged grin.

It's not like I expected her to get all dewy-eyed or anything, but I don't think it would be bragging to say that I can still muster a certain amount of boyish charm. She looked me over like I was the last brassiere on the sale table.

"And you would be?" Blanche DuBois on Valium.

"Leo Waterman. I'm with convention security."

I presented my ID, which she passed to the guy leaning on the drapes without so much as a glance.

"Yes," she said. "Sir Geoffrey Miles himself called."

Drapeman passed my ID behind the door.

She looked over at Drapeman, who looked behind the door and nodded. "Won't you come in," she said with a degree of warmth and enthusiasm generally reserved for a yeast infection.

The suites were, indeed, mirror images of each other. What I had presumed to be an armoire in Jack's suite was, however, actually an entertainment center, with a big-screen TV and a videotape player. The Kansas City Chiefs were playing the San Diego Chargers. A lank-haired kid was stuffing his face with Chee-tos and watching the game.

Al Michaels was doing the play-by-play.

"*. . . third down seven on the KC thirty-six . . .*"

The guy behind the door was pretty much another Drapeman. Both were about forty, well groomed, and had mastered that stone-faced professional sheen so often seen on Secret Service agents.

"Spaulding," she said, "please turn that off."

"Why do I gotta?" he whined. "You guys go out in the hall."

"*. . . three-step drop, Bono flares a little swing pass . . .*"

"You can watch the game in your room," she tried.

"Go talk in *your* room," he insisted.

"*. . . Allen finally steps out at the San Diego fifteen.*"

Drapeman crossed the room to the entertainment center and pushed the power button. The big screen went blank from the center out. The kid jumped up from the couch and tried to get at the controls. Working like a cutting horse, Drapeman kept his body between the kid and the button as the kid jumped wildly about.

Frustrated, Spaulding Meyerson turned my way.

"Yeah, Gordo here's a big man when it comes to kids," he said, jerking a thumb over his shoulder at Drapeman. "A real big man. Ask him about how Rickey Ray cleaned both their asses up in about five seconds. Ask them about that, whydoncha? How he sent the stooges here crawling back holdin' their 'nads and crying like little girls."

"Spaulding," she snarled. "That's enough."

This time she got his attention. Mine, too. He shut up, jammed his hands in his pockets and started to stalk from the room. Halfway across, however, I could tell he wasn't going to leave. He wasn't going to give us that satisfaction. Instead, he ducked in behind the bar, pulled a can of Coke out of the fridge, popped the top and took a healthy swig. The room was silent except for swallowing.

"Please excuse my son, Spaulding," she said. "I assure you he doesn't always act this way."

Sure he didn't. Unless I missed my guess, Spaulding Meyerson was well down the road to a lifetime of serious assholery. As if in confirmation, Spaulding belched and gave us a toothy grin.

"These gentlemen are Mr. Francona." She nodded toward Drapeman. "And Mr. Hill." Neither man made a move to shake hands, so I stood still. "They handle all of my security needs. As I told Sir Geoffrey, beyond their able services I have no need for special security assistance."

"Except for when Rickey Ray beats the holy hell out of them, that is," Spaulding added.

I was getting the brush-off, so I waded right in.

"I was hoping we might be able to put our heads together on how best to stop Mr. Del Fuego's—uh—" I stammered.

She helped me out. "Barbecue."

"Yeah. The barbecue."

"Old Jackeroo is gonna roast old lardass." Spaulding smirked.

She shot her son a quick, murderous glance.

"I assure you, Mr. Waterman, no such event shall take place."

"You sound pretty confident," I said.

"The Lord works in mysterious ways."

"Care to share?"

"I'm afraid not," Abby said. "For my daughter's sake, for the sake of decency, this abomination must surely be stopped. Bunky must be saved. I have faith." She said it like a chant.

"But . . ." I looked around the room. "What if Bunky is already, you know . . . shrink-wrapped."

"Have you seen today's paper?" Abby inquired.

"Haven't had the chance."

She stuck out her hand like a surgeon waiting for a tool. The one she'd called Hill slapped a section of newspaper into her small hand. She held the newspaper under her and let it unfold. It covered half of her petite body.

"Come On Down, Folks. Feed Yer Face at the FeedLot," was all it said. It was the picture. That and the facial expressions. Ol' Jackeroo held a carving knife in one hand and a leash in the other, his face a slanted mask of malignant mischief. The leash was attached to the halter of an enormous black bull, whose liquid eyes seemed to say he somehow had an idea of what in hell was going on and didn't like it one damn bit.

Worse yet, someone had taken a piece of white chalk and divided the animal's gleaming black hide into a series of irregularly shaped quadrants. The sections were labeled. The one at the rear read rump. T-bone, porterhouse, sirloin, short ribs, chuck, tri-tip and London broil, they were all there. I changed my mind. The bull didn't look worried; he looked embarrassed.

When I was a kid, I used to wonder if the cattle knew their fate. If maybe each herd didn't have at least one cynic who walked around the pasture going: " They're gonna kill us, ya know." While the other cows went, "Oh, Larry, chill out, you're so paranoid. We're pettts."

"I have it on good authority that the setting of that picture is here in Greater Seattle."

"Gasworks Park," I said. "About a mile or so north of here."

No doubt about it. The abandoned apparatus of the old gasworks rose from the hillside like the conning tower of some buried battleship.

"Mr. Francona spoke with the photographer."

I waited.

"The picture was taken two days ago," she said.

I shrugged. "Why? Wouldn't it be a whole lot easier to just have the animal dressed out? I mean, that's gotta be less trouble than keeping it alive."

"Obviously, you don't understand Mr. Del Fuego," she said.

"That's probably true," I admitted. "So why is he going to all this trouble? I hear he's got enough problems of his own."

"Because he hates me. He blames me for his business failures. He claims I've been spying on him."

"Have you?"

"Certainly not." She seemed genuincly insulted. "This is a difficult market. Not at all like when we began."

According to Abigail Meyerson, Jack had merely ridden a wave of prosperity, using the initial success of every new restaurant to finance the next, and so forth, on down the line, creating a nationwide pyramid scheme, rather than a self-supporting corporation.

"It's easy enough as long as interest rates are high," she went on. "Nobody wants their investment back. Why should they? They're making a fortune on the interest. Nowadays . . ."

Abigail Meyerson treated me to a five-minute primer on the trials of restaurant ownership in the late nineties. Skyrocketing real estate prices, the perils of the pluralistic workforce, the added strain of just-in-time inventory, the heartbreak of psoriasis. I waited her out.

"Abby's Angus can provide its customers with a full-pound, three-inch porterhouse steak which is less than four percent fat. Did you realize that?"

I confessed that it had escaped my attention.

"That's the market, Mr. Waterman. It's the fats against the skinnys and, unlike the generations preceding us, it's the skinnys who have all the money. Mr. Del Fuego is a relic from the CB-radio period. I can't imagine what he thinks he's doing in a health-conscious market such as Seattle. It's lunacy. I have no need to sabotage Mr. Del Fuego."

"Besides which," I said, "you're not that kind of girl."

Without altering either her voice or her facial expression, Abby replied, "On the contrary, Mr. Waterman, I'm exactly that kind of girl. I readily admit that it is my intention to drive Mr. Del Fuego from the industry. I have been opening restaurants right on top of him for over two years. I consider it to be my civic duty. I make no bones about it."

"A little steak joke there," I tried.

I regretted the words the minute they escaped my lips.

"Oh," she said. "A joke. Yes. Bone." Silence. "Well, here's a bone for you, Mr. Waterman. The only reason I'm not buying up Mr. Del Fuego's back paper and demanding immediate payment is that somebody else is saving me the time, trouble and expense."

It took a moment for me to process this. "You're saying that somebody out there is trying to put Jack out of business, and it isn't you."

"No. I'm saying that somebody *in addition* to me is trying to put Mr. Del Fuego out of business. And doing quite well at it, too, I would expect."

"How so?"

"I've been told that his Toledo store was forced to close

when a three-hundred-fifty-thousand-dollar note was suddenly and quite unexpectedly called due. When Mr. Del Fuego was unable to meet his obligations, the property reverted to the noteholders, who then proceeded to auction it off down to the last rivet. They're supposed to have walked off with almost eight hundred thousand."

"And Jack thinks it's you who's doing this to him."

"Which is why he's started this preposterous charade with that poor animal and why he must be stopped."

"Still seems like a whole lot of trouble, without much reward."

"Mr. Del Fuego, beneath all that rural charm, is one of those unfortunate creatures who harbors what used to be called a good old-fashioned mean streak. Nowadays, they probably have some other name for it and count it as a disability, for which one can collect a government dole. But that's how it is. It's how he's operated since the very beginning. You only have to look at how he got his first restaurant and at that poor woman and her family."

I knew who she meant, but I played along.

"What woman is that?"

"His first wife. I believe her name was Sheila Somers. She had a nice little steak house where she used to play the piano and sing."

"Where and when was this?"

"Austin, Texas," Abby said. "What . . . eighteen, twenty years ago. She made the great mistake of marrying our friend Willie Wogers."

"Who's that?"

"That's his real name, you know. Long o—Wogers. Willie. He was just another small-time hoodlum and gambler."

"Interesting," I said.

"She killed herself. Hanged herself in the garage, or . . ." Abby eyed the room. "At least that's what the authorities ruled," she finally said.

"Really."

"Less than two years after they were married."

Her tone suggested she considered it a minor miracle that the woman had lasted that long.

"And Jack got the business?"

"And I'll give him this," she said. "He had sense enough to see that the market was ripe for expansion. In those days, venture capitalists were coming out of the woodwork trying to give away money. There was a real gap in the upscale steak business."

"You said something about her family."

"She had two children by a previous marriage. A boy and a girl. In their early teens. They lived with their father."

"Probably for the best," I offered lamely.

She sighed. "One would have thought so."

I knew what my line was supposed to be. "But?"

"Oh, I hate to gossip."

Oh, yeah. I held my piece. She didn't disappoint.

"Sometimes," she mused, "bad things come in threes."

"What was next?" I prodded.

"The father dropped dead."

"And Jack ended up with the kids?"

"Hardly," she scoffed. "Mr. Del Fuego is without a nurturing bone in his entire bloated body."

"She have family? "

"Just some trailer-trash sister who wouldn't take them."

"So?"

"He farmed them out to foster care, where, as I understand it, they came to bad ends."

"Bad ends?"

Abby showed me a small palm. "I can say no more," she said, then took my elbow and turned me toward the door.

"I assure you, Mr. Waterman, my security needs are under complete control. Would you please remember to thank Sir Geoffrey for his concern." I was getting the boot.

"Mr. Del Fuego denies vandalizing your property."

She stopped in her tracks. Drapeman and Doorman stood in the middle of the room. That's when she told Spaulding to get the tape.

When Spaulding reappeared, he wasn't alone. Brie Meyerson was not at all what I expected. First off, she wasn't a kid. Contrary to rumor, Brie Meyerson was a full-blown woman of about twenty. Not beautiful, but pretty in an old-fashioned sort of way. She smelled of soap and her hair was still damp.

Her mother introduced us and then turned toward the entertainment center, where Frick and Frack were trying to get the tape to play. "Is there a problem?" Her tone suggested that problems were only for the lame and the halten.

When she didn't get an answer, Abigail Meyerson walked over and began to add her two cents to the problem. Spaulding called them a bunch of spazzes and popped another Coke.

Brie asked me, "And what part in this circus do you play?"

I told her, and then turned the question around.

She was entering her junior year at Bryn Mawr College. Her mother had insisted that both she and Spaulding, who had just flunked out of either his fifth or sixth prep school, accompany her for the summer to get a feel for the business. It had been a nightmare.

"Two weeks to go," she whispered. "Bye. Nice to meet you."

She slipped out the door and was gone just as Spaulding couldn't take it anymore. "Jesus. Here, let me in there."

He crossed the room, knelt before the VCR, pushed a couple of buttons and stood off to the side, grinning for all he was worth.

Me, I readied my poker face. I was the man of steel.

"I hope, Mr. Waterman, that this will give you some idea of the depths of perversity to which this man has sunk."

The picture flickered on. Color. Good production values. Probably made for a promotional or training film. Abigail Meyerson stood behind an oak podium, speaking into a microphone. Over her left shoulder, the head of a neon Angus bull winked down in good-natured invitation, and the familiar red letters spelled out ABBY'S ANGUS.

"It is with great pleasure," she intoned. "That here, on the occasion of our thirty-fifth restaurant, we take a moment to acknowledge those . . ." The camera angle widened. Spaulding stood up on the dais, shifting his weight from foot to foot and picking his nose. Brie wore a white sundress the way I always thought one ought to be worn. I chastised myself for impure thoughts and tuned back in to the speech.

Before I could pick up the thread, however, it happened.

With an audible pop, the whole sign flickered and died. And then, just as quickly, recovered its former brilliance. Except for the G. The G stayed out. The sign now read ABBY'S AN US. And the good-natured wink of the bull was suddenly a perverted leer.

As for me, if you didn't count the throbbing of my temples and the almost obscene fluttering of my nostrils, I held it together pretty well.

8

"**W**hat else have you got?" he shouted through the
door.

I checked my drooping wallet. "My library card."

"Has it got a picture?"

"Nope."

"What good is that?"

"Books."

I'd already held up, and then passed under the door, my
convention security ID card, my PI license, my driver's license and my VISA and COSTCO cards. I could only hope
that eventually Mason Reese would open the door and return my identity. If he decided to go shopping, I was in
serious trouble.

"It's not much," he complained.

"I'm not much of a joiner."

A room-service waiter pushed a cart up the hall in my
direction. He was a handsome fellow with dark curly hair
and a wispy mustache. Both levels of the rolling cart were
covered with silver-lidded chafing dishes, which chattered
slightly as he rolled along. A designer ice bucket showed
the tops of a champagne bottle and three soft drinks, whose

black screw-on tops stared back at me with green jungle eyes. Before moving the cart behind me, the waiter stood upright. His gold badge read Rodrigo. "Something I can help you with, sir?"

"No, but thanks," I said.

Only his five-star service training prevented him from asking me what in hell I was doing there in the hall, standing in front of a door with a DO NOT DISTURB sign hanging from the handle. As it was, he kept throwing glances over his shoulder as he pushed the cart the length of the hall, knocked on the last door on the left and disappeared inside.

The door to eight-fourteen suddenly banged open on its chain. Mason Reese peered out through the crack at me. He was a puny little guy of about fifty, with a bald pate and narrow eyes. "I can't be too careful, you know," he said. "I'm dealing with lunatics here."

Normally, I would consider a statement such as this as merely stress-induced hyperbole. Today, however, I was inclined to agree.

"I understand," I said. "I can get hotel security up here to verify my identity, if you want."

"Don't bother," he said. "I have nothing to say to you."

He slid his index and middle fingers out through the crack. I pulled my identification from between the fingers and took my time putting them back from whence they came. When I looked up, the door was slowly closing.

"Is any of that story about Abigail Meyerson and the pork chop bone true?" I blurted.

The door stopped moving and an eye reappeared. "What story?"

"That she had it gold plated."

"She had two of them made. One for a key chain and another that hung from the mirror of her Mercedes. She used to pass out these little replicas. In the corporation, they called it being 'slipped the bone.' If you were 'slipped the bone,' it meant you were on your way up the corporate ladder."

The door eased toward closed again.

"Meyerson sort of indicated that she thought Jack had maybe killed his first wife. Any truth to that?"

The door again banged on the chain. "She was a lush. That's why the courts gave the kids to the father. Jack had nothing to do with it." Reese almost grinned. "Unless you count his just being ol' Jackeroo and driving her to it, of course."

"What about her kids?"

"What about 'em?"

"Ms. Meyerson said she heard . . ."

"That 'bad ends' crap of hers."

"Yeah."

"Crap," he snapped. "She always makes it sound like Jack set 'em loose on an ice floe or something. He paid the freight. Maybe he wasn't the paternal type. Maybe he never laid eyes on those kids. But he saw to it that they went to good homes. I know, because it was my job to take care of it. The girl, Sandy was her name, went to these people in Pennsylvania. The foster parents kept in touch with me for years. Sent me her college graduation picture. The boy, Richard, went down south. Georgia someplace. A wealthy farm family."

"Big of Jack."

"You've met Jack. What do *you* think was best?"

I had to admit, Mason Reese probably had a point. Spending one's formative years with a guy who referred to himself exclusively in the third person might not have constituted a particularly sound foundation for successful citizenship.

I had slipped my toe into the crack, so I took a deep breath while I considered my next option. "What about all this stuff about The Meyerson Corporation spying on him?"

"I know nothing of that," Reese said. "I have not been in Mr. Del Fuego's direct employ for several years now. I know he's let go the whole staff it took us twenty years to build."

"Why'd he do that?"

"Paranoia. He kept weeding traitors out of the organization until there wasn't an organization."

"Is that what you're going to say at your news conference?"

"That remains to be seen, now, doesn't it?" He leaned lightly against the door.

"Abby and ol' Jackeroo have really got your ass in the wringer, haven't they?"

He sneered at me. "The way I see it, I hold the initiative."

"How can that be?" I scoffed. "It's your credibility that's at stake here, isn't it? And either way, you lose. I mean, if you claim your rating is on the up-and-up, Meyerson will probably add your name to the court case. God only knows what sort of damages that woman will ask for. And if you admit it was all a gag, you become an industry embarrassment, a pariah. Hell, your airline accounts just might sue you, too. You're damned if you do and damned if you don't."

"The situation is under control," he said.

"Seems pretty volatile to me," I countered. "As I see it, just about everybody would be better off if you took a hike."

He leaned heavily against the door. When it failed to budge, he looked down at my foot. "Kindly remove your foot. I have nothing further to say to you."

I kept the foot where it was. "Jack had some questions about the death of Ms. Meyerson's husband."

"That's just Jack talking through his ass as usual."

He leaned harder on the door.

"I'm staying here in the hotel. If anything interesting develops, feel free to give me a call."

He pressed his weight against the door and turned sideways so I could see the thick black automatic that he held down along his right leg.

"I'm prepared to defend myself," he said.

He was nervous and apt to do something stupid. I showed him my hands. I could feel the leather sole bending from the pressure of the steel door, so I pulled my foot out. The door snapped shut with a rush of hot air. End of interview.

The door at the end of the hall reopened. The waiter eyed me suspiciously as he rolled the now empty cart back up the hall. I waited until he'd passed me and then followed him on his way. After he rolled the cart into the elevator and turned around, I stepped in. I stood facing the rear as the door slid shut. That always drives 'em crazy.

9

For organizational purposes, I'd mentally reduced the afternoon's festivities to simply The Three H's: hygiene, hair and haberdashery. A trilogy of tasks which, I felt quite certain, would be best accomplished in precisely that order.

I got lucky. Seattle is a white-collar town with lots of folks having latitude as to their hours. During the week, the freeways begin to clog at two-thirty. Fridays it's an hour or so earlier. Holiday weekends, it starts on Thursday afternoons. I found a diagonal parking spot on James Street and backed in.

Downtown Seattle parking meters are calibrated to parcel out their time in nanoseconds. Eight nanoseconds per twenty-five-cent piece. I thumbed quarters into the meter until I risked carpel tunnel syndrome and was rewarded with a maximum thirty minutes of grudging forbearance. My relationship with the Parking Enforcement Patrol was such that last spring I had purchased a T-shirt emblazoned with the words: "Meter Maids Eat Their Young," which I proudly wore whenever both circumstances and the weather permitted.

I leaned forward and allowed gravity to pull me down the steep face of James Street. Halfway to the corner, I jay-jogged across both James Street and a suddenly empty Fifth Avenue and headed uptown toward the Y. At Cherry, I pointed myself downhill again, and there she was . . . the good Dr. Duvall, right in front of me, striding purposefully along in a shiny new pair of Air Jordans and a green-and-white Adidas running suit that made whisking noises as she walked.

I skipped down the hill, into the entrance to the cop's garage, until I was just off her inside shoulder.

"You believe in the hereafter, honey," I growled.

Rebecca answered without turning. "I certainly do."

"Then you know what I'm here after."

"Where does that come from? That's so corny."

She reached back, slipped an arm around my waist and yarded me up next to her. I stuck my nose behind her ear. She smelled like the great outdoors, according to Coco Chanel.

"*Laugh-in*," I said. "Remember? Arte Johnson used to putter along behind Ruth Buzzi, muttering all this suggestive stuff."

"And she'd beat the heck out of him with her purse."

"Couldn't have that now, though, could we? Not here in the latter stages of the sensitive nineties."

"Oh, no, sexual harassment and all that," she said.

"Why is everything sexual harassment these days?" I asked. "What happened to regular old run-of-the-mill harassment? Like when I just bust your balls because I think you're a jerk. Everything's got to be sexual these days. I don't understand it."

She said, "You're a truly unique thinker, Leo," and kissed me on the cheek. "It's your best feature."

"My best? You must be joking."

"Sorry, big fella. The other one's like a baseball pitcher." She nudged me in the ribs. "You're only as good as your next outing."

"I thought it was your *last* outing."

"Not in a buyer's market," she said.

Arm in arm, we gravitated down Cherry, skidding to a stop on the corner of Fourth Avenue. The crew was visible now. A blot on the urban landscape, milling around on the corner a block north. While a couple of bums in one place were hardly worthy of mention, a full dozen degenerates shuffling around the same corner had, not surprisingly, attracted official attention. A blue-and-white SPD cruiser was pulled to the curb on the east side of Third Avenue, its pair of officers out and milling about, enjoying the late sunshine and trading pleasantries with the crew.

"Uh-oh," Duvall said.

"Not to worry," I assured her. "They can handle it. They get a lot of practice."

By the time we'd covered half the distance, Norman had stepped up on the low brick wall surrounding the Rainier Club and was waving his arms wildly about.

"What in pity's name is Norman doing?" Rebecca asked, picking up the pace and dragging me along.

"Preaching, I suspect. That's what they do when they're told to disperse. They claim they're having a church service."

I could hear the voices now. Norman, usually quite soft-spoken, was orating at top volume.

"Also in the day of your gladness, and in your solemn days, and in the beginnings of your months, ye shall blow with your trumpets over your burnt offerings . . ."

The older cop was leaning back against the fender of the cruiser, enjoying the show as the rookie tried to assume command.

"I'm not tellin' you again, Red. You get your big butt down from there or you're goin' to jail," the young cop hollered.

He was peach-fuzz-fresh out of cop school, his hair still cut military-short. He didn't have to shave more than a couple of times a week and his training hadn't prepared him for anything quite like Nearly Normal Norman. At six-seven and about two-sixty, Norman cut an imposing figure. The rookie kept looking over his shoulder at his partner, who was using a pen knife to clean his fingernails.

Norman saw me coming and stopped spouting.

"Brother Waterman," he bellowed. "Will you witness and testify for the children of the Lord?"

I raised my right hand. "I will," I swore.

The cop turned on me like a rabid Chihuahua.

"You want to go with him?" he demanded. "You looking to spend a little time in the lockup?"

"I've got a better idea, Officer," I said. "How's about if they all go with me instead?"

"Where would you be taking this . . . this . . . group?"

Red Lopez's voice rose above the crowd. "Your momma's."

"Who said that?" The cop strained to see over the crowd.

"It was Joe," said Ralph solemnly.

"Joe who?"

"Joe Mama," they yelled in unison.

While they yukked it up, the kid stiff-legged it over to his partner and began whispering heatedly in the older man's ear. The veteran cop just smiled and shook his head. Not in my patrol car. No way.

Normal hopped down from the wall. "How was I doin'?" he asked.

"You oughta have you a TV program, Normal," Mary said.

"I didn't know you could quote Scripture, " I said.

"I been prayed over a lot," was his reply.

I counted noses. George, Harold, Ralph, Normal, Mary, Earlene, Flounder, Red Lopez, Billy Bob Fung, Hot Shot Scott, Big Frank and Heavy Duty Judy. The gang was all here.

"Let's go," I said, taking Rebecca's arm and starting up the street. Rebecca giggled at my side.

"I can't believe we're doing this," she said.

"Look at it like they're your scout troop, or something."

Wide-eyed, she peered back over her shoulder at the crew, silently mouthed the words "scout troop" and nearly collapsed with laughter. I dragged her up the street.

Normal strode out ahead, using the parking meters like conveniently placed walking sticks. The rest of the crew followed along piecemeal. Scott, Billy Bob and Red lagged behind, passing a bag-shrouded pint bottle among them. I pretended not to notice.

I stopped on the next corner and waited for stragglers. When the multitude had reassembled, I gave them the program.

"Everybody here is going to get paid a hundred bucks a day plus expenses," I said. Always start with the good news. That's my motto.

As expected, this statement was met with wild acclaim.

"Everybody gets a whole new set of clothes."

More cheering and calls for a drink.

"You've all done this before, so everybody knows the drill." I had them eating out of my hand. Now for the bad news.

"But," I continued, "this job is a little different than anything we've done before, because of the neighborhood we're going to be working in. It's a bit outside our usual stomping grounds."

"Where's that?" Frank asked.

"Up at the top of University. The Olympic Star."

"Oh, hoity-toity," Earlene said, dancing about.

The cruiser rolled slowly by. The older cop was behind the wheel, leaving the young guy free to glare out over his arm at us.

"I'll remember every one of you," he promised out the window.

"That's what she said," yelled Red.

I waited while the group shared another moment of madcap mirth.

"First thing, we're all going to go across the street"—I

pointed—"to the Y and everybody is going to take a shower.
On me," I added. "Then . . ."

That was as far as I got before being shouted down. There
were several barnyard epithets, a couple of anatomically un-
feasible sexual suggestions and at least one serious aspersion
of my parentage. I let them vent. I'd expected as much. What
I hadn't expected was what Harold said next.

"You said 'we' and 'everybody,' " he said. "That mean
you and Miss Duvall are gonna shower, too?"

A mutinous rumble rose from the crowd. Rebecca
squeezed my arm hard enough to break the skin. Her eyes
were the size of hubcaps.

"Sure," I said.

Forty-five minutes later, I was back on the sidewalk, feeling the chill of the evening breeze as it ran through my wet
hair, and knowing beyond question that the image of Ralph
would surely go to the grave with me. The girls showed up
about five minutes later.

"Okay," I said. "All in our places with bright, shiny
faces."

"Stuff it, Leo," said George. "What next?"

"Haircuts," I said, and started up Third Avenue. As the
crew shambled along dispiritedly behind us, Rebecca spoke
into my ear.

"*If,* and I stress the *if,* I ever talk to you again . . . we
shall *never, ever* speak of this," she said.

"These people know we're coming?" I asked.

"They know someone is coming."

"Kind of you to spare them the details."

"If I'd told him whose hair it was they were going to cut,
he never would have agreed to it. This is not a sheep ranch,
Leo; it's a salon."

Turned out she was right. The crew waited outside Mai-
son de Paul while Duvall and I went in. Mr. Paul himself
was waiting.

He confronted Rebecca. "Surely, Mees Duvall, you cannot
expect my staff to—"

She cut him short. "They're all clean," she said.

"But, madame . . ." he insisted in his phony accent

I pulled out a wad of hundreds as thick as his wrist.

"Fifty a head," he said with a sudden Bronx lilt. "Plus tip."

Rebecca supervised the styling. I took the first shift next door to The Owl Tavern for beers while we waited for the rest.

It was nearly seven before we were completely reassembled. The last line of sunshine burned candy-apple red out over the Olympics as we marched uptown to Westlake Center. Without the sun, the air was more like fall and the electric breeze from the passing busses the sole source of warmth. I stopped outside the espresso stand.

"Okay. George, Frank and Judy, you guys go with Rebecca. The rest of you come with me."

"Where they goin'?" asked Ralph.

"We're going to gussy them up so they can work inside the hotel. They need some different stuff."

By this time they were pretty much grumbled out and resignedly went along with the program. An hour later, it was all over, and they were splendid. They now carried their old clothes in a motley collection of paper sacks, which littered the bricks.

I'd equipped them from the ground up. New shoes, socks and underwear. Shirts and slacks. New winter jackets, maybe a bit much for the current weather, but something that would serve them well in the coming months.

They were still prancing around, high-fiving and modeling their new outfits, when Rebecca showed up with the others. The crowd went wild.

Big Frank wore a gray pinstriped suit with a blue tie. His tasseled loafers squeaked as he walked across the pedestrian mall. Heavy Duty Judy was resplendent in a flowered silk pantsuit, bright yellow shoes and a matching bag. The transformation was remarkable. Together, they looked for all the world to be a wealthy out-of-town couple in town to see the sights. And George was even better.

In a dark blue double-breasted wool suit and red power tie, George looked so good he could have been the mayor. "Oh, Georgie," Earlene trilled, "what a babe you are."

"This monkey suit hurts my neck," he complained.

"You were a banker. You always wore a tie. I remember."

"I had less necks then," he said.

"Okay," I hollered. They ignored me. Red Lopez and Hot Shot Scott were waltzing. Norman held Billy Bob Fung under one arm and Flounder under the other. Mary appeared to be helping George tuck in his shirt. George appeared to be enjoying it. Somebody was doing a Bert Parks impression.

"There she is . . . Miss America . . ."

"Could I have your attention, please?"

". . . there she is . . . your ideal . . ."

"This calls for a drink," I screamed.

It worked every time. They sang my praises and took me literally. Turned out no less than nine of them had something to nip on secreted somewhere on their persons.

I held up a hundred-dollar bill. "I'm going to get you all back to The Zoo by cab," I announced. More hosannas. "The rest is for a couple of rounds on me when you get there." I took several bows and waved like the Queen.

"Bonnie says you can use the old cooler out in back to change clothes in. It's important that you keep what you're wearing now in real good shape. For the first couple of days, it might be best only to wear the outfit while you're working; otherwise, if you look bad in that neighborhood, you're going to get pinched for sure. Okay?"

The mob was fickle. As quickly as my stock had risen, it now plummeted. No way were they putting that old crap back on.

"Okay, okay," I relented. "But you gotta stay neat and clean."

Scout's honor, all of them. Behind them, at the corner of

Pike and Third, Rebecca had corralled three cabs. Two Gray-Tops and a Yellow. "Ladies and Gentlemen," I announced, "your chariots await."

I slipped George a hundred and watched as they thundered over toward Duvall and the cabs. In the gloom, an even dozen bags of old clothes squatted among the rough stones like fungi.

10

We drove separately, which was fine with me. I was in no hurry. As I turned right onto Eastlake and the traffic thinned, I found myself behind one of those new Honda vans, sporting a yellow bumper sticker that read "HONK IF YOU **ARE** JESUS." What the hell. I gave a little toot. The driver stuck an arm out the window and shot me the finger. I figured it came with the martyrdom territory, so I honked again.

I tried to recall the last time I had laid eyes on the family digs. I've reached that point in life where I constantly underestimate how long ago it was that something happened. If my first instinct is three years, it's always been at least five. Worse yet, my confusion seems to exponentially worsen the longer the time frame involved. Any utterance of mine concerning something as ancient as, say, ten years or so ago can instantly be translated into a span considerably closer to twenty. My first instinct said Bill and Ellen Levine had lived there for six years, so, using the new and revised Waterman approach to time estimation, I figured that made my last visit to this neighborhood, conservatively speaking, about ten years whence.

I crested the side of the hill on Taylor and drove down until I almost ran into Crockett Avenue. In the driveway, my mind's eye saw the shadows of the various low-slung chariots of the fifties and sixties that my old man had owned and that we'd washed out here on Sunday afternoons. In the streets, I could imagine the nights of the parties. The cars of my parents' friends lining the narrow street on both sides, leaving only a thin nerve-racking slot for passersby. But what were the neighbors going to do? It wasn't like you could call the cops on my old man or anything.

The younger guys drove gleaming triple-finned Pontiac convertibles half a block long, while the more substantial drove big, three-porthole Buicks with plush seats and wide white tires. But it was the Caddies that interested me. The vast fleet of Cadillacs, black or dark blue, resting nose to tail around the hill like chrome Conestoga wagons, belonged to the real downtown movers and shakers.

The recalled smell of gasoline reunited me with a forgotten fascination concerning the gas tanks of certain Cadillacs. The ones where you pushed a little button in the taillight and the whole light assembly swung straight up, revealing what was to me, for some childish reason, a precious pearl of a gas cap. I'd wait until the party was in full swing, then sneak out of the house in my pajamas to circle the block, looking for the right models, and I'd try them all, just to make sure they worked.

Rebecca's blue Ford Explorer sat square and high in the driveway. Duvall, on the other hand, slouched curved and low on the front steps, leaning back against the risers, staring out at the street.

I took a seat beside her. "Hiya, Toots."

She looked over her shoulder at the house. "It's huge," she said. "When I came up before, it was full of people; there was all this scaffolding over it and all these trucks around. It didn't seem so big and imposing then."

I threw an arm around her shoulder. "It's just a house."

"I can't believe your mother didn't like it."

"She liked it just fine. It's just that it wasn't up on Capital Hill, where she figured a swell like the old man should be."

Rebecca dangled the keys in front of my face. "Shall we?"

I rose and offered her a hand. "After you, madame."

I pulled her to her feet. She got the keys right on the first try, swung the big rounded door open and disappeared, I took a deep breath, stepped inside and was stopped in my tracks.

The place bore almost no resemblance to the theater of my childhood. The house, as I remembered it, was a place of heavy drapes and dark wood, where silence and shadow were valued above all. A place to whisper rather than shout. To turn on more lights rather than open the drapes. All that was gone. Hell, the stairs were gone.

Used to be that when you walked in the front door, you were faced with a wide expanse of stairs leading to the second floor. To what my mother called the Ballroom. To the right of the stairs was the front room; on the left, the parlor; and behind the stairs, the kitchen and servants' areas.

They'd gutted the place. Now all was light and airy. What appeared to be a rough-textured plaster had replaced the dark wood. The narrow, twelve-pane windows had been removed, the openings expanded and new white windows installed. We stood in the middle of the gigantic front room, which now rose above us for the full two stories of the house. Whatever the upstairs looked like, one thing was for sure: the Ballroom was long gone.

"How's your checking account?" Duvall asked.

"Pretty good," I said. "Why?"

"Because everything you and I own, separately and collectively, doesn't begin to make a dent in furnishing this room. The other eleven rooms I don't even want to think about."

"We'll do what me and the old man did after she died."

"What's that?"

"We just decided what parts of the house we were actually going to live in, and closed off the rest of it."

A chill ran down my spine as I recalled the disconnected

feeling that the old man had once described as "like living in a museum."

I'd come back only long enough to lay him out in the front room, before the mile-long funeral procession took him up by Volunteer Park to the Lake View Cemetery and laid him next to my mother while the fire department band played "Across the River and Far Away." I'd never set foot inside this house since that day.

The stairs now came down in two stages, on two sides. The kitchen was where it had always been, but was completely renovated into something out of a magazine, with a half-acre center island and enough recessed lighting to land airplanes.

The back of the house, which hung out over the cliff, was now completely glassed in, offering a panoramic view of Lake Union, the west side of Capital Hill and the glistening Cascade Mountains beyond. My parents had no interest in the view. The help lived on the view side. My parents had no interest in looking out; what they wanted was to make damn sure others couldn't look in.

Rebecca took my hand. "Come upstairs," she said.

I let her pull me to the second floor. We started at the top of the stairs and worked our way through the maze of skylighted conversation areas, bathrooms, walk-in closets, and as nearly as I could tell, about six bedrooms. At the far end of the hall, a master suite hung out over the corner of the house, looking both east over the freeway and north over the urban sprawl of Seattle. The room was furnished.

"What's this?" I said.

"It's our new bedroom furniture."

"It's beautiful," I said honestly.

The bed was an antique. Walnut. Ornate and rounded all over in an Art Deco sort of way. The footboard was decorated with intricately carved seashells. The matching nightstands and the trunk at the end of the bed were part of the same elaborate set.

I put both arms around her from behind.

"How'd you get all this stuff up here?"

She squirmed out of my arms and escaped. "I got Tyanne's boyfriend and a couple of buddies to do it."

"How'd you know where to tell them to put it?"

"I called the architect," she said smugly, sounding just like she used to in school when she was the only one who knew the answer.

"Oh, well, missy, I guess that big-time education of yours is paying dividends now, isn't it?"

"Except in my personal life."

"Oh, yeah?" I patted the bed. "Howsabout we try this thing out? A little test drive. You know, just to make sure it's not defective."

She closed the nearest Levolor. "I wouldn't dream of keeping you from your fancy hotel room. What did you call it . . . a godsend. That was it, wasn't it?" If she hadn't been working her way around the room, closing the blinds, I would have been worried.

I said, "I think I should tell you . . . I'm really not that kind of girl."

She killed the lights. "You can be the girl later, if you want."

Dixie and Bart were the first to show. By my watch it was nine forty-nine A.M. when they came out of the elevator arm in arm and headed directly for the escalator. Dressed in a gray herringbone sport coat over a black silk T-shirt, Bart looked like the kind of kid you hoped would show up to take your daughter on a date. He kept his eyes pointed forward as if walking down a tunnel. Dixie Donner was a sight to behold.

If the brown suit hadn't been spray-painted on, you couldn't have been absolutely certain that she wasn't wearing drawers, and if the shoes hadn't had four-inch heels, which forced her to place one foot directly in front of the other, the unfettered thrashing of her buttocks would surely have been less noticeable than it was. The crowded lobby ground to a halt as she wobbled across the marble floor.

When I gave George the sign, he fell in behind the pair and rode down to the street not three steps behind.

Frank and Judy were having coffee in one of the conveniently located conversation areas around the lobby. Big Frank cocked an eyebrow my way, letting me know he was ready if anything happened before George got back. It didn't.

Five minutes passed before George was again at my side. "Who was that?"

I told him. He wrote it down.

"You mean the kid ain't her son?"

" 'Fraid not," I said.

"They took a cab. Normal and Billy Bob are on 'em," George announced.

We'd given each of the crew a hundred bucks, a notebook and a pencil to keep track of comings and goings, and a stirring admonition to stay alert and sober. I could only hope.

Mason Reese was next. At ten-twenty, he poked his head out of the elevator, twitched his whiskers, then darted across the lobby toward the reception desk, like a possum crossing the interstate.

"Mason Reese," I said to George. He made a note.

Reese strained up over the counter as he spoke with Marie, who lifted the phone, spoke at some length and hung up.

His business completed, he jammed his hands into his pants pockets and made for the great outdoors, with George in hot pursuit.

I strolled over to the desk. Marie looked up with a smile. "Mr. Waterman, what can I do for you?"

"What did Mr. Reese want?"

Her eyes darted to the right and then seemed to look inward.

I tried to make things easier on her. "You can check with Ms. Ricci, if you want," I said. "I won't be insulted."

The idea seemed to terrify her. "Oh, no, sir. N-no," she stammered. "Mr. Reese wanted to check on a voice-mail message he'd received late last night."

"What did he want to know?"

"He wanted to know why he hadn't heard the ring."

"And?"

"The operator said the party had requested voice mail

because it was so late. The party hadn't wanted to disturb Mr. Reese."

"Does the hotel still have a recording of the message?"

"That's the same thing Mr. Reese asked."

"And?"

"No. Not once Mr. Reese saw the red light flashing on his telephone and listened to the message." She shrugged. "It automatically erases and starts over."

I thanked her and turned around to find Marty Conlan standing right behind me. "Something I can help you with, Leo?"

Clapping him on the back, I said, "Thanks anyway, Marty. We're running like a well-oiled machine."

"Yeah," he snorted. "Well oiled being the key phrase."

Standing over by a pair of bellhops and a luggage cart was our boy Lance, his right hand encased in a white plaster cast the size of a volleyball, his eyes locked on mine in an open challenge.

"If your boy doesn't stop looking at me like that, I'm going to wet my pants," I said as I started back toward my position by the potted palms.

"Look at him," Marty whined. "What else am I gonna do with his big ass? Security is supposed to be discreet. Jesus, look at him."

"Paint the cast with Day-Glo and have him hail cabs."

"Very funny."

"I don't know, man. Just get him out of here, will ya? He sticks out like a sore thumb."

"Oh, har, har."

George was waiting for me. "He took off on foot. I sent Red and Mary after him."

At eleven-ten, the brass doors slid open and Drapeman stepped out.

"That's one of the Meyerson security guys. His name's Francona."

"Should I—" he started.

"No, let him go. He's not going far without the rest of them."

Ten minutes later, the rest of the Meyerson contingent left in a knot. Hill stepped out of the elevator first, took a quick inventory and moved aside as Abigail Meyerson led her brood across the floor. Hill brought up the rear. When I held up two fingers, George nodded and followed them down.

It wasn't long before he returned. "Had 'em a big stretch limo with the Francona fella drivin'. I sent Earlene and Harold in a cab."

"Who's left outside?"

"Ralphie, Flounder and Hot Shot."

"The only ones still upstairs are Jack Del Fuego, his driver and his girlfriend. They've also got a limo in the garage. I don't see them splitting up much. We'll send Flounder and Hot Shot after them. We'll keep Ralph around here in case something comes up."

I walked over to the concierge and arranged for Frank and Judy to be able to charge food to my room. Then I went over to their table.

"You guys go downstairs and have some lunch. George and I will take care of things here."

They didn't take a lot of convincing.

Forty minutes later, they reappeared looking fat, sassy and, unless I was mistaken, completely looped.

"My mistake," I said to George as they slithered back to their table. "From now on, it's room service."

"They're all right," George assured me.

Jack came off the elevator first. I checked my watch. Twelve-twenty, just like Rickey Ray had predicted. Today's suit was four acres of baby blue over the same type of ruffled tuxedo shirt he'd been wearing yesterday. Rickey Ray and Candace trailed along behind him as he bounced across the lobby.

"Del Fuego," I whispered to George. "The girlfriend, the bodyguard."

George's eyes were locked on Rickey Ray. "Jesus Christ, Leo, what happened to his face?"

"Car accident, I think."

"Jesus," he repeated as he started after them.

"Bring Ralph back in with you."

I stood and watched George glide down to the ground level.

I walked over to Frank and Judy. "You guys okay?" I inquired.

"Okay, shit, Leo. We're fantabulous," Judy slurred.

"Marvelous," Frank agreed with a bleary-eyed leer.

"I'm going to take George and Ralph upstairs and get them some lunch. You two think you can handle things for an hour or so?"

"Fantabulous," Judy said again.

"You remember what everybody looks like?"

"Sure," they said in unison.

"So tell me," I insisted.

And, by God, they did. They ran down all the players in elaborate detail. Judy even included several trenchant comments on what she called Dixie's May-December relationship. I was pleasantly surprised.

"It's in the bag," Frank assured me.

"That makes three of you," George said from over my shoulder, his voice dripping with envy. Ralph stepped in closer, hoping to soak up some of their fumes.

"Come on," I said, walking toward the elevators. "Let's get you boys a little lunch."

I pushed the button for nine.

"I'm going up to see the client," I announced. "You guys have keys. There's a room-service menu in the drawer under the phone. Order whatever you want." I made sure I had eye contact. "Don't get shitfaced, okay? I need you guys."

"Just a phlegm cutter," George promised.

As I watched them hustle down the corridor toward the room, I made a mental note to call room service and arrange for no more alcohol to be charged to the account. I then fished the security key out of my pocket, slid it into the slot in the elevator wall, moved it one half-turn to the right and pushed sixteen. Up, up and away.

Rowcliffe opened the door. "Ah, Mr. Waterman, won't you come in, please," he said as he stepped behind the door. He led me through the elaborate sitting room, into the master bedroom.

Sir Geoffrey was more or less where I'd left him. In bed. The burgundy silk sheets were now slate-gray silk sheets and he was reading instead of eating, but otherwise, everything was pretty much the same.

He folded *The Western Canon*, by Harold Bloom, across his middle and looked out over his half-glasses at me.

"Ah, Mr. Waterman," he said, using his left hand to prop the book. "Have you had the pleasure of reading Mr. Bloom?" he inquired.

When I allowed how I hadn't, he let the book fall.

"A pity," he said. "A most ambitious work. Unless I'm mistaken, Mr. Bloom makes quite a credible argument against any and all ideology in literary criticism. These days, a most unpopular notion, you know. Pluralism and all that." He made that shooing movement with his fingers again. "And, of course, his assertion regarding the loss of aesthetic and artistic standards is obvious to all but the most purblind supporters of this wave of multicultural jingoism." He said "multicultural" like he was saying "stool sample."

I kept in mind that this was the same guy who'd said that I was a PI of some renown, that money was no object and that the ten thousand bucks was just to get the operation off the ground. The rest was easy.

"Everybody is out for the day," I said.

"Report," was all he said, so I did.

I gave him the whole thing. Who left, how, and when. When I finished, he said. "This evening should be easier."

"Are most of them going to the opening ceremonies?"

"All of them. Señor Alomar assures me that Mr. Reese and both contingents have reservations at the banquet."

"Which starts when?"

"At nine."

He was right, which was good. Once the quarry was back in the coop this afternoon, I could let most of the crew go. This was ideal, because they tended to get drunker and less responsible as the day went on. That way they'd have plenty of time to get hammered, sober up and get back here in the morning. Timing is everything.

Sir Geoffrey Miles picked up his book, adjusted his glasses and began to read. Years of training has taught me that when people begin reading in your presence, it's probably time to go, so I headed out. "Bravo," Sir Geoffrey said to the book as I cleared the doorway.

Rowcliffe miraculously appeared at my side. The guy was scary.

12

George and Ralph were at the far end of the room, mauling their room-service order. George had removed his suit coat and rolled up his sleeves. Ralph had shucked off his jacket and tucked a hand towel into his shirt as a bib. In a touching display of responsibility, they'd ordered just one six-pack between them. A Les Schwab tire commercial blared from the TV. Ralph, his mouth stuffed with cheeseburger, waved a bottle opener at the screen.

"Bel Fuero," he gargled.

"What about him?"

He chewed hard and tried to swallow. No go.

"Ob tb."

"He was on TV?"

He nodded and lifted two of the Heinekens out of the silver ice bucket. He opened one and took a long pull. I watched a ball of food the size of a gopher move down his throat and disappear.

George was bent low over the table, a plate in one hand and a domed silver cover in the other, his nose working like a bloodhound's. As he sniffed, his scalp reddened between the rows of his pure white hair. He put the cover down and pointed at the plate.

"Who yakked on my fish?" he demanded.

"That's pesto," said Ralph, opening another beer. "You know, basil and olive oil and stuff like—"

George pointed with the sterling fork. "Hey, I want to hear from you, Drunken Hines, I'll let you know."

It was not surprising that George was getting a bit testy. He had, after all, been up working since eight A.M. and was still sober at one-thirty in the afternoon, a happenstance of such profound rarity as to rival the millennial appearance of certain comets. He grabbed the dripping bottle from Ralph and downed it in a single gulp.

"Aaah," he murmured enthusiastically.

"And lots of garlic," Ralph added.

George looked disgustedly my way. "Like I'm gonna be takin' my culinary advice from Mr. Mighty Dog here, right?"

Ralph's grin grew wider. "And sometimes pine nuts, too."

"You hear this, Leo? The proud inventor of the Little Friskies Burrito is lookin' to trade recipes with me. Pine nuts, my ass," he muttered. "Can you believe that? Pine nuts."

"You don't want it?" Ralph asked, reaching for the salmon.

George quickly pulled the plate back. "I didn't say I wasn't gonna eat it, man. I just wanted to know what that green stuff was." He peered at it again. "Kinda looks like those little piles Flounder used to leave all over the place."

"Remember that time?" Ralph asked.

George leered. "The teapot."

"And Jimmy Young just added water."

"Said it had an earthy flavor."

They shared a touching moment of remembrance.

Ralph stuffed the other half of the cheeseburger in his mouth and chewed contentedly; suddenly his eyes grew wide.

"Bere bere." He pointed.

It wasn't Jack himself. It was that picture of Jack and Bunky from today's *Post Intelligencer*, blown up into a life-sized cardboard cutout. It was Monday. It was *Afternoon Northwest* with Lola King. Jesus.

Lola King was our homegrown afternoon slime queen. Has your mom been giving it up to sailors? Tune in today. Got gay grandparents into bondage? Next Monday. Women who love men who love mastiffs? Check your local listings. Lola was a champion of the public's right to know . . . whether they wanted to or not.

She was a boilerplate blonde with a bony, washboard breastbone which, for some reason, she had always been determined to share with the universe. She'd been on local TV for all of my adult life, and during that time nearly everything she had worn had pointedly emphasized this remarkably barren and ever-expanding part of her anatomy. The annual expansion of chest acreage had, over the years, spawned wide speculation, including omnipresent whispers that *she* was actually a *he*. L-O-L-A Lola.

Bruce Gill, a guy I know at KOMO-TV, claims that, because she received a number of unflattering letters regarding her drooping cleavage back in the late seventies, she now tucks her tits under her arms while she's on the air, a notion which I choose to offhandedly dismiss, since the image of her winking out from behind is more than my tortured psyche can bear.

She held the mike in one hand while she patted Bunky's massive cardboard rump with the other. "For those of you just joining us, we are here today and for the rest of this week on a special mission of mercy." She then stepped to the right and threw her free arm around Bunky's neck. "We are here on a mission of mercy, a mission to save a life, a mission to save a heart," she intoned.

Without warning, she slid down to the far end of the cutout.

"Yes, heart, Mr. Del Fuego." The camera panned Jack's demonic countenance while Lola continued the narration.

"But you wouldn't know anything about hearts, would you, now, Mr. Jack Del Fuego, because you don't have one, do you? At least not in the sense that the rest of us have a heart."

Jack kept right on smiling and winking as Lola King stared at the teleprompter and recited the whole poor-little-girl, 4-H, family-pet nightmare in unrhymed iambic pentameter. Her recitation was punctuated by periodic spasms of lamentation from the studio audience, which had unwittingly assumed the role of the classic Greek chorus.

"*Afternoon Northwest* invited Mr. Del Fuego to appear on the program this afternoon, but he refused."

"Ooooh," from the audience.

"Here with us this afternoon . . . representing NUTSS, which as most of you know stands for Neighbors United To Stop Suffering, an organization whose sole purpose is to guarantee the rights and safety of our four-footed, our finned and our feathered friends. Let's have a warm *Afternoon Northwest* welcome for . . . Clarissa Hedgpeth."

A recorded version of "Walk with the Animals, Talk with the Animals" blared out of the set as the Hedgpeth woman strode onstage, leading her signature white standard poodle, Bruce. Wild applause.

She looked like Carol Channing with clinical depression. Same white-haired, wide-eyed wonder, but without any of the fun. Just an abiding confusion. Clarissa Hedgpeth always appeared to be whistling in the dark, as if only her trembling smile held back the impending floodwaters of disaster.

She waved at the audience. "Thank you. Thank you," she said.

Bruce flopped down on the floor at his mistress's feet and stared stupidly at the audience. His body was shaved and waved in typical poodle fashion, a puff of hair here and a knot there, including a tennis-ball-size hairball at the tip of his tail. The camera panned back to include the coiffured mutt in the shot. As if on cue, the dog lifted his leg and began to vigorously lick his shaved privates. The camera quickly panned back to close-ups of the two women. The audience tittered.

"I wish I could do that," said Ralph, pushing a fistful of fries into his already stuffed mouth.

"You probably ought to try to pet him first," George suggested.

They yucked it up, stomping around the floor, repeating, ". . . pet him first . . . you better pet him first . . ." and pounding each another on the back.

Much as it pained me, I interrupted the revelry.

"I'm glad you fellas are enjoying your lunch so much, but do you think maybe you could snap it up a bit so Judy and Frank aren't down there all alone for too damn long?"

"What are you gonna do?" Ralph complained.

"I'm going out looking for Bunky."

"Ain't nothin' for us to do downstairs," Ralph said.

"I want to know when everybody comes back and how," I lied.

With these guys, idle hands were truly the devil's workshop. "It'll take all four of you to do that," I said. "Write it all down."

They gave me the silent treatment as they finished up.

On the tube, Clarissa Hedgpeth was dripping sincerity and holding forth on the merits of all creatures great and small.

"Animal liberationists do not separate out the human animal, so there is no rational basis for saying that a human being has special rights. A rat is a pig is a dog is a boy. They are all mammals."

With the possible exception of Lola, of course.

Lola looked concerned but continued to smile and proffer the mike. Clarissa went on. "During World War Two, six million Jews were killed in concentration camps. But do you realize that next year, over six billion broiler chickens will be slaughtered so that Americans can . . ."

I watched as thirty-five years in the business passed before Lola King's eyes. She could see it. This was the end. If she wasn't careful here, they'd crucify her for this one. I'd read in the paper about how management had tried to replace her with one of the weather girls and that the ensuing age-discrimination suit had kept them from turning her out to pasture or, even worse, from sending her back to the beginning, doing the inclement-weather spots, standing out in Ocean Shores in her parka, screaming into the mike while an eighty-mile-an-hour gale blew ice spicules up her ass. No, thanks. She jumped in.

"But surely, Clarissa, you can't be equating poultry to people. We wouldn't want our viewers to think that you were saying . . ."

Clarissa did her best wide-eyed space princess. "Oh, but I am, Lola. There's no difference between Bruce and us . . ."

Bruce looked insulted. Lola stared to the left of the camera and narrowed her eyes to mere slits as a sudden commercial break cut Clarissa Hedgpeth off in mid-slur. Now for a word from our sponsor.

George and Ralph wiped their mouths, hiked up their britches and started across the room. As they walked, I thought I heard little bells, but I was so involved in wondering how many angry letters the station was going to get that I pushed the thought aside.

I went over to the desk, pulled the phone book out of the drawer, thumbed through it and began removing pages. As I started to replace both the phone book and the room-service menu, I noticed a gold key on a chain, resting on the bottom of the drawer. The mini-bar key.

That's when it hit me. The goddamn tinkling. I bent, opened the little door and found what I'd expected. They'd excavated the sucker, taking about half of it and spreading the rest out neatly on the shelves to cover their tracks. Excluding the pop, of course. They'd left all the pop. That stuff'll kill ya.

I went into the bathroom, brushed my teeth, washed my face and hands, then changed into a pair of jeans and an old Huskies T-shirt.

The station must have run seven or eight minutes' worth of commercials, because when I came back into the room, the program came back from the break, just in time to sign off. "Thank you, ladies and gentlemen," Lola said. "We're out of time today, but tune in tomorrow as we continue our investigative report on animal rights. Tomorrow's guests will be Steven Drew of the NVS—the National Vegan Society—and Konrad Kramer, spokesman for the ALF, which is the Animal Liberation Front. Until then, I'm Lola King and *this* is *Afternoon Northwest.*" Fade to black.

I turned off the tube, stuffed the Yellow Pages into my pocket and pulled the door closed behind me.

B

It was five forty-five when I rolled the Fiat around the circular drive of the Olympic Star and crawled out. Squatting there among the gleaming luxury sedans, the Fiat stuck out like a wart. I handed the nearest uniform the keys and two bucks, then stood on the sidewalk and stretched myself out as he peered dejectedly at the little car. I was still readjusting my lumbar vertebrae while he raced it out into the street and disappeared.

Across University Avenue, the crew was spread out, doing what it does best, lounging on a set of concrete stairs in between the Delta Airlines office and the side entrance to Rainier Square. I counted noses. All eight of them were there. Five on the stairs. Billy Bob, Mary and Hot Shot Scott asleep on the upper landing. Forgetting he was undercover, Flounder gave me a small, wasted wave as I turned to enter the hotel.

George was picking his teeth with a matchbook cover and rocking on his heels at the top of the escalator. As I stepped from the moving track, he lurched over and threw a playful arm around my shoulder.

"You find the cow?"

His eyes were bleary; he smelled like a distillery. Having spent the afternoon kicking turds around stockyards and boarding stables, I was in no mood for further fertilizer.

"Just the part that's stuck to my sneakers," I answered.

If he got the joke, he didn't let on. "All the pigeons are in the coop," he reported. I looked around him, toward the tables at the far side of the lobby.

Ralph had joined Frank and Judy at their table. The cocktail hour was in full swing. Ralph's movements had that loose-jointed quality he gets when he's out of it.

"I want you and Frank and Judy to stick around for a bit. Pay everybody and send them home. Tell them to be back at eight tomorrow morning, looking and smelling good."

"How long we gotta stick around?"

"Seven. Maybe a little after. They're all going to the same shindig this evening. Once they're all out and about, you guys can go."

He stuck out his hand. I slapped six hundred dollars down on his palm. "Pay yourself while you're at it, big fella," I said.

Even at my most limber and malleable, I don't believe what George suggested I do next would have been possible.

I moved to the right, pushed the up button and waited. Three elevators down, the door opened. I hustled over and stepped in.

The room had been straightened and the room-service cart removed when I got there. I smiled. Although it made no sense, I was always vaguely insulted when I left a room a wreck and then returned to find it still in disarray. Despite the fact that no one had ever cleaned up after me, I had always been filled with the all-abiding belief that someone should do it. That it was natural and preordained. That whatever little piles and wrinkles I might leave in my wake should miraculously be returned to their previous states, thus eliminating all record of my passing.

I emptied my pockets onto the sideboard and was removing my jacket when I noticed the blinking red light on the phone. I threw the coat on the bed and picked up the receiver. Following the printed directions, I dialed six-three. An electronic voice said, "You have one message, left today at two-ten. To listen to your message, please push one." I followed along. And they said I wasn't a team player. "This is Mason Reese," the recording said. "Yesterday, you said if anything interesting developed . . ." He actually chuckled into the phone. "Maybe you better give me a call." Click. "End of message," the electronic voice droned. "To listen to this message again . . ."

Without thinking, I depressed the button and dialed eight-one-four. I let it ring about twenty times. When I replaced the receiver, the red light on the phone went out and the one in my head went on.

Sometimes I like to tell myself that, if nothing else, middle age has taught me to follow my instincts. If it feels right, do it. If not, don't. A creed as simple as that should be easy to follow. And it would be, except for the other guy. My lifelong companion. The one who pokes his nose in where it doesn't belong. That guy. The one who just has to get in the last word, no matter what. Every time. Always. The one who hits my golf shots into the trees when I'm not looking. Him. He and I took the stairs, figuring we'd be there long before the elevator arrived.

I stepped onto the eighth floor in time to see a gray-clad maid backing into a room at the far end of the hall, leaning way back, dragging her heavily laden cart over the threshold.

As I strolled down the carpeted hallway, I tried to figure out what tune she was whistling as she worked. I was sure I'd heard it before. I hummed the melody to myself, hoping that would help. That's probably why I'd already knocked on Mason Reese's door a couple of times before I noticed it was slightly ajar.

Down the hall, the whistling continued. She'd left the cart in the doorway, propping the door open as maids are taught to do. A brown arm reached out and grabbed a spray bottle from the cart and disappeared back inside.

I won't lie. My submarine dive horn was blasting in my ears. *Ahoooga Ahoooga.* Dive! Dive! Every instinct in my body screamed for me to turn around and go quietly back from whence I had come. Instead, I checked the corridor again and elbowed the door open.

The light from the hall traveled only about six feet into the room, but that was far enough. On the carpet, midway between where I stood and the elegant little two-seater couch against the rear wall, a slick patch of goo glistened like black obsidian in the half darkness. I'd seen it before and knew what it was.

I used the back of my hand to flip the switch on the left side of the door. It was already up. I flipped it down. Nothing. I took a deep breath, trying to calm my stomach. I would have walked away, I swear I would have, but . . .

The whistling stopped. I quickly looked to my right. The cart was moving back into the hall. I could see both of her arms and one foot. In a single motion, without a single thought, I stepped into the room and closed the door behind me.

I leaned back against the door. The room wasn't totally dark. A muted luminance filtered under the doors leading to the bedroom. I could see the white plastic DO NOT DISTURB sign on the floor to my right, and I could still make out the wet patch on the carpet. Even better, now I could smell its heady, metallic scent. I kept my stomach in place with a series of deep breaths. I waited.

The whistling resumed, louder now. It was Abba. "Dancing Queen." The Hispanic maid was whistling "Dancing Queen." Talk about a global village. A key scraped in the lock. The door opened an inch before I leaned back hard and growled, "No. Not now. Come back later."

I heard the key slide out. I kept taking deep breaths and counted to sixty before turning around and peering out through the magnified peephole. She stood in the hall with her hands on her hips staring at the door. I put my back to the door and waited. Three hundred this time. When I peeked again, she was gone.

Keeping as far from the slime as possible, I crossed the room and switched on the table lamp. In the harsh light, the slop was no longer black but a deep rust red, sprinkled here and there with bits of what looked like oysters. I decided not to think about the oysters, instead focusing on several small gray-and-white feathers, whose airy arms fluttered in the artificial breeze.

I used my knuckles to push the bedroom doors apart. The light was coming from under the bathroom door. I walked over the threshold carefully, staying out of the occasional blood trail. The bed had been turned down far enough to expose the pillows, one of which now sat in the middle of the flowered bedspread, its pillowcase gone, bleeding goose feathers from a nasty-looking hole in its striped middle.

I kept my eyes on the floor and my hands in my pockets as I sidled along the length of the room, my butt dragging across the face of the dresser. No body on either side of the bed. Reaching the far side of the bed, I knelt down, took a deep breath, lifted the bed skirt and peeked under. Nothing.

I unbuttoned the cuff of my shirt, drew my hand back inside and used the cuff to try the bathroom door. Locked. I leaned my weight against the door and discovered one of the few drawbacks of five-star hotels. Nothing is cheap. I reached in my pocket and pulled out the electronic key for my room. I knelt by the lock, wiggled the thin piece of plastic into the crack between the door and the jamb, covered my right hand with the cuff again and gave the door a hard wiggle. On the second try, the plastic key began to bend and then moved forward a quarter inch. With my left hand I held the card in the lock; with my right hand I tried to pull the door open. Nothing doing.

Careful to keep the cuff between my hand and the crystal doorknob, I gave it another series of tremors, concentrating this time on pulling down on the knob. With a rush, the card slipped all the way between the door and the jamb.

I was smiling inwardly as I pushed myself to my feet and jerked the door open. I swallowed the smile in a hurry, using my mouth to breathe instead. Lo and behold, there was the missing pillowcase, presently holding not a pillow but what appeared from the doorway to be the lion's share of Mason Reese's brains.

He sat on the toilet fully dressed, his head thrown back and his mouth wide open as if singing arias to the balcony. The bottom third of his face was starting to show beneath the hem of the pillowcase as the weight of the glutinous material dripping from the back of the sack gradually pulled it off his head.

He'd been shot just beneath the nose. Most of his yellow upper teeth, some still connected to bone, now rested haphazardly on and around his thickening tongue. I reached over and touched him on the shoulder. He was just beginning to stiffen, and the body waved like that of a drunk. I held my breath, not daring to move until the corpse settled down and stopped rocking.

I left him as I found him, sitting there agape, losing his bag under the bright lights. The door relocked itself as I closed it slowly, then retraced my steps through both rooms to the hall door.

I leaned against the door again and took stock. I figured this was the point of no return. Sooner rather than later, I was going to have to step out into the corridor. I'd already made up my mind that if I was seen by anyone, I was going to go back to my room and call my attorney and the police, in precisely that order, and then sit down and wait to see who showed up first. I was betting on Jed. These days you can get food delivered before the police show up.

I cracked open the door and looked out toward the elevators. Nothing. I put my ear to the crack and listened. Again nothing. One . . . two . . .

In one fluid motion I yanked open the door, stepped out into the hall and shut the door behind me. So far, so good. The smell of rusting iron swirled about my head and then lost itself in the sterile air of the corridor. I turned and beat feet down the hall.

I took three steps before the elevator bonged. I thought about sprinting but decided against it. I was still seventy feet from the stairway door, so I stopped, put my hands on my hips and turned around. The cast came out first.

None of this thumb-and-fingers-sticking-out crap. The doctor had encased the whole damn hand in a five-pound ball of cement. The rest of Lance appeared next, followed by his buddy, Mr. Lincoln Aimes. The sight of me standing in the hall drew them up short. Lance stuck out his left arm, keeping Aimes in the elevator.

"Go down and call the cops, Linc," Lance said.

Aimes pushed the red button on the walkie-talkie he held in his right hand and opened his mouth to speak. Lance beat him to the punch. "No. Go downstairs, man," he said, pawing at the device.

The doors began to close. Aimes, looking confused, used his forearm to force them back open. "What are you—" he started.

"Just do it, man. Go down and get the cops."

Lance turned my way. "I've got something to settle with Waterman here. Waterman here is going to resist being taken into custody."

Linc didn't like the idea one bit. "Aw, now, Lance, man, remember what Mr. Conlan said. We should just—"

Lance was a poor listener. Using both hands, he pushed Aimes deeper into the elevator. "Marty's not here, man. He took his old lady to a movie. You just call the cops. You're out of it, okay?" I heard him say. "He didn't bust your thumb," he added, reaching in and pushing a button.

Lincoln Aimes was still protesting as the doors hissed shut.

The sleeve of Lance's blue blazer had been split up the seam to allow for the cast, with only a safety pin at the wrist keeping the thing from flapping in the breeze. He jerked the pin loose and started shuffling down the hall in my direction with the torn sleeve hanging straight down, feeling around the floor with his lead foot like he expected a trapdoor or something. I held up a hand.

"This may not be the time for this, kid." I said.

"Oh, it's the time, all right," he said.

He held his left arm forward like a ram, allowing the right one to dangle down by his right knee as he moved slowly forward.

One thing was for sure. If he hit me with the cast, I was going to the graveyard, not the hospital. The more swings he got, the better his chances became. No doubt about it. This was going to have to be short and sweet.

I let him get within about eight feet and then began to match him shuffle for shuffle; every one he took forward, I took one back, until I sensed we'd found a rhythm, and then, as he lifted his lead foot to plod forward, I closed the distance in a hurry.

He brought the cast up and over the top, not so much trying to punch me as to drive me through the floor. I was one step too quick and took his forearm high on the shoulder. The force jammed my neck into my torso, sending an electric shock racing down my spinal column and momentarily loosening my joints.

I could smell the old coffee on his breath as I grabbed both of his ears and drove my forehead upward, aiming at an imaginary spot about a foot behind his face. I remember the sound of impacted flesh as bone met bone with a wet crack, and a brief recognition that Lance had a head like a rock . . . then, only the giddy feeling of flight.

I saw a green dragon kite darting in a clear blue sky, one moment climbing hard, the next angling dangerously toward the whitecaps. The dragon needed a longer tail. I reached to jerk the string hard, to turn and run toward land, when, without warning, the dragon hovered for a moment above the waves, looked me right in the eye, then shimmied tail-first down into the blue water. The string had broken.

14

I overheard one of the uniforms telling a new arrival that they'd found us lying on the carpet with our legs entwined, both of us out cold. I wasn't a bit surprised. I had a knot on my forehead the size of a bread box and a brain-tumor headache.

I didn't know what the hell had happened to Lance. He was gone when the smelling salts cauterized my nasal passages and dragged me back to consciousness. All that remained were two small bloodstains on the hall carpet. At his end, not mine, I was glad to see.

It was six-fifteen; I was sitting with my hands cuffed to a wide leather belt which was locked around my waist, so I could still read my watch. It was odd to be sitting there, doing nothing, in a room two doors down the hall from Mason Reese, while an army of cops and technicians scurried about the eighth-floor corridor.

I'd given the two SPD detectives my name, rank and serial number and then completely clammed up. My attorney, Jed James, had arrived thirty minutes later and was now making waves somewhere down the hall. For the Seattle law enforcement community, Jed James was a nightmare come true. Jed's ten years as the ACLU's chief litigator in New York had cultivated a confrontational manner seemingly designed to appall the average, ever-polite Seattleite. No cause was too unpopular, no infringement too slight. To my knowledge, if you counted appeals, his record remained unscathed.

I heard his voice rise from somewhere in the hall. I could only catch the words "brain damage," but was comforted to know he was thinking of me.

The door opened and Jed began to back in. He was still talking to someone I couldn't see. "I can't promise anything, Detective," he was saying. "Let me have a few words with my client and I'll get back to you." The other person said something, but I couldn't make it out.

Jed closed the door behind him and walked over and sat on the edge of the bed, pushing his face in close to mine, speaking softly.

"You really did tell them nothing."

"Correctomundo."

"And when we talked before, you told me everything." He made it a statement but meant it as a question, so I told him again.

"Well, then," he said, "I know this is going to sound weird coming from me, Leo, but, all things considered, my best advice is to tell them everything you know."

My head throbbed as I raised it to look in his eyes. He didn't look drunk or stoned, so I said, "I'm found lying stone cold outside the door of a guy with his brains blown out, and what's supposed to be the most incisive legal mind in the Pacific Northwest is advising me to spill my guts?"

He folded his arms across his chest. "They don't make you for the murder, Leo. They keep saying they do, but they don't mean it. They sure as hell are going to keep pretending they do, though, unless you give them a hand. If we give them what we have on the murder, they'll back off the rest of the shit. You know the game as well as I do, my man."

"What rest of the shit?"

"The first-degree assault, the tampering with evidence, the breaking and entering, that little shit, you know. The shit you're actually guilty of."

"The kid attacked me."

"We'll worry about that later. Whadda you say?"

"I don't want to admit to being in the room," I said.

"You said you didn't touch anything."

"I didn't. But they're really not going to like me being in there."

"They've got a maid who says somebody was in eight-fourteen about five minutes before she reported it to security. If you tell them that wasn't you, it changes the whole direction of the investigation."

"They're gonna go rat-shit," I insisted.

"You let me worry about that. We'll trade them what you know for what you did."

I thought it over. He was right. "I'd have to talk to *my* client."

Without a word, he left the room, leaving the door open. SPD uniforms leaned against the wall on either side of the door. Through the opening I saw a medical examiner's assistant named Morris scurry by and realized that I'd never been sure whether Morris was his first or his last name. I was still ruminating on this quirk of nature when Jed re-entered the room carrying a standard black desk phone, which was, I suspected, the same one they'd taken out of here earlier.

He attached the cord to the jack in the back of the phone, stretched the cord out and set the thing in my lap. With his left hand he held the receiver to my ear. "Number," he said.

"One-six-zero-zero."

He dialed. I listened as Rowcliffe answered.

"Sir Geoffrey Miles's suite," he said.

"Rowcliffe. It's Leo Waterman."

"Good evening, sir."

"I need to talk to Sir Geoffrey."

"Sir Geoffrey is dressing, sir, and, if I may say so, having a rather dreadful time with his tie. This might not be an altogether propitious moment."

"Tell him Mason Reese is dead," I said.

The guy was amazing. "Very good, sir," was all he said.

Jed was staring intently at me. I nodded my head.

Miles came on in a rush. "You say?" he huffed.

"I do."

"Report."

He never interrupted for the ten minutes it took me to give him the whole ball of wax. When I'd finished, he said. "You are indubitably correct. I'm amazed the police have not been at my door already."

"It won't be long," I said. "Too many people know."

I heard him take a deep breath. "Better here than at the banquet, I suppose." he said finally. "Yes, Mr. Waterman, by all means. We have no choice but to cooperate fully with the authorities." Another deep breath. "I leave the matter to your discretion." With a click, he was gone.

Jed replaced the receiver and unplugged the phone, allowing the cord to fall upon the carpet.

"Tell the cops I want to chat," I said.

He carried the phone with him out of the room. I sat there and fiddled with the pair of handcuffs that connected my hands to the thick leather belt around my middle. Jed appeared in the doorway.

"They've got a stenographer downstairs," he said.

I nodded as someone spoke in the hall. The two cops on the door came in, took me by the elbows and hoisted me out of the chair.

Jed still held the phone when I was propelled out into the hall and up toward the elevators. On the far side of the bank of elevators, a yellow police ribbon was stretched across the hall. About five thousand dollars' worth of SPD overtime milled about the corridor in small groups.

The underlying buzz of conversation ground to silence as I walked up the hall with my escorts. The county Mountie stepped away from the doors as we approached. As the cop on my right let go of my arm and reached for the button, the light came on, the bong sounded and the center door slid open. George Paris stood swaying in the car, his tie loose at the neck and his new blue double-breasted suit buttoned wrong.

His bleary eyes took me in. He got half a step forward before the King County cop bounced off the far wall and pounded him in the chest with a stiff arm, sending him staggering back into the darkness at the rear of the compartment.

The county cop turned to my keepers. "I've told this joker three times that he can't come up here. I'm taking him in." As the two cops grunted their approval, he reached behind him for his handcuffs.

"Officer George," I yelled. "You and your friends better get out of here, You hear me? Get lost, Officer George."

His hand hesitated at the snap to his handcuff case. He looked quizzically in my direction. "My name's not George."

I suddenly ran toward him, dragging my escorts with me. I heard the muted bell as Jed dropped the phone. The county cop took three quick steps in our direction, put both hands on my chest and stopped me in my tracks. The elevator doors slid shut.

"Shit," he said, looking over his shoulder. I pushed hard against his hands, again diverting his attention.

Jed was at my side. "Don't hurt him. Don't hurt him. He's had a blow to the head. He's delusional."

From the doorway of eight-fourteen a short man in a blue suit hurried our way, pulling a uniformed SPD officer in his wake.

"What's your name?" he demanded of the county cop.

"Jacobson, sir."

Blue Suit pushed the down button several times as he spoke. "Get on your radio and tell your boys downstairs to stop and detain that man—and anybody he's with," he added.

Jacobson opened his mouth and then changed his mind, opting instead to do as he was told. Using the radio on his shoulder, he relayed George's description to somebody named Bobby in the lobby.

"Sixty to sixty-five, maybe five-ten, one-fifty or so. Little skinny guy, white hair slicked straight back. Blue suit, red tie. Yeah . . . Yeah, that's right."

The elevator arrived with the usual fanfare and the SPD officer started down after George. Jacobson looked pained.

"Is your name George Jacobson?" Blue Suit asked.

"No, sir. Jeff."

"Then what do you suppose all that Officer George crap was about, Officer Jacobson? Got any ideas? Take your time now."

Jacobson traced a design in the carpet with his toe. "He was telling the old guy to get lost, wasn't he?"

"Very good," was all Blue Suit said to the cop. Then, he stepped close to me, pushing his face in mine. "You think you're pretty cute, don't you?"

"I have a fairly positive self-image."

"My client has had an extreme trauma," Jed began.

"When we get your little friend back up here, we'll see about your self-fucking-image, pal."

I turned to Jed and said in my best Bugs Bunny voice, "He said a baaaad word." Jed's mouth twitched, but he hung in there.

"See, I told you," Jed said to the cop.

"Tell me about the rabbits, George. Tell me again about the rabbits," I said to Jed. Unable to keep his face together, he stepped over and pushed the down button. Just to make sure.

Blue Suit stood there staring at me in stony silence, playing some sort of mind game with me, he imagined. I think maybe I was supposed to get all mushy and then beg him to let me kiss his ring and confess. My head hurt too badly for any more snappy repartee, so, in an unusual show of restraint, I shut up.

Jacobson's radio was squawking, He turned away so we couldn't hear. Blue Suit hustled over. I watched as Jacobson filled him in. Blue Suit listened for five seconds and then began barking orders in a strangled whisper. As he spoke, the county cop leaned away and poured the translation into his shoulder. I couldn't hear what was said, but one thing was sure. They didn't have George. I could tell by their body language. George should have been in the lobby and in custody by now, and he wasn't. The old dog was running.

Another elevator arrived. The cop in charge of my left elbow put out a hand to hold the door open and said, "Lieutenant Driscoll."

Blue Suit glanced over disgustedly and nodded. "Tell them I'll be down shortly," he said. The last image I captured before being led into the elevator was that of Blue Suit whispering heatedly into the county cop's ear. Jacobson just kept agreeing and checking the carpet for clues.

We got off on M, for mezzanine, turned left down the deep red carpet and then up a short flight of stairs into what the hotel called Embassy Row, a series of elegant meeting rooms lodged between the second and third floors on the north side of the building. With all the movable walls in place, there were three rooms on each side of the hall. The common area between the rows of rooms was littered with both city and county officers, who stopped their banter to watch me go by.

The last door on the left held a gold plate that read SENATE ROOM. The cop on my right held my elbow with one hand while he opened the door with the other. Jed slid by the cops and entered first, ranting as he walked. "What kind of inquisition is this?"

There were three people in the room. Alone on the left side of the long table was a woman of about fifty-five with hair more salt than pepper, done up in a kind of Lady Bird Johnson double flip. She had a glass of water and a court stenographer's machine in front of her.

Except for the extreme corners, the table was covered with

a spotless white linen. At the far end, between the suits, the cloth was covered by the contents of my wallet and card case, spread out in rows. The bare corners were occupied by a man and a woman. Each had a neatly arranged assortment of pens, pencils, highlighters, notebooks and pocket tape recorders laid out and ready. Looked a lot like the first day of school.

The man was pushing forty and already bald. Hawk-faced, he had an athletically trim figure that, even as he sat, spoke of fitness. A gold name tag read Det. Sgt. Rob Lobdell. One of the new breed of detectives, I guessed. Probably had a law degree and probably would never pull his piece in anger. Kind of made me nostalgic for thugs.

The woman was a bit younger and rather heavyset. A redhead with one of those almost pure white complexions prone to freckles. She wore a simple blue dress with a wide skirt. She spoke first. "Mr. Waterman, my name is Martha Lawrence. I'm an assistant district attorney for the City of Seattle." She gestured slightly toward her right. "This is Detective Lobdell of the SPD." She looked at Jed for the first time.

Jed was not prone to wasting time on introductions.

"I trust that since my client has offered his full cooperation, you will now be able to see your way clear to remove these morbid manacles from his person."

Lobdell curled his lip. "Like hell. This man is—"

Lawrence waved him off. While the cops disconnected me from both the belt and the cuffs, Lobdell sulked and pretended to check his notes. I thought he was going to object again when she told the officers to wait outside, but he settled for shaking his head in disgust.

"Mr. James," she said with a sigh.

"Ms. Lawrence. So nice to see you again," he said.

"You're sure of that, are you?" she inquired

"Oh, but I did so enjoy our last little tryst."

"Yes . . . I'll bet you did."

"It *is* so much easier when one wins," he admitted.

She burned a hole in his brain with her green eyes and then shifted her gaze to me. "Mr. Waterman, I don't know what happened upstairs, but I'm going to advise you of your rights. Forgive me if you've heard this before." She did it without reading it off the card. I was impressed.

"Please have a seat."

Jed and I sat across from the stenographer.

"I am told that you wish to cooperate with us in the matter of the death of Mason Reese." She spelled out the last name.

I let Jed do the talking. "I wish to make a statement on behalf of my client," he said.

"Then do so," Lawrence said.

"My client wishes to state, for the record, that he has no knowledge of, and was in no way party to, the death of Mason Reese. Like any other concerned citizen of our republic, Mr. Waterman, of course, wishes to cooperate with the duly appointed authorities in any way possible and to aid in the speedy disposition of this affair."

"Is that it?" she said when he'd finished.

Jed said it was.

"Well, then, please allow me also to begin with a statement." Again she leveled her gaze on me. "Mr. Waterman, I am given to understand that you have become accustomed to preferential treatment by nearly all the city agencies." I opened my mouth to protest, but she added, "Including law enforcement agencies. I give you fair warning, Mr. Waterman. None of that is going to happen here. Both Detective Lobdell and I are fairly new to the Seattle area. Unlike you, we have no history here, and as far as we are concerned, neither do you."

"Are you threatening my client?"

She ignored Jed. "Mr. Waterman, you are about to be charged with first-degree assault, unlawful entry and accessory to murder. I don't have to tell you that these are serious charges." She rambled on for another three minutes about how I was both literally and metaphorically fucked, since all the evidence against me was airtight and I was surely going to spend my declining years as a sperm-drenched sex toy in a maximum-security prison. I couldn't make up my mind whether she was trying to scare me or to show Lobdell what a hard-ass she was. Probably both.

"You skipped a bunch of stuff," I said.

"And what would that be?"

"You left out the whole part where you ask me the questions and I give you the snappy answers."

Jed was giving me the shut-up squeeze.

"They always ask me dumb-ass questions before they threaten me. It's in the cop book somewhere. First questions, then threats. Look it up. It definitely needs to be done in that order."

"I wish to confer privately with my client," Jed said suddenly.

Lawrence rose. "As you wish," she said. Lobdell walked up to the stenographer's side and helped her with her chair.

Jed waited until the door closed behind them before he spoke.

"It's damage control."

"I thought we were going to deal."

"We're in rough company."

"The Lawrence woman?"

"We have a history," he said. "It would be fair to say that her past dealings with me have—how shall I say—somewhat steepened her career path. You might be better off with different representation."

"Not a chance."

"You may be tarred with the same brush."

"Sounds like I've already been tarred with my own brush. Hell, it sounds like my brush may be worse than your brush."

He nodded. "You've never met her before?"

"Never."

Jed took a deep breath. "If they had any intention of dealing, they wouldn't have sent her. They're gonna do this by the numbers."

"Then, as you said, it's damage control."

Damage control meant that we told them as little as humanly possible. That we had to protect against information erosion. We wouldn't specifically lie about anything, except what it was we remembered. Nobody can prove what it is a person does or does not remember. We would answer their questions in as succinct and specific a manner as possible, carefully avoiding telling them anything more than what they asked. Jed would jump in and take any questions that he thought required his attention. When in doubt, we'd do the old Ollie North Tango: *To the best of my recollection* . . .

When the authorities decide they want to get serious, it's best to have an ace in the hole. It's no skin off their noses one way or the other whether you go home or you go to jail. Either way, they go home and eat their young. Like everything else, it's just a system of trade-offs. If you expect them to look the other way on your transgressions, you damn well better have something good to trade.

Jed walked to the door and invited our tormentors back into the room. Lobdell got the stenographer settled and then picked up where Lawrence had left off. "Were you operating as a private investigator during your stay here at the hotel?"

"Yes."

"By whom were you employed?"

"Sir Geoffrey Miles."

The pair exchanged a short glance.

"With a *J* or a *G*?" Lawrence asked.

I spelled it out for them.

"Where will we find this gentleman?" Lobdell asked.

"Room sixteen hundred."

Lobdell excused himself and stepped out in the hall for a moment. Lawrence waited for him to return and get settled before she asked, "What were you hired to do?"

"Security."

"For whom?"

"What," I said.

"What what?" Lawrence tried.

"I was handling security for a what, not a who."

They waited. So did I.

"Well?" Lobdell said.

"Well what?"

"Which *what* were you handling security for?"

"The convention that's going on over in the convention center."

"The foodfest," Lobdell said.

"Le Cuisine Internationale," I gave it my best Pepe Le Pew French accent.

"What, specifically, were you hired to do?" Lawrence asked.

Jed threw me a little nod, saying that I should give them this part of the story, so I did. I ran down the whole Meyerson, Del Fuego, Reese soap opera. I told them how I'd interviewed the parties.

Lawrence interrupted once. As I finished describing my interview with Reese, she said. "So, Mr. Waterman, you're saying that you didn't enter Mr. Reese's room?"

I looked to Jed. "Yes," I said. "That's right." And then I told them about Rodrigo, the room-service waiter who'd seen me in the hall.

"I have a few questions," Lobdell announced. Turned out, so did Ms. Lawrence. They picked at the story like fussy vultures, tearing off one bite-sized nibble at a time before moving on to the next. It took an hour to go back over the story to their satisfaction. I was losing my patience.

"Go on," she said.

I explained about how, the next morning, I'd kept track of their comings and goings. About stomping around boarding stables and cattle yards all afternoon and returning to the hotel.

"And what time did you get back here?" Lobdell asked.

"I just told you that. Right before six."

"And there was a message."

"Yes."

"From?"

"Mason Reese."

Lawrence was getting a little antsy, too. "Survey says . . ."

"He said I should give him a call."

"And you did," the cop prompted.

"Yeah, but I got no answer."

They were good. They were able to take complex events and reduce them to a series of single actions which could then be either verified and dismissed or disputed and investigated. One halten step at a time, they documented me from my room to the door of eight-fourteen.

"I elbowed the door open," I said.

"But you didn't go in," Lawrence said immediately.

If I answered, the jig was up, so I treated it as a statement and buttoned my lip.

"Is that correct?" Lobdell asked.

"Is what correct?"

"That you did not enter Mr. Reese's room, after you pushed open the door."

"I didn't say that."

She paged backward in her notebook. "You certainly did."

Jed took over. "In the citation for which you are searching, Ms. Lawrence, you asked Mr. Waterman, *in the context of his interview with Mr. Reese,* if he had entered Mr. Reese's room. You did not ask him if he had entered Mr. Reese's room at *any* time."

"That's pathetic," the sergeant snapped.

"Actually, it's poor grammar," I suggested.

Lobdell kept picking. "After receiving the message, after going downstairs, after pushing open the door, did you enter Mr. Reese's room?"

"Yes."

It took another half hour to cover the three minutes I'd spent in the room. When I'd finished, Jed said, "My client was concerned for the well-being of Mr. Reese. He was aware of the animosity inherent in the dispute between Mr. Del Fuego and Mrs. Meyerson and was concerned for Mason Reese's safety."

Lobdell sneered at us. "So it was as a public-spirited citizen that Mr. Waterman unlawfully entered and disturbed a crime scene."

"Would that we had more of his ilk," Jed said.

"What he said," I added.

"What sort of gun did Mr. Reese have?" Lawrence asked.

"A black automatic."

"Just a black automatic. That's the best you can do?" Lobdell prompted.

"Most of it was in his hand."

"And he brandished this weapon?" Lawrence persisted.

"No. 'Brandished' is too strong a word. It makes it sound like he waved it at me. He just let me know he had it."

Lobdell jumped back in. "When you entered the room in your capacity as concerned citizen, was the gun there?"

"Not that I saw."

Lawrence again. "Do you own a handgun, Mr. Waterman?"

"Two."

"Where are those weapons at this time?"

I'd left them locked in the trunk of my car, but there was no chance they were still there. By now, the cops had long since been through my room and my car. These two were fishing for lies.

"I'm betting you've got them," I said. "Make sure you don't miss the licenses. Those are in the glove box."

"And immediately after exiting the room is when you assaulted Mr. Kenny?" Lobdell said.

"Immediately after exiting the room is when I defended myself from an unprovoked attack by Mr. Kenny."

"What reason would Mr. Kenny have for assaulting you?"

"Yesterday I broke his thumb."

They looked bewildered, so I told them the story. When

I'd finished, Lawrence said, "Even granting that your version of the incident is accurate"—her tone indicated that hogs would sing opera first—"there would appear to be very little difference between the impropriety of Mr. Kenny's actions and that of your own."

"The difference, Ms. Lawrence, is that I'm a professional thug and Lance is not. A professional would never use any more force than is necessary. Nothing could be dumber. That kid just wanted to show off for his buddy. Unfortunately for him, amateurs operate at their own risk. That's all there is to it."

"And when he saw you in the hall, he summarily assaulted you? Is that what you're selling us, Mr. Waterman?" Lobdell again.

"Sure is." Before he could speak, I said, "Try his partner. A guy named Lincoln Aimes. See what he has to say. I rate him as a pretty good kid. He'll stick up for his buddy at first, but if you press him, I'll bet he'll tell you the truth."

Lobdell was losing his patience. "If it's all right with you, Waterman, we'll stage our own investigation. If I had my way, you and the rest of these clowns would already be downtown."

As they scribbled in their pads, the door opened and one of my elbow uniforms came in with a folded piece of notebook paper, which he set down next to Sergeant Lobdell. Lobdell finished his scribbling and then picked up the note. I watched as his eyes moved over and down the lines and thought I detected a slight smile hiding in his thin lips.

He leaned over and whispered in the woman's ear, and then they agreed on something. "Mr. Waterman, in the matter of recording the comings and goings of the principals, did you act alone or did you employ the help of others?"

He had me in a vise. Was the note from the blue-suited Lieutenant Driscoll, telling him of my ploy to get rid of George? That I could deal with. Or did they actually have George? If I outright lied and they had George in custody, I'd be guilty of obstruction. Time to Ollie.

"I hired a guy."

"What guy?"

"A guy named George."

"Does this George have a last name?"

"Probably, but I don't know it."

"You don't know his last name?"

"He's an old friend of my father's. I've known him all my life. He's always just been my uncle George. That's how I think of him."

Lobdell jerked a thumb in the direction of the hall, and the cop hustled out. "Perhaps we can help," Lobdell said.

His white hair hung down in front of his face, but with his arms handcuffed behind him, George couldn't do anything about it.

Lobdell addressed him. "Mr. Waterman says your name is George but that he can't remember your last name. Is your name George?"

"Maybe it is. Maybe it ain't," George said.

"I'd like to speak to my client privately," Jed said.

"You already did," Lawrence objected.

"This gentleman is also my client."

"My ass," said Lobdell.

"The gentleman's name is George Paris, and if you will check the county court records, you will find that I have represented Mr. Paris in a number of matters both criminal and civil. You will, as a matter of fact, find that I am Mr. Paris's attorney of record, and as much as I hate to repeat myself, I want to talk to my client alone."

Before Lawrence could speak, Lobdell jumped to his feet. "And you shall, Mr. James. Just as soon as we get these gentlemen booked into the King County Correction Facility, you will be afforded ample opportunity to confer with either or both of your clients."

I could see that Lawrence had more questions, but didn't want to make a scene. She took the professional approach.

"Good evening, gentlemen." Gathering her gear into a

pile, she prepared to make her exit. "I expect we'll be seeing one another again in the morning."

"Count on it," said Jed.

Lawrence cleared her throat. "And, ah, Mr. Waterman . . ." She lifted my PI license from the pile of documents before her and waved it in the air. "Until this matter is satisfactorily resolved, the county is pulling your PI ticket, retaining custody of your handguns and revoking your 'right to carry' permits. Consider yourself to be at least temporarily out of the private eye business. Good evening, gentlemen."

I f you go to the King County lockup, you spend at least six hours. No matter if your mom is standing there with the bail money clutched in her little hand when they bring you in. Whether it's littering or larceny, mopery or murder, you still spend at least six hours. King County doesn't get reimbursed by the state for stays of less than six hours. Need I say more?

They drove us singly and then locked us up together. Go figure. After separating us from our belts and shoes, and taking a couple of those glam photos with the handy number on the bottom, they left us in a small cell with a black telephone on the wall.

The turnkey was a pear-shaped guy on the verge of retirement. His bald head gleamed like an egg in the overhead lights, and his two-tone brown uniform seemed in danger of being rendered asunder by the onslaught of his burgeoning body as he waddled us along the corridor.

"Make your calls," he said, leaving us alone.

"Where are Frank and Judy?" I asked as soon as he was gone.

"They beat it. I give them the high sign first time I come down from the eighth, after I seen all them damn cops."

I clapped George on his bony shoulder. "Good man. How much info did you have in your notebook? Did you write down where everybody went today?"

"Hell, no," he said. "Never even got a chance to talk to anybody else. I just got done payin' people when the place was crawlin' with cops."

"Good. So all they've got is the cames and wents."

"They probably ain't even got that."

"They didn't get your notebook?"

He gave me a sly grin. "Fat chance."

"Tell me about it," I said.

He did. When he finished, I threw an arm around his shoulder and gave him a shake. "You're the best, George. The best."

"As good as Buddy used to be?"

Nobody had mentioned Buddy in a long time. I was suddenly filled with that cold feeling I got whenever his name came up. I took a deep breath. I used to think it was sorrow that froze my innards, but have come to see it as a kind of permanent rage for which there is no suitable outlet. Buddy Knox had been the de facto leader of the crew before George. He was stubborn, and I was careless. On a job down in Tacoma, the combination cost Buddy his life. What his death cost me remains to be seen.

"Better," I said. "You keep your shit together better than he did. I couldn't trust him the way I can trust you."

I gave him a small hug.

He struggled to escape. "Leggo of me, ya gorilla," he growled. "Christ, in here they'll be thinkin' we're engaged."

"You could do worse," I lisped.

George looked grim. "We gonna call anybody?"

"Not unless you've got a girlfriend."

Ten minutes later, the jailer reappeared. "You boys call your mamas?" he asked as he pulled open the cell door.

"Called yours instead," George snapped.

"One of them psychics, are ya?" he said affably. "Follow me."

We walked along the gray corridor, past a half-dozen individual holding cells and down around the corner to the left.

Even from the outside, it was obvious that the big general holding cell was where the action was. Beneath the bright lights, twenty or so men were divided into three distinct groups. At the far end of the cell, six or seven Hispanics sat close together in sullen silence. Something about their clothes and haircuts told me they were probably waiting for the immigration van. Their quiet eyes followed George and me as we shadowed the jailer down the hall to the orange door.

The middle of the cell was held down by the African-American contingent, which lounged on the benches and the floor like they'd signed a lease. Sitting with his back to us was a huge specimen with a three-ring neck. As George stepped into the cell, he was just finishing up a story. ". . . and so I axed the bitch. I said, 'bitch, you want me to come upside your head again?' and she say . . ." He looked over at George. "Hey, Granpaaaw," he hollered in a put-on drawl, to the delight of his audience. "Come ova hea . . . ah got somefin' fo' ya. Ah bettcha you kin pull them teeth right out, can't ya, Pops? Got nothin' but smooth gum for cool Poppa here."

George ignored him, instead slipping over by the far wall, leaning back against the blocks with his hands stuffed in his pockets. The white man's section was just inside the door. Two long-haired rednecks about thirty sat side by side on the metal bench while a third lay snoring on the floor as I entered.

"Ooh, you got you a bodyguard, huh, Gramps? He be guardin' yo body fo' you, old man?"

The turnkey snapped the door shut behind me, but didn't seem to be in any hurry to leave. I think maybe he'd seen this particular movie before and had been looking forward to the sequel.

From this side, Mr. Bigmouth was mostly flab. One hell of a lot of flab, but still flab. He was no more than a biscuit away from three and a quarter, but soft and out of shape. He had a big, square head and eyes that were nearly squeezed shut by the pressure of his blossoming cheeks.

"How 'bout you?" He pointed a fleshy finger my way. "Got some fo' you, too, honey."

The jailer was still in sight, so I decided to take a chance. At least I didn't have to worry about whether Lardass was armed. These days a guy can't pick a fight with a nine-year-old, for fear that the little shit will have an Uzi in his backpack. Besides which, fighting in jail is like fighting in school. It tends to get broken up before it runs too far out of hand.

I looked down at the nearest butt-rocker on the bench. He wore a tight black Metallica T-shirt, a pair of ratty jeans about two sizes too small and yellow socks with holes in the toes.

"Has that fat piece of shit been running his mouth all night?" I asked in a loud voice.

The jailer stopped sauntering and smiled. George pulled his hands from his pockets and stood up straight along the wall. The redneck ran his eyes between Bigmouth and me and then back again, but said nothing.

"What you say?" Bigmouth demanded. He looked out at his audience in disbelief. "That honky motherfucker call me names?"

"Call you a fat piece of shit, my man," somebody said.

In order to drag his big ass up from the bench, Bigmouth had to reach up and grab the bars with both hands. Even so, his pants did all they could to stay behind. As he rose, his unbelted drawers slid down to reveal a section of ass the size of a car hood.

He looked at the crowd, stuck his arms straight out and cleared his hands of imaginary dust. The mob loved the show, dissolving into a series of whistles, waves and high fives. The Mexican guys grinned and moved as far toward the back of the room as the bars would allow.

He was still mugging at his boys when I stepped over the guy on the floor. "If you think your hands are clean enough now, fat boy, what say we get down to it, because no matter what, I'm here till about ten in the morning, and I've got no intention of spending the night listening to your big fucking mouth."

Not only did the room go silent, but the first sign of doubt crept into his narrow little eyes. This was not the way it was supposed to go. I was supposed to be hollering for help by now. And then the jailers were supposed to come and bail my ass out, and then he could bust our balls for the rest of the night. A beginning, a middle and an end.

"I bust you up, motherfucker," he said.

"Only if you fall on me, Lard Bucket."

He wasn't sure anymore, but the expectant looks on his pals' faces convinced him he had no choice. As he waddled forward in what I'm sure he imagined was a quick rush, I bobbed my head to the left and let his big fist sail harmlessly over my shoulder. While he was still coming forward, I hooked him hard to the side, just under the ribs, burying myself to the wrist in his torso. When he grunted and reached for the spot, I pushed off on my right foot, winging my right hand straight in from the shoulder, moving forward until I was standing on my left foot.

It hit him right on the button. My whole arm went numb. Either this was National Hardhead Week or I was losing my stroke. He wobbled but stayed up, staggering a few steps and then slowly rubbing his hand over his face, checking for blood. While he stared stupidly at his palm, I shuffled in and gave him another hook to the ribs. This time the grunt was more of a scream, as he howled and bent toward the blow.

I butted him up against the bars and worked his body like the heavy bag, doubling up on every other hook while he flailed away harmlessly at my back. In less than a minute I had him moaning at every blow and desperately trying to slip his elbows into his hip pockets. As I felt him begin to slide down the bars, I took one step back and hit him in the forehead with the heel of my hand. His head snapped all the way back, banging off the bars with a muted clang.

I gathered myself again as he stepped toward me. When I saw his eyes, I backpedaled into the center of the room. Bigmouth reached out as if to pull a lamp cord, twirled once in a pirouette and collapsed onto the concrete floor. The turnkey waited to see what was going to happen next.

"Anybody else?" I asked the assembled multitude. No takers.

"You ladies, settle down now," the jailer admonished as he left.

It took twenty minutes and a bucket brigade of water cups from the sink in the rear of the cell for the homeboys to get the big fellow over to his perch on the bench.

"Little testy tonight, Leo?" George asked.

"Assholes like that, it's do it now or do it later," I said, without believing it.

It was eight-twenty. The rednecks rose and offered George and me the bench. At first we demurred, but when they insisted, we eventually had no choice but to acquiesce. We spent the night alternately watching each other's backs and napping.

I was swimming upstream in that river that flows between wakefulness and sleep, the place where the mind sorts out the day just past and prepares for the next, when they came for us. Everybody was issued a nifty pair of orange coveralls and a pair of little white booties, kind of like the slipper socks my mother had insisted on buying for me, right up until the day she died. That and a lovely pair of steel bracelets, and we were ready for court.

George and I shuffled into courtroom number four at ten-o-six the next morning and walked out the door on bail at exactly eleven-twenty. Judge Ellen Gardner had not been amused by Martha Lawrence's attempt to deny us bail. Jed had let her ramble on about what dangerous characters we were until the judge interrupted her litany.

"You keep mentioning an ongoing murder investigation,

Ms. Lawrence. Am I to take it that these gentlemen are to be charged in that investigation?"

"We believe these men have material knowledge which is pertinent to—"

"Are you charging them or not?" the judge interrupted.

Lawrence took a deep breath. "Not at this time, Your Honor."

"Mr. Waterman is released on his own recognizance." Bang.

"Mr. Paris's bail is set at ten thousand dollars." Bang-bang.

Rebecca was waiting with Jed when we came squinting out into the sunlight on Third Avenue. I availed myself of a handshake from Jed and a long hug and a kiss from Duvall.

"Is the phone working in the new house?" I asked her.

"As of this morning."

"What's the number?"

I wrote it in my notebook, then threw my arm around George's shoulder and pulled him down the street, away from Jed and Rebecca. Jed was an officer of the court and Rebecca worked for the county. The way I saw it, there was no sense compromising their respective positions.

I wrote the new number on the back of one of my business cards and handed it to George. "Find everybody who worked yesterday," I said. "Find out where everybody went and write it down. Then call that number and leave the info on the machine. Then—and this is real important—throw away whatever you wrote it on." I pointed at the card in his hand. "That, too. Memorize the number and get rid of that thing."

"How come the spy shit?"

"In case either or both of us get picked up again, which I think is real likely." I told him why, then reached into my pocket again and pulled out the rest of the cash. "Divvy up the money and get lost. All of you. I mean stone-lost."

"Ain't you worried about cops and your phone?"

"It's a brand-new number," I said.

"How come we gotta get lost?"

"Because we know something the cops don't. We know where all those people were all day yesterday. That's our edge, my friend. That's what we've got to trade."

He eyed me up and down. "Ya know, Leo, watchin' you in the cage last night and listenin' to you now, I got to say that the older you get, the more you remind me of your old man."

16

never meant to break his nose. I just didn't want to get hit by that damn cast. The sight of Lance standing at the rear of the lobby as I walked in, now sporting not just the cast but a crosshatched mask of tape and gauze, almost made me feel bad. Almost. Even from this distance I could see the deep discoloration around his eyes and the cotton packed in his nostrils. I waved as I headed for the reception desk.

Marie wasn't working today, but Molly was.

"Can I help you, sir?"

I threw my electronic room key up on the desk. The magnetic strip was nearly peeled off and hung down, while the card itself had been remolded into a C shape by the door lock.

"I'm Mr. Waterman in nine-ten," I said. "My key won't work in the door." I meant it as a little joke. Sort of an ironic comment on the dreadful state of the key. Instead, Molly took me seriously and began a detailed explanation of why and how electronic keys operated. It was my own fault, so I let her ramble on while she made me another. As she babbled, I was again reminded that technology divides people into those who care *why* and *how* the technology works, like Molly, and those who care only *that* it works, like me.

"Thanks," I said when she handed it over.

"Remember," she sang to my back, "the little brown plastic strip needs to stay connected to the card."

I decided against writing this down.

I could feel Lance's eyes on me as I pushed the up button and the doors to my immediate left slid open. I stepped in and pushed 9.

On the ninth floor I got off, watched as the doors closed behind me and listened as the elevator hummed off. I pushed the up button. Twenty seconds later, the same elevator I'd just gotten out of reappeared. Shit. I needed the elevator on the right.

I waited several minutes before pushing up again. This time the doors on the far left yawned open. No good. It took the better part of ten minutes before I was able to summon the elevator on the far right, and even then it was full of German tourists. I rode to the ground floor with them, *ja, ja,* and then quickly pushed the close-door button before an elderly couple could get on board. What a guy!

On my way back up to nine. I checked the red-and-white sticker on the box mounted below the elevator buttons which read: "TELEPHONE—In the event of emergency, insert your room key and lift receiver. You will automatically be connected to the operator." I pulled my handy-dandy new room key from my pocket, inserted it in the slot, and as directed, opened the little door. Momentarily I pondered the fact that, apparently, only guests were allowed to have emergencies in these elevators. George's blue notebook was tucked inside the phone box, just where he'd left it, the golf pencil still stuck in among the spiraled wire. I pocketed it and stepped out.

The next order of business was a shower. I have always had the same reaction to those infrequent occasions when my work has landed me in the pokey. I invariably have an incredible urge to shower and generally completely deplete the available hot water before I am able to stop. Today wasn't a problem. I stood there with the steaming water rolling down my body for the better part of forty minutes without detecting even the slightest variation in water temperature. Let's hear it for good hotels.

By the time I stepped out of the glass shower stall, the walls of the bathroom were dripping like a rain forest, so I grabbed two towels and walked out through the bedroom into the sitting room with a cloud of steam dogging my trail.

The digital clock read twelve fifty-eight. I picked up the remote control and pushed power. The credits from a game show rolled by as I dried myself and began to dress.

I was zipping up a pair of black gabardine slacks when the logo for *Afternoon Northwest* appeared on the screen. The cardboard cutout of Jack and Bunky was still front and center on the set. This was strange. *Afternoon Northwest* was usually on once a week, on Mondays, yet here it was, airing again on Tuesday.

". . . and now, ladies and gentlemen, your host of *Afternoon Northwest* . . . Miiiiiss Loooollla Kiiiiiing."

L-O-L-A Lola tromped onstage wearing pretty much the same thing as yesterday. Today the skirt was a deep brown and the cutaway jacket a watered-down yellow. Otherwise it was the same. She must have found one she liked and taken it to a tailor and told him to make her forty of them. The crowd hooted and hollered.

She was the color of old custard and had on her somber face. The one she used to use for airplane crashes during her brief tenure as a news anchor. "Before we continue our weeklong special on cruelty to animals, ladies and gentlemen, I feel it is incumbent upon me to state"—she shook her head for emphasis, like Nixon used to—"clearly and unequivocally, that neither this show nor this station endorses the views of yesterday's guest, Miss Clarissa Hedgpeth."

The crowd gave her a tentative hand.

"As our loyal viewers know, we make every effort to

bring our audience, both in the studio and at home"—she looked beseechingly at the camera—"a wide variety of opinions on a wide variety of issues."

I had to go with her there. Who, after all, could ever forget programming like "Homicidal Postal Workers Speak Out," "Espresso Ruined My Life" or the immortal "Felching for Fun and Profit"?

I lost what she was saying as I went into the bedroom in search of shoes. When I came back out, a graphic detailing the addresses and phone numbers of both Clarissa Hedgpeth and her organization, NUTSS, was on the screen, and Lola was doing the voice-of-doom narration. "Once again, that's area code 206-328-6540 for those of you who would like to comment directly to Miss Hedgpeth."

Lola King looked to her left, got some sort of signal and then plowed ahead. "Today, ladies and gentlemen, *Afternoon Northwest* will continue our investigation of animal rights issues. Our guest this afternoon is Steven Drew . . . president and founder of the National Vegan Society. Please, a big Northwest hello for Steeeeven Drewww."

I got the belt all the way through before I realized I missed a loop in the back. *Arrrg.*

Steven was short, with a full head of corrugated hair pulled back into a thick black ponytail. When he turned to plant the obligatory peck on Lola's cheek, I could see that the hairs on the back of his neck grew completely down into his collar, giving rise to the possibility that our boy Steve was completely haired over like a gibbon, a malady which I imagined at least subconsciously fueled his crusade on behalf of our furry friends.

Lola beamed at the camera. "Can you tell our viewers, here and at home, exactly what a vegan is, Steve?"

Steve gave a nervous smile and locked in on the wrong camera.

"I certainly can, er, Lola," he mumbled. "A vegan—pronounced *vee*-gun, by the way—is someone who does not consume animal products. While vegetarians avoid flesh foods, vegans also reject the exploitation and abuse inherent in the making of dairy and egg products, as well as clothing from animal sources."

"Well, isn't that asking a lot of people, Steve? I mean, how many people are going to be able to lead a lifestyle like that?"

Steve, who had by now found the camera with the red light, was nodding his head. "We understand that, Lola. While leading a purely vegan life may be difficult for many, we encourage those who strive toward this goal to consider themselves to be practicing vegans."

Kind of like Catholicism, I thought as I went to find myself a tie in the bedroom.

It took me four tries to get a good knot in the tie, so I missed the introduction of the second guest, which turned out to be something of a handicap since the guy was masked. He had one of those terrorist scarves wound around the lower part of his face and a pair of wraparound sunglasses covering his eyes. He was saying, "We encourage people to take action. To look around their areas for targets. They're everywhere. Laboratories where animal testing takes place, factory farms, hunt kennels, meat-packing plants, fur shops, abattoirs."

Lola wanted to comment, but the guy was rolling. "ALF members in Michigan recently freed eight thousand mink from the farm of the president of the American Mink Association. There's a seventy-thousand-dollar reward out for them right now, as we speak, Lola."

Lola tried again, "But, Konrad, isn't it . . ."

"I'll tell you what it is, Lola. It's flattering. When militants blew up those eight trucks in Sweden . . . it's flattering, is what it is."

As I grabbed my jacket and looked around for the remote, Steven Drew managed to get a word in edgewise. "We see it as a matter of individual conscience, Lola. We believe that individuals can make a difference. Leading a cruelty-free life is—"

Konrad Kramer jabbed a finger in Drew's direction.

"Hey, tofu boy. Where were you and your hippies when we were monkeywrenching the sea lion traps at the Ballard Locks? If it weren't for committed ALF commandos, those poor devils would have been mukluks."

I spied the remote lying camouflaged on the bedspread and put an end to the dazzling repartee. I stopped at the gilded mirror on the wall and gave myself one last inspection. My forehead still had a puffy Neanderthal bulge, but other than that, I looked pretty good.

The first elevator to stop was packed, but I got in anyway. The more the merrier. As the doors closed, I inserted my key for the security floors and pushed sixteen. As I'd expected, the rabble was struck dumb by my magnificence.

Once again, Rowcliffe answered almost immediately.

"How do you do that?" I asked.

"Do what, sir?"

"Answer the door instantly, like you've been camped out the whole time waiting for somebody to knock."

"Practice, sir," was his reply.

I waded through the carpet, following the butler into the bedroom. The current book was *Full House* by Stephen Jay Gould. Pink silk jammies and sheets today. No comment.

"Ah, Mr. Waterman," Sir Geoffrey said. "Apparently, you were indeed in competent legal hands."

"Yes, sir."

"Rowcliffe spoke with your spousal unit, a Ms. . . . ."

The butler appeared in the doorway. "Duvall, your lordship."

"Of course . . . yes. Ms. Duvall assured us that you were being well represented and would be expeditiously liberated."

"It's an occupational hazard," I assured him.

He looked peeved. "I must say, I myself found the experience unsettling, to say the very least."

"Cops give you a hard time?"

"They were as rude to me as they dared," he sniffed.

"Certainly not as peremptorily as the others were treated, but . . ."

"What others?"

"That whole dreadful knot of Meyersons and Del Fuegos. They questioned us all until nearly dawn. Where had we been. Whom had we seen. It was interminable. They seemed to be convinced that someone in that room was responsible for Mr. Reese's demise."

"It's a good bet."

"They went so far as to suggest that I, of all people, also had reason to wish Mason Reese dead. They even questioned Rowcliffe at great length."

"I'd pay good money to watch that."

"It was rather amusing," he conceded.

I didn't even bother to ask about the details of Rowcliffe's interview. Instead, I asked Sir Geoffrey, "What did you tell them?"

"Regarding?"

"What I was doing for you."

"Merely that you had been retained as security liaison for Le Cuisine Internationale."

"That's it?"

"They were highly objectionable young fellows."

"You didn't tell them that we were following people?"

He folded his arms high across his chest. "Certainly not. I had no way of knowing what your situation was. God only knew what you were telling them. I had no choice but to quibble."

"You'd make a good crook, Sir Geoffrey."

He made that noise with his lips again. "They inquired about someone named George. I told them I had no knowledge of your exact arrangements and had never heard of the gentleman in question." He showed me a palm. "Which was technically true, of course. That seemed to satisfy them."

"Not for long."

"You think not?"

"They're going to go through the staff like locusts and when they do, I figure it's a good bet one of the valets is going to remember George and the rest of the crew. Or they're going to find out from the desk personnel that I had extra keys made to my room. They're not stupid. It's going to get sticky before it's over."

"Of course, you're right." He sighed. "It's tempting to think of the police as a pack of bumbling boobs."

"They're not," I said. "As a matter of fact, they tend to be quite good at what they do."

He pursed his lips and marinated the idea for quite a while, finally breathing out hard from his nose and saying, "As I see it, we are still holding the trump cards."

"No doubt about it, Sir Geoffrey."

"We know what they'd like to."

"But pretty soon they're going to know that we know."

"And they will surely ferret out these men of yours."

"Yes, they will."

I had no illusions about it. Nobody on my crew was spy material. They all drank too much for anything clandestine. These were the kind of people who, while supposedly hiding out, get hammered and brag to anybody who'll listen that they're hiding out. It shouldn't take long.

"You said that both you and Rowcliffe were present when the Meyerson and Del Fuego contingents gave the cops their stories about where they'd been and when."

"Certainly. The swine kept us all sequestered in a single large room downstairs. Imagine, if you can, being retained in the same space with that malignant mob. It was hideous."

"The good news is that the papers are carrying it as a hotel murder. The convention wasn't even mentioned in the morning edition."

This morning's *Post Intelligencer* had chronicled the whole sordid history of the great Meyerson-Del Fuego dispute. For the better part of two full pages, years of outrageous accusations and heartfelt denials had made for exceptionally lively reading.

"A pity we cannot keep it so."

"Maybe we can."

He arched a knowing eyebrow at me. "What have you in mind?"

"Maybe we can get this whole thing over with before it spills over into the convention."

"By handing them the murderer," he said.

"All we've got to do is compare where they said they were between two forty-five and five or so with where they each actually went and when they actually came back. Whoever lied is probably a good candidate for a murder rap."

17

Rebecca moved the last chanterelle mushroom around her plate in a clockwise direction, plowing little furrows in the last of the dill sauce.

"You look tired," she said.

"Nothing a good night's sleep won't cure."

We were the only diners at Cool Hand Luke, a great little hole-in-the-wall restaurant in Madrona Park, a section of Seattle which was, depending upon your outlook, either the best part of the ghetto or the worst part of the high-rent district. In Seattle, it all depends upon whether or not water is visible. In a single block, you can crest a hill, find one of the lakes or the Sound suddenly come into view, and move from Thunderbird in a bag to an audacious little '93 zinfandel.

Four-thirty is a bit late for lunch and a bit early for dinner. In an hour or so, a table would involve a thirty-minute wait.

"Your lunch was good?"

Duvall put the fork down, leaving the mushroom to drown, and reached over, dropping her hand on mine.

"Not that I don't appreciate it, Leo, but you seem to be very concerned about whether or not I liked my lunch."

She was right. I'd asked her about six times. I hate it when women are observant. "I guess I feel like I ought to apologize for having all this crap going on right in the middle of when we're moving."

She shrugged. "So apologize."

"You'd have to meet this group to know what I mean, but I really thought they were just a bunch of idiots with more money than brains. I took the talk of"—I drew imaginary quotation marks with my fingers—" 'mortal danger' to be . . . you know . . . the worst sort of overstatement for effect. I mean these people take themselves pretty damn seriously. I figured what we had here was a bunch of habitual self-dramatizers." My turn to shrug.

"But somebody's dead."

"Yeah. Somebody's dead. The cops have pulled my license. They've got me for obstruction and tampering, if they want to pursue it. They're probably out looking for the crew by now. Fearless Fosdick here has failed to stop exactly the kind of disaster he was hired to prevent. And on top of this crap, the whole thing makes me look like I'm getting cold feet about our move."

"Are you?"

"No. Are you?"

"A little."

"Me, too."

"Under the circumstances, I think a little apprehension is an appropriate response," she said.

"You do?"

"Certainly. It's a big move for both of us."

"Good."

"Good what?"

"Good that we're of the same mind."

"Are we?"

"I hope so."

"Me, too."

I began to chuckle to myself. Duvall shook her head.

"Listen to us," she said. "We sound like the Marx Brothers."

"Abbott and Costello's 'Who's on First?' "

"You know, Leo, sometimes I worry that two grown people shouldn't have this much trouble talking about their relationship."

"I'm not good with 'should,' Rebecca. I mean, is there a standard out there someplace that we're falling short of? I mean, like, are we being plotted on a graph somewhere?"

"Not that I know of."

"Good, because one of the first things I learned from being a private eye is that there are no perfect people out there. I used to think there was this class of people who skated through life. Who made all the right moves, who played the game the way it was intended to be played and in return got to forgo the pain and suffering that marked the rest of us."

"And then you saw the light?"

"And then I got a peek behind their closed doors. They started hiring me to find their runaway kids and thieving chauffeurs. And you know what? They were the same as us, but with lots of money."

"And all the money didn't help."

"Sometimes it did; sometimes it didn't. Mostly, it just postponed the pain."

"I'm kind of lost on the point here, Leo."

"The point is that what we *should* be doing is whatever we *are* doing. If we were supposed to be some other way, we'd be that way."

"Isn't that just a wee bit circular and convenient?"

"Maybe, but as far as I'm concerned, you and I are a special case, not a statistic. I mean, how many other couples in our situation have been dating for the better part of twenty years?"

"Hopefully, not too many."

"We've had a lot of practice at pretending. I figure it's going to take a bit of practice to stop."

"Pretending? What pretending? I'm not pretending."

"Oh, come on, Dr. Duvall," I joshed. "Think about it. Let's be honest here. You and I missing each other was a classic case of overthink. Two otherwise intelligent people managed to rationalize themselves all the way past the exit to truth and into the next county. How did we do that? It was always obvious to everybody except us. My mother—I mean, what—we were in the sixth grade or something and she used to tell me to latch onto you." I waved a finger and used my shrill Wicked Witch of the West voice. " 'That girl is going somewhere, Leo,' she'd say. Then she'd shake her head in wonder and go. 'And she likes *you,* Leo.' Even the other kids always teased us. Remember?"

"That was because we always had to dance together because we were taller than everybody else."

"Even when I was married to Annette, my aunts still used to ask about you. Hell, they still know everything we do. They always knew. Why didn't we?"

"It was more complicated than that."

"Don't I know it. Hell, I married a woman pretty much just to get my old man's attention."

"And I listened to the 'worked my fingers to the bone' stories for so long I started to believe them. So what? That's all ancient history."

"I makes me nervous, is all. If I was that stupid then and didn't know it, how can I ever be totally sure I'm not doing it again and don't know it again?"

She patted my hand once more. "Neither of us exactly came from a background that was an ad for connubial bliss."

"Yeah, I used to think that, too. Until I met these Del Fuego and Meyerson clans. These people have a soap opera going on that makes our childhoods look like *The Partridge Family.* They've got old grudges. They've got new grudges. They've got husbands and wives dead under suspicious circumstances. Meyerson's got a daughter named Penny she hasn't spoken to in years."

"Do you know why?"

"It seems Mama Meyerson felt the girl married considerably beneath her station."

"But all women do, Leo."

I decided I didn't like her smile, so I ignored her.

"Del Fuego's got an ex-wife who follows him into the bathroom. A girlfriend young enough to be his daughter. A bodyguard who looks like the *Creature from the Black Lagoon*. A couple of stepkids running around out there somewhere who nobody seems to have a clue what happened to. These are some seriously strange folks."

"See," Duvall said. "We're not so screwed up after all."

"Yeah, but think of all the gas we could have saved."

"You're such a romantic, Leo."

I changed the subject. "The cops aren't going to leave me alone until they get this thing solved."

"Meaning?"

"Meaning that I better not be going out to the house anymore. I think I can pretty much expect to be under surveillance soon, and I don't see any sense in adding the cops to the moving mix."

"We can't postpone, Leo. Rhetta's van full of stuff arrives on Saturday morning. I've got to be out by then."

"The move goes off on schedule," I said. "The boys will be at your place at eight in the morning on Wednesday."

We'd hired a sixteen-foot truck, along with my nephew Matthew and three of his burly fraternity brothers to do the actual lifting and toting. One full day should move us both.

"But you're not going to be around."

"Probably not. You think you can handle it?"

"The problem is not whether I can handle it, but how I feel about having to."

"I guess this gets me to the apology part," I said. "Sorry. I didn't mean for this to interfere."

" 'Sorry' is a good description of it," she said, rising.

It was a quiet ride back to the hotel. I had her leave me a block up from the hotel, on Seneca. "What's the remote code for the voice mail at the house?" I asked as she pulled the car to the curb.

Rebecca reached behind the driver's seat and dragged her briefcase into her lap. "I don't have it memorized yet," she said while rooting around in the bag. She pulled out her day planner.

"Keep it that way," I said. "Until this thing is over. Next time you're at the house, unplug the phones. Use your cell phone. The voice mail will still take messages."

She read me the number. I turned to the front of my little notebook, to a series of notations that were several months old, and wrote the number in the margin.

"One more thing."

"What?"

"Thanks," I said. "I'll call you later."

"On my cell phone, of course," she said.

I settled for escaping with my life.

18

"We don't believe you've been completely truthful with us, Mr. Waterman." Martha Lawrence had all of her stuff symmetrically arranged in front of her again. Today, she was in a three-piece knitted green suit that matched her eyes, with her red hair held atop her head by a big tortoiseshell clip. No Lobdell. I guess he didn't want to play with me anymore.

We were back in the Senate Room. I'd come into the hotel through the Seneca Street doors and gotten no more than a dozen steps across the carpet when a couple of dicks took an unhealthy interest in my elbows. My feet barely touched the ground on our way up to the mezzanine, where they plopped me in a chair and now stood one pace to the rear.

"Am I under arrest?"

"Would you prefer to be?"

"If you're going to detain me, arrest me."

"We're not detaining you, Mr. Waterman. We are merely giving you the opportunity to exercise the kind of public-spirited cooperation which Mr. James assured Judge Gardner you were prepared to provide. You do, after all, have such close ties to the community."

Talk about a snappy rejoinder. The good Ms. Lawrence was giving me a chance to dig my own grave. If I walked, she'd request another bail hearing in the morning. She'd trot the bruise brothers in to swear I'd refused to cooperate, and they'd reset bail up in Charlie Manson land.

"What's your story, Lawrence? How come I seem to have your undivided attention? You strike me as a competent person. Unlike your friend Lobdell, I might mention. You know I didn't kill Mason Reese. What's the deal here?"

"Let's just say I have an aversion to people who think the rules don't apply to them."

"People who think the rules don't apply to them are responsible for most of the scientific and artistic breakthroughs."

"Somehow, I don't think that applies to low-rent private eyes."

"There you go with those aspersions again, Lawrence."

The color was rising in her cheeks. I could see her freckles now.

"You don't even have a valid PI license. You have a judicial variance, whatever legal travesty that may be."

"So what? So twenty years ago, my old man pulled some strings and got me a ticket. What's that to you? I've been at it for twenty years. I've got a good reputation."

She heaved a sigh. "Please."

"You know what I did for the first three years? I served process. Divorce papers. Eviction notices. Bond revocations. Repossession notices. Ever slapped an eviction notice in the palm of an unemployed shipfitter with four kids, Lawrence? It's a real treat, believe me."

"You have no credentials whatsoever."

"Is that what this is about? Credentials?"

"Most of us earn our way, Mr. Waterman."

As I'd apparently left my capacity for guilt in my other suit, I said, "What say we get on with this?"

She hesitated. She wanted to argue some more. Instead, she said, "Your answers had best get better, Mr. Waterman."

"Maybe if you ask better questions, I'll have better answers."

"Perhaps," she said. " Let's see if I can learn from my own mistakes." She leaned over and put both hands on the table. "Mr. Waterman . . . yesterday," Lawrence began.

"That would be Monday," I interrupted.

Her green eyes narrowed. "Yes, Monday."

"I just wanted to do my part for being clear."

She gave me a smile thin enough to pass for a scar. "Yesterday . . . Monday," she began again. "In the course of your work for Le Cuisine Internationale, did you have occasion to have a number of people followed?"

I could read the gleam in her eye. If I said no, I was going straight to jail, without passing Go or collecting two hundred dollars.

So I said, "Yes."

Her disappointment was palpable. "You did?"

"Maybe you ought to write this stuff down so we don't have to keep repeating ourselves."

"Whom did you have followed?"

" 'Whom' is a terrible word, you know."

"What?"

" 'Whom'—it's one of those snob words people use to tell other people that they're educated. It gives language mavens something to feel snooty about. I think maybe only credentialed folks use the word. It doesn't work any better than 'who,' and it sounds funny."

"Are you refusing to answer my questions, Mr. Waterman?"

"Certainly not. I was merely making an observation, an aside, a minor digression, as it were."

"Well?"

"Mason Reese, the Del Fuego group and the Meyerson group."

"Were they followed singularly or in groups?"

"Except for Reese, they left in groups."

"Do you have a record of when the various parties left the hotel yesterday morning?"

"Some of them left in the afternoon."

She stayed calm. "Do you have a record?"

She picked up a stenographer's pad and a pencil.

"Yes," I said. "Dixie Donner and her traveling companion, whose name is Bart something-or-other, left on foot at nine forty-nine. Mason Reese left on foot at ten-twenty." She scribbled away. "At eleven-twenty the Meyerson crowd left by limousine, and the Del Fuegos came down at twelve-twenty. They also left by limo."

When she finished writing, she leafed backward in the notebook until she found what she was looking for. She marked the spot with her middle finger as she looked back and forth between the pages.

"All right, then. Let's start with Mr. Reese. Where did Mr. Reese go?"

"I have no idea."

The gleam returned to her green eyes. "You don't expect me to believe that, do you?"

"I don't have any control over what you do or don't believe, Lawrence. All I can do is tell you the truth. I don't know where anybody went because I haven't had a chance to run down the operatives and find out. Every time I set foot outdoors, you guys arrest me."

"You're very close to having that honor again, Mr. Waterman."

"Besides, if I were to go out and find all those people. I'd be operating as a private investigator, wouldn't I? And we couldn't have that, now, could we? Not with me without a license and all."

"Very cute," she said, without meaning it.

She readied her pencil. "I want the names and addresses of these operatives of yours."

"I don't know that either."

"You hired these people, and you don't know their names?"

"I didn't hire them."

"Who did?"

"George."

"Then give me his address and phone number."

"He doesn't have either. You know that. You were in court this morning. It's a matter of public record. That's why his bail was so high."

"You're serious, aren't you? You're actually trying to tell me that . . . that gentleman was—is—homeless?"

"Yeah, I am. It's like I told you before—George was a friend of my father's. What can I say? He drinks. He's fallen on hard times. He flops wherever he can. Once in a while I have a need for day labor. When that happens, I try to use George and his associates if I can."

"Because you're such a charitable sort."

"Because they work cheap and they make great surveillance operatives. Think about it, Lawrence; who better to have hang around outside a building all day long than a bum? They're perfect for it."

She considered her options. "When you want to contact Mr. Paris, how do you do so?"

"I leave him a message at this bar he hangs out in."

"What bar is that?"

"The Zoo, on Eastlake."

Scribble, scribble. She kept at me for the better part of an hour, worrying the issue like a terrier with a rat. Writing down everything I said. Finally, she dropped the notebook on the table and looked at me. She wasn't mad anymore. Beulah the Bureaucrat was back.

"Mr. Waterman, despite your protestations of harassment, we're going to do this by the numbers. We are going to follow up on every lead you've given us. If at any point it appears that you have been untruthful, if it appears that you have been withholding information pertinent to this investigation, I am going to charge you with obstruction of justice and I am going to permanently pull your judicial variance. I hope I'm making myself clear."

When I failed to respond, she shifted her gaze to the cops. "Take Mr. Waterman over with the others."

"Come on, Lawrence," I whined. "I'm tired. I want to go to my room. What over? What others?"

All the others, it turned out. Across the hall, they'd opened the doors between the individual rooms, creating a single large meeting space. Tension hung in the air like fog.

Directly in front of me, a serious clutch of suits leaned toward one another. Lieutenant Driscoll was on Marty Conlan's right. On Marty's left was Detective Lobdell.

Lawrence's voice came from behind me. "Excuse me, please, Mr. Waterman."

I moved out into the middle of the room so that she could enter. She walked by me and stepped up onto the dais. The conversation stopped. When she began to speak, she had the suits' undivided attention. I headed for my client.

In the right rear corner, Sir Geoffrey Miles, Rowcliffe and Señor Alomar huddled together in a tight knot. Rowcliffe stood one pace to the rear, offering no expression whatever, while Miles sat with his hands clasped across his midriff, his chin high and gaze haughty. Alomar surveyed the room with the bemused ease of a man on vacation.

To my immediate right, the Meyerson contingent had redeployed the furniture, turning two tables sideways, circling the wagons, cutting that corner off from the rest of the room. Abigail Meyerson sat placidly between Hill and Francona, her back to the front wall and her hands in her lap. Behind them, Brie skittered back and forth along the west wall of the room, rubbing her shoulder against the surface as she paced like a shooting-gallery duck. Spaulding was clear over in the opposite corner, grab-assing with Rickey Ray.

The Del Fuego mob was situated directly across from Sir Geoffrey. Dixie sat front and center with her hand resting on Bart's right leg, way too high for polite company. Bart appeared not to notice. Jack Del Fuego and Candace sat behind a long pink-covered table. Jack wore an abstract-patterned sport coat that looked like the international symbol for bad taste. Candace gave the impression of being slightly amused.

I grabbed a loose chair from the corner and sat down next to Sir Geoffrey. "What's going on? Things seem a mite tense."

"Sir Geoffrey has fomented insurrection," said Rowcliffe.

"He has rallied the masses," added Alomar.

I didn't have to ask. "These fools have been niggling at us all day," Sir Geoffrey spat. "They had the gall to offer us prepared sandwiches. Tuna on wheat. Ha! I have sworn to remain mute until properly fed. The remainder of the rabble followed my lead and are, for once, holding their tongues."

"Dinner, sir," Rowcliffe said.

He was right. A liveried waiter stepped into the room, shot the bolts, top and bottom, and opened both doors wide. When he stepped aside, an armada of carts rattled forward. I counted them. Twelve carts full of food and drink. The door opener directed traffic.

"Meyerson order." He pointed. Four carts broke off the train and headed that way. "Miles." he nodded in our direction. My old friend Rodrigo pushed the lead cart free of the melee and headed toward us. He seemed surprised to see me in such esteemed company.

With a grand flourish, Rodrigo skidded the cart to a stop in front of Miles and Alomar. "At your service," he said. This got him a barely perceptible nod from Sir Geoffrey, while Alomar yawned into the back of his hand. Rowcliffe stepped forward and began to set the table.

I moved back out of the way, allowing the crew to hover and dart around, delivering two bottles of wine, a basket of assorted breads, rolls and muffins, another basket of gleaming fruit, plates, glasses, silverware. As if by magic, the trappings of a banquet appeared around the two men. These were guys who knew how to order from room service.

Rodrigo removed the silver cover from one of the dishes

on his cart. "The shad roe with Creole sauce," he announced.

Alomar waggled a doubtful finger. As Rodrigo set the plate before him, Alomar dropped a hand on the waiter's shoulder.

"You spoke to the chef, as I instructed?"

"Yes, sir," Rodrigo replied.

"About the pimiento?"

"Yes, sir. I told him what you said. A mere rumor of pimiento."

"Good fellow."

Rodrigo turned back and produced lamb kidneys bourguignon, which Rowcliffe took from his hand and set before Sir Geoffrey. Sir Geoffrey bent and sniffed the air above the plate.

"This time the shallots are fresh?" he asked.

Rodrigo held up a hand. "The chef, he swears."

Miles made a resigned face and pointed at the wine bucket.

"Rowcliffe, let's begin with the Merlot."

At the front of the room, the city contingent was drinking coffee and tea from a collection of silver urns, still deep in discussion, only now Lobdell was doing most of the talking.

A water glass of scotch had loosened Jack's tongue. I could hear him from where I was sitting. As he held his plate aloft, a huge gob of mashed potatoes and gravy began to slide down his face.

"Will ya take a look at this dry little piece of shit for twenty-nine dollars?" he bellowed. "Hey, Abby. This must be one of your sawdust specials."

Dixie waved her fork in the air. "I told you we're not charging enough, Jack. Haven't I told him that?" she asked nobody in particular. "We're givin' them too damn much for too damn little."

The Meyerson group pretended not to hear. Sir Geoffrey and Señor Alomar were in rapt concentration. Only Rickey

Ray wasn't eating. He still stood near the center of the room, taking it all in.

I walked over to his side. "What, no pressed duck for you?"

He chuckled, allowing a broken grin to nearly pull his face back into order. "No way, Leo. You eat that shit, you look like old Jack." He looked me over. "You don' look like you eat too mucha that crap neither."

"More than I should."

He dug a finger into my rib cage. "You're holding it pretty good."

"Holding too much of it, is what I am."

He nudged me with an elbow, "Well, you know, you get older . . ."

"Oh, it's like that, is it?"

Amid the quiet clatter of silverware and working jaws, we shared a laugh. "That's a wild flock you got over there," I said.

"You ain't just kiddin'."

"How long you been baby-sitting Jack Del Fuego?"

"Couple of years or so."

"How'd you come to know Jack?"

"I went right after him, podna. That's how it is with me. I always gotta go for it. Got limited career choices, ya know. That's what the Army guy tol' me when they turned me down. Said he figured I'd got limited career choices."

"You were still fighting when you met Jack?"

"Yeah, and gettin' damn sick of it, too."

"Tough way to make a living."

"Aw, hell," he said. "You got you a good look at my face. I been fightin' my whole life. Never seemed like I had any choice. I used to be real sensitive about it. All you had to do was look at me a little bit too long and I was all over you like a cheap suit. By the time I started to fight for money, I figured, you know, what did I have to lose, anyway. Wasn't like I was gonna get uglier as I went along."

"Jack see you fight?"

He nodded. "I had a month off till I had to defend my title back in Dallas. I heard they was having tough-guy matches down Oklahoma City way. Givin' away five grand every Friday night. I figured, you know, what the hell, might as well make some cash. I seen him around the fights with the other high rollers, you know. Didn't take much imagination to see he was one of those guys who was always gonna have to own the biggest dog. That's how come he had the meatball brothers. All the other wads just had one gofer chauffeur, but the Jackeroo just had to have two. Anyway, fella I knew tol' me how much Jack was paying the Galante brothers to watch his big ass, and I figured, shit, I might as well be the one takin' his money as that pair of mud pies. So, you know, one Friday right after the fights, I walked up to him at this big barbecue he was throwin' for his golf buddies and tol' him, right in front of God and everybody, how I was fixin' to become his bodyguard and companion."

"What did he have to say about that?"

"He had him a good laugh and then told the Galante brothers to take me on t'other side of the park and teach me some manners."

"Didn't work out that way, did it?"

"Not hardly, Leo." He grinned. "After a while, he come lookin' for the suet brigade, and, you know . . ." He showed me a palm.

"The rest is history," I finished for him.

"Yeah. I piled 'em up, belly to belly, and was sittin' on 'em like a bench when he got there. The Jackster, he liked that. Said it showed imagination. Been with him ever since."

Spaulding Meyerson was heading our way.

"Can't get rid of that Meyerson kid," Rickey Ray said.

Spaulding stopped in the middle of the room, pulled his feet underneath him and leaned into the burger he was holding before him.

"You're his hero for whatever it was you did to his mom's bodyguards."

A font of refuse erupted from the bottom of the bun, plopping down onto the rich brown carpet. Spaulding wasn't quick enough to react and ended up with half a lettuce leaf and a glob of mayonnaise resting atop his right shoe.

"That was back in Cleveland. Right after she hired 'em. Took all Jack's stuff off the luggage dolly and left it in the garage. Bunch of it got stole. The old Jackster was right put out about it. I just cuffed 'em around a little, is all."

"Don't they ever speak?"

"I heard Francona talk."

"What did he say?"

His lip curled. "He say, 'Please, no more.' "

Spaulding shook his foot like a dog walking in snow for the first time, sending a hail of condiments flying out in all directions. From the far corner, I heard Abby Meyerson tell her son that she wished to speak with him. He ignored her and headed our way, the dripping burger now held out to the side. "Hey, big guy," he said to Rickey Ray.

He had a piece of pickle on his front tooth.

"I think yo' mama wants you, buddy," Rickey replied.

Spaulding leaned in and gave Rickey a leer.

"You get lucky yet, big guy?"

Rickey Ray pinned him with a glare.

Spaulding winked. "Rickey's sweet on the Jackster's girl toy."

"I tol' you before, kid," Rickey growled.

"He's got big wood for her," Spaulding assured me.

As they bantered back and forth, I could tell that they'd run this scene before, and I finally understood what it was Spaulding Meyerson did well. He got under people's skin. He had an uncanny instinct for intuitively knowing just how to be optimally obnoxious. He probably had a future in law.

He kept at Rickey Ray, but now talked to me. "All Natural for Men," he said, pointing at Rickey's head. Then he cupped the same hand to his mouth in mock discretion. "Dyed his hair so they'd match." He put a finger to his mouth. "Shhhhh."

I hoped to God the kid wasn't counting on me to save

his ass if Rickey Ray started on him, because the best he was going to get out of me was shrieking for the police. Rickey Ray was a couple of counties past anything I was looking for. To quote Dirty Harry Callahan: "A man needs to know his limitations."

Spaulding kept nodding and grinning his pickle-toothed grin.

I could feel Rickey Ray's blood pressure rising

Abby's low voice rolled our way. *"Spaulding!"*

"She looks pretty pissed off," Rickey chided through clenched teeth. "Don' wanna make yo' mama mad there, Spauldo."

Spaulding didn't bother looking. "Walter—he was one of Dixie's dicks before Bart—Walter used to say Momma always looked like she had a Dove Bar up her ass."

A resonant voice came from behind me.

"If she does, it's the only thing that's ever been up there."

Brie Meyerson took a wide arc over to my side, maintaining her distance from the seeping burger.

"Mother wants you back, Spaulding," she said, taking a sip from a plastic pop bottle and then screwing the top back on.

Her brother chomped down on the second third of his burger and began to chew with his mouth open. I glanced away and resorted to idle chatter. "How are you, Miss Meyerson?" I asked.

"Bored," she said.

Not for long. Having expertly removed the meat, Jack now held the steaming T-bone aloft. "Abby darlin'," he bellowed. "Here, take this thing. Use it on that boy of yours. Time to face it, honey. You've done the best you could with him, but that one just ain't a keeper."

Abigail Meyerson answered without looking up. "At least my children are still with me, Mr. Del Fuego. At least I didn't force them upon strangers."

Jack answered through a mouthful of steak. "Other than that one you drove off." He swallowed. "Ya didn't forget about that one, now, did ya? I know she been gone a long time and all, but—"

"Oh, yeah," Spaulding yelled at the top of his voice. "Old Jack don't drive 'em off; he strings 'em up. Better check those drapes behind the old Jackster. Make sure he hasn't got the cords in his pocket. The Jackster's got a way with a rope."

Jack shot Spaulding a disgusted look and began to wave the bone around in earnest, as if painting grease letters in the air.

"Come on, now, Abby. You still remember how. I know you do, and I'm even donating my bones. It's for the good of the species, darlin'. For the good of the species."

For the first time, Candace seemed embarrassed by Jack's antics. She was sitting bolt upright, her hands gripping the edge of her plate like it was a life preserver, her lips invisible.

Jack waved the bone at Rodrigo, who had been observing from the far wall. "Hey, Lorenzo," Jack drawled. "Take this here Meyerson tongue depressor over to the little lady there."

Rodrigo hesitated. Jack stayed at him.

"Let's go. Chop-chop."

Rodrigo skipped across the room and took the bone from Jack's hands. He held it at arm's length, using only the tips of his fingers. He turned to walk away.

Francona and Hill rose as one. Abby continued to eat.

Rodrigo got the message. Any attempt to deliver the greasy scrap to their table would probably involve a prolonged need for physical therapy. He turned imploringly back toward Jack. No help there.

Candace was furiously whispering in the Jackalope's ear, but the old boy just wouldn't quit. "Go on, boy. Abby's puttin' on airs, is all. She's one of the finest bone artists on the planet."

Rodrigo was flushed with color, his free hand pumping into a fist.

I walked over, took the bone from the waiter's hand and deposited it in the nearest trash can. The room was silent as I returned to my roost next to Rickey Ray. I turned to Brie Meyerson and broke the silence.

"So how are you holding up under all of this?" I asked as if nothing at all had happened. She seemed relieved.

"I'm used to it," she said. "They do it all the time."

"No, I mean . . ." I searched for a sentence that didn't include both "Bunky" and "cook." "You know, the whole . . ."

"You mean that whole barbecue thing?"

"Yeah."

She checked over each shoulder and then leaned in very close. She might have reminded me of spring, but she smelled of cologne.

"I couldn't care less," she said. "That's Mother's thing."

"Really?"

"I'm not supposed to say anything, but, you know . . ."

"I thought . . ."

"Oh, you mean the whole grand opera, little-girl-and-her-beloved-pet thing?" She rolled her eyes heavenward. "Spare me. It's a cow. It didn't exactly sleep on the edge of my bed. I was raised on that farm. I know what happens to cows. Mother thinks it makes good copy, is all. It's all hype. I think she watched too many Shirley Temple movies as a child. So dull."

Trying not to be dull, I pointed at the bottle in her hand. The black plastic top featured those green panther eyes.

"What is that stuff, anyway?" I asked. "I keep seeing it around."

"That's because it's all the rage, you know," she mocked.

"It is, huh?"

She held the label up to my face. Red background, yellow banner with the word "Josta," and a sinuous black panther prowling across the top.

"It's Josta," she said.

"Josta 'nother soft drink?"

She laughed. "Very good, but no." She pointed to the label. "See, it's made with the guarana berry, and the guarana berry is supposed to have medicinal properties. In Brazil, they say it's an aphrodisiac."

Spaulding waved the burger in our direction. We both tensed.

"Shit tastes like cough syrup," he offered. "Her Majesty just orders it because nobody's ever got it on hand, and she likes to see them have to run all over hell and gone to find it."

"Stuff it, Spaulding."

Dixie's voice rose above the throng. "Be a sweetie, Bart, and get Momma a cup of coffee from over there in the cop section."

Bart rose and skirted his way behind Candace and Jack, moving into the middle of the room from a break in the tables.

"Step it up, sweetie," Spaulding brayed.

"Shut up, you moron," his sister whispered.

Spaulding grinned and brought the burger up to his mouth. It arrived ahead of schedule. Just as he was about to take a bite, Brie reached out and pushed the sandwich hard into her brother's face, twisting her wrist from side to side, mashing the mess into his face. I wanted to applaud, but decided it would be unprofessional.

Spaulding jerked his feet back and allowed the mess to drop onto the carpet. "You bitch." He reached for his sister.

I stepped between the pair. "Easy, kid. Easy."

Spaulding tried to move forward, but Rickey Ray had him by the belt. "Just a little joke there, podna. Don't be gettin' your panties all in a wad now."

Rickey Ray grinned over Spaulding's shoulder. "Got us a real hellcat here, Leo. Whip any girl on the block."

All I saw was Rickey Ray's hand lose its grip on the belt. Spaulding lurched forward, stepped in his own hamburger mess and nearly fell. Francona grabbed the kid by the elbow and pulled him upright.

"Well, looky here," I heard Rickey Ray say. "Somebitch touched me." He looked over at me. Hill was standing on his toes, two paces away from Rickey. "Somebitch done slapped me on the wrist. You see that, Leo?" I told him I hadn't, but I somehow knew it wasn't going to matter.

In an instant, all vestiges of the friendly cowboy disappeared from his face, and I saw a frightening ability to switch gears. The ancient Scots liked to speak in terms of becoming fey. Of succumbing to a self-induced battle trance, in the midst of which the warrior was a virtual killing machine. All hell broke loose.

As Rickey started for Hill, Francona, in an amazing display of stupidity, started for Rickey. Fortunately, Lieutenant Driscoll and Marty Conlan arrived at just about the same time. As if magnetically drawn together, the five of them formed a lurching knot of screaming, pushing humanity.

"Rowcliffe. The Mondavi Reserve, please."

Alomar agreed. "The Merlot lacked substance."

"Mr. Waterman," Sir Geoffrey said without looking up, "would you be so kind as to inquire when we shall be permitted to leave?"

"Sure," I said.

Marty and Driscoll were starting to get things calmed down as I turned and walked toward the corner of the dais. Lawrence and Lobdell were going nose to nose.

His face was red. "That's not what we'd do with any other group. We'd brace her and check everybody's reaction. I don't see why—"

"I'm merely saying that, considering the long-standing animosity among these groups . . ."

He was shaking his head. "It's standard procedure."

"This is not a standard situation. As I see it—"

She noticed me and stopped abruptly.

"Yes, Mr. Waterman?"

"Sir Geoffrey wants to know when he and Mr. Alomar can leave. Also, don't drink the Merlot; it lacks substance."

My boyish charm seemed to be at an all-time low. She sighed.

"We have transcriptions of their statements for them to sign, and then everyone can be on their way."

Francona and Hill were shepherding both Meyerson kids back to the family fort. Spaulding left a trail of squashed burger all the way across the room.

Rickey Ray had flipped his switch the other way. He showed Driscoll his palms. "Just funnin.'"

Marty Conlan was jerking at his pants and tucking in his shirt. He looked winded. That was the most action he'd had in years. I could see the excitement in his face.

Brie Meyerson was nearly back at the table when Lobdell spoke. "Miss Meyerson."

She turned to him. "Yes?"

"I'm afraid we have a problem with your statement."

"What? Oh." Brie had not inherited the family stoneface from her mother. The girl looked terrified. Forks poised in mid-stroke. Wine went unswallowed.

"I remind you, Miss Meyerson, this is a murder investigation."

When the girl didn't speak, he played his card.

"Perhaps I should tell you that the security floors in this hotel are monitored by surveillance cameras and that, while everyone else's coming and goings are confirmed by the tape, you do not appear on it until five-twenty P.M."

"I don't understand," the girl stammered.

"It's very simple. You told us that after returning to the hotel at two-thirty, you went straight to your room for a nap because you were feeling poorly." He drew the words out. "You do not appear on the tape, Miss Meyerson. So . . . if you weren't in your room, where were you?"

The girl instinctively turned toward her mother for help. Some help. Abigail Meyerson sat at attention. "Well?"

Brie glanced across the room toward the Del Fuego delegation.

"I . . ." She started to speak.

Lobdell began yapping. "I repeat, Miss Meyerson, this is a murder investigation. Where were you?"

In a touching display of sibling support, Spaulding piped up. "Leave her alone, dick face."

Lobdell gave it the voice of doom. "Miss Meyerson?"

From the corner of my eye I caught the movement as Candace Atherton put her napkin on the table and stood.

She spoke directly to Brie. "He's right. I'm afraid we'll have to tell them. I'm so sorry."

Whereas all eating had stopped a couple of minutes back, all breathing was now temporarily suspended.

"We . . ." The girl seemed to be slipping into vapor lock.

Candace now turned to Lobdell. "This is going to be somewhat awkward, Detective, and I must apologize." She cast a quick sidelong glance at the Meyerson contingent. "Miss Meyerson went to the movies with Mr. Tolliver and myself. We didn't say so before because we were afraid her mother . . ."

"Nonsense." Abigail Meyerson was on her feet.

Candace kept talking. "Up at what's called the Broadway market. A film named *Bound*. None of us liked it much. We left before it was over."

"My daughter went absolutely nowhere with these—"

Lobdell cut her off. "Well, Miss Meyerson?"

We had a mass exhale and waited.

The girl had gathered herself. "All right. All right. It's true."

A couple of hundred pins dropped.

Sir Geoffrey seemed amused. "Indeed."

They'd been right to worry what Abby Meyerson would think. As she dabbed at her lips, it was hard to tell where the white linen napkin left off and her face began.

She stood and picked her black purse up from the table. Her expression held no clue. She may well have been the coolest cucumber I can ever remember. Must be that Dove Bar, I mused.

"I apologize for my daughter," she said to Lobdell. "I had

no idea." She straightened her spine even more. "I assure you that my daughter will have no further contact with these people, and as of this moment, I shall require any further contact whatsoever with me or my family to pass through my attorney."

She pulled a business card from her purse and laid it on the table. Spaulding grabbed his crotch on the way out. Brie tried to linger.

"Brie," was all her mother said from the doorway. Abby never looked back as she closed the door behind them.

Rickey Ray whispered. "She's in the frying pan now."

His lordship had his hands folded over his middle and his lips pursed. He spoke without opening his eyes.

"There are, I suppose, worse places to be."

19

"There's a couple of necks out there in a white Chevy," Terry whispered in my ear. "They been in asking for you and Georgie by name. Got descriptions of the rest of your crew. They got uniforms out pushin' the neighborhood hard for the last couple of days."

I put my mouth to his ear. "Actually, there's probably more like four of them out there now. I just dragged a couple more of them with me from the hotel."

I'd picked them up right away. A couple of bulls in a blue Ford Taurus, hanging about five cars back and two lanes over as I rolled up the freeway toward The Zoo. Trying for all the world to look like a pair of weightlifters on their way to the gym at ten-thirty in the morning. Sure. The minute I ducked down the Lakeshore Drive exit, they allowed the gap between us to widen. They knew where I was going.

I motioned for Terry to lean in closer, but he shook his head, turning instead toward the far end of the bar, staying completely rigid as he moved. I followed him down the length of the bar.

"The back's still bad?" I inquired as I walked.

He waved an arm at me, telling me to follow. He wore

the same black polyester pantsuit he'd worn every day for the past fifteen years or so. It was the white patent leather belt and shoes, however, that made the ensemble.

"Killin' me, Leo. Doc says I got a disintegrating vertebra."

Terry lifted the hinged section of bar and headed toward the back of the building, pushing chairs out of his way as he shuffled along.

"Wants me to go under the knife," he continued. "But I don't know, man. You let people be cuttin' into your back, you could end up on a creeper with a cup full of pencils, if you know what I mean."

I told him I understood and followed him out the back door, onto the rickety back porch of the bar. He left the door ajar behind us.

The plywood floor sagged from the weight of the recycling barrels. Three for brown glass. Two for green. Terry checked the area.

Satisfied, he put a hand on my shoulder. "Those two outside was in for a while yesterday. I don't know what they was doin' back there." He shrugged and pointed to his ear. "You never know."

Two battered brown Dumpsters gagged on the oversized loads of refuse that had been packed into their mouths, leaving the covers now propped agape on the chain-link fence that separated this space from the peeling yellow house beyond.

"George said you would know what he was talkin' about if I said he was with Piggy and Roscoe and that they had a camp that was right back in the same place as the old camp. He said for you to remember the place where Cappy burned his truss."

Oh, yeah, like I was ever going to forget the smell of that thick yellow smoke rising to the roaring ceiling and then spreading out in both directions as the old man limped around the fire humming opera.

"I'm gonna leave from here," I said. "After a bit, the necks are gonna come in to see what the hell happened to me. You can handle it?"

"Be my pleasure to Schultz 'em, Leo. Hell, it's about the most fun I can have with this back," he replied.

"I'm gonna need a couple of candy bars," I said.

Terry nodded. "Always a good idea." He pulled the door open and eased himself inside, placing his white feet with great care, as if walking on hot coals. The steel door bumped twice on its cylinder and then snapped behind him. For some reason, the Dumpsters smelled worse in the silence.

The way I saw it, I had a case of Rickey Ray's limited options. The longer the heat looked for the crew, the more of them they were going to find. I had no illusions. This was not the Double-O Section. Some of them were going to get shitfaced and run their mouths to somebody who was going to flap his gums to somebody else who was going to make some folding money out of it. I needed to see George, and I needed to see him now. The good news was that the camp was within easy walking distance of where I stood.

The bad news was that I was about to use up one of my free Lose The Cops cards. Any damn fool can dump a tail if the tail doesn't know he's been spotted. About the time tails decide they don't give a damn whether or not you know you're being followed, it becomes exponentially more difficult. Once you make them look bad, and the four guys outside were going to be up shit's creek for losing me, then you become subject to all the high-tech, tag-team surveillance they can muster. It can still be done, but it takes quite a bit more finesse.

If they were smart, one of the cars would be parked halfway up Lynn, facing downhill, with a nice view all the way to Lake Union, while the other would be along the curb on Eastlake Boulevard, covering the terrain north to south. Sadly, that left only the Dumpsters and the fence.

The door opened; Terry's hand appeared and dropped a Snickers bar and a bag of M&M Peanuts into my hand.

"Thanks," I said, but the door had already snapped shut.

I stashed the goodies in my jacket pocket, then stepped off the porch. I wiggled sideways into the space between the Dumpsters and levered them apart. Each box had two sets of U-shaped ears welded to the side, lift handles for the garbage trucks that slipped their hydraulic tongues into the slots.

Reluctantly gripping the edge of each Dumpster, I boosted myself up onto the lower set of handles. The yellow house on the other side of the fence had a ragged backyard barely big enough for a faded blue wading pool, partially collapsed and sagging under the weight of green water and sodden leaves. Several pieces of ancient firewood, some cross-hatched with the bite of the ax, littered the yard, along with a white bleach bottle, whose bottom was cut out. No dog-house. No food dishes. No bones. Good.

I considered a number of methods by which I could possibly climb up and over the garbage without touching a single exposed surface, but eventually said screw it and propelled myself up to the higher set of handles and then up onto the top, careful of my footing lest I slide down the lid and into the Dumpster, in which case suicide would surely be the sole remaining option.

I sidestepped to the top of the lid and jumped. About halfway down, I felt pretty good. That was before I realized that what I had taken to be the ground was merely the top of waist-high field grass. The resultant glitch in my athletic timing drove my knees up under my chin with a crack and then catapulted me back into the lower part of the fence like a missile. The fence groaned and rattled.

I sat in the damp, rough grass with my palms up, as if hoping to stem the torrent of dead leaves showering down upon my head and into my lap from the shaking blackberry bush which had woven itself into the fabric of the fence. I blinked once and then remembered where I was.

I struggled to my feet, stepped around the sad little pool and followed the cracked cement path which led around the right side of the house. Nobody had walked this way in quite a while. I could tell because, two steps in, I took a three-pound spiderweb full in the face. If the thing had been any bigger and stronger, I'd have had whiplash.

By my reckoning, a good, fresh spiderweb in the mug is one of life's least endearing experiences. I rank it right up there with getting parking tickets and stepping in dog shit as serious day killers. Imagine how other insects felt about it.

I squatted and duckwalked the rest of the way, using my hands to hack an imaginary path into the air before me. At that point, I was not prepared to consider how stupid it certainly must have looked. *Arrrg.*

I was still rubbing and picking at my face when I emerged onto Eastlake Boulevard, a block north of the white Chevy Blazer. After checking both ways, I dipped across the street and started up the hill, where I leaned back against a storefront and pawed at the imagined maze of filament which my central nervous system insisted was still stuck to my face, but which my fingers could not detect. Nothing short of a shower was going to suffice.

Resigned, I trudged the two steep blocks up to Boylston and then turned right. The Taurus was just where I thought it would be, straddling the little grass island on the right of the street. I turned up my collar and crossed Lynn a block and a half behind the two cops, taking my time, making sure that if they happened to snatch a rearview look at me, there'd be nothing sufficiently remarkable about my presence to command their attention.

Three blocks in front of me, Boylston Avenue seems to allow but two choices. You can go straight ahead onto the Interstate, or you can duck left under the bridge and run along the face of Capital Hill and the high-rent homes looking out over Lake Union from the east. Either way, you're a long way from terra firma. I took the third route.

Under the overpass, the ground falls off sharply as it works its way in a series of gullies down toward the lake, and for about half a mile, all twelve lanes of the freeway are held aloft by a forest of cement columns and buttresses that stretch forward into the darkness farther than the eye can follow, a woodland excavated and exposed to the air for the first time in centuries.

What it was mostly, though, was about five acres of roof. A roof that roared, but a roof nonetheless, and a roof in a place where it rains most of the time is a valuable commodity indeed.

The city and the homeless have been duking it out over this particular section of real estate for as long as I can remember. I've formulated a theory that says it's a question of what year it happens to be. If it's between elections, city officials wage an unceasing battle to keep the less fortunate from building their shantytowns and hobo jungles under the bridge. As fast as they build them, the city sends in the cops and the bulldozers. As the elections approach, however, the harassment stops. Seattle is a liberal, socially conscious town. While vilifying the poor may be acceptable in the burbs, downtown it will get you voted out of office in a heartbeat. This was an election year.

I stood on the sidewalk at the top of Boylston. Gray pillars grew in clutches of three, supporting the overhead roadway with enormous pinchers of concrete and steel. The columns seemed to grow downward from the road above like smooth, symmetrical stalactites. The inconsistent rise and fall of the hill skewed the perspective all out of whack, so that I slid down a short embankment even though it looked like I should be moving at a level.

The ground was a morass of stunted vegetation and metallic debris. Only the blackberry bushes flourished, and it was among these brittle, armored survivors that the well-worn paths wove. Few natural objects could protect your back like a good blackberry thicket. A cozy cul-de-sac with an overhead roof to keep out the insistent rain and two-inch thorns to discourage intruders was to be both cherished and defended. It had been a long time since I'd been down here. Last time I'd walked down to the bottom, where the highway and the hill come together, I'd had to shoot a man to get back out. That probably explained why, permit or no permit, the little .32 auto was strapped to my right calf this morning.

I knelt, pulled up my pant leg and removed the gun from its holster. After checking the safety, I slipped it into my jacket pocket and looked around. The area was as I remembered it. A wide central path wound crazily among a labyrinth of thorny mounds, into which had been hacked a veritable jigsaw puzzle of cul-de-sacs and courtyards. At the base, the mottled red vines were nearly as big as my wrist, providing solid support for the twisted arches of thorn. The smooth path glittered with bits of glass and crunched underfoot. I slipped my hand into my pocket, resting it on the little automatic, and started down the path.

In the distance I could hear yelling. High-pitched yelling and the sound of a hammer hitting something over and over. On my left, a battered piece of cardboard had been drawn across an entrance. The smell of burning trash hung in the air.

I kept my eyes straight ahead as I wound down the path, past maybe a dozen camps sheltering maybe thirty people in all, some still in the sack, others up and around the fire. Above the tinking of the hammer, I heard the hoarse call which now preceded me down the hill. They thought I was the cops. I kept moving downward, toward the darkness at the far end of the structure and the incessant sound of the hammering, feeling more like Dante with every step, as the roaring of the overhead roadway began to drown out all other ambient noise in a pool of rushing air and falling dust.

The woman sat way up top on the embankment, with her head no more than a couple of feet below the roof and a boulder between her knees, using the remaining claw of a hammer to batter away at the brown rock. Steadily. In four-four time. One . . . two . . . three . . . four. Despite the abnormally warm weather, she was wearing everything she owned. Under a leaking down vest, I counted three different sweaters. No telling what was under that. She was barefoot, and her rough, clawed feet waved to the beat of the hammer.

Below the bird feet, nestled back in the farthest reaches of the jungle, was, by bum standards, a high-class hideaway. Five makeshift benches surrounding a rock-lined fire pit, where some small animal was, at this moment, roasting. All nice and dry. Empty, too. Only the sounds of the metal chipping away at the rock and the roar of the tires.

"George," I hollered. "It's Leo."

"Comin'," I heard him growl from somewhere on my right.

I could hear the sound of boots on packed earth before I noticed the movement in the bushes. George came out first. His new suit was in ruins, stained through at the knees and ripped at the cuffs. Then came Piggy and Roscoe Radamacher.

At one time I might have known Piggy's real name and maybe even why they called him Piggy, but neither came to mind right now. As bums go, Piggy was generally neat and clean. Comparatively speaking, anyway. And he wasn't particularly overweight either, just that sort of pasty quality they get from too much junk food.

George stepped out into the cleared area and took a seat on the nearest plank and bucket bench. His hands were dirty; he looked haggard and drawn.

"Piggy, you remember Leo, doncha?"

"I remember," he said.

I had no doubt. I'd been part of a phalanx of cops and volunteers who'd swept down through this jungle like locusts about five years ago, searching for Alice Ann Royal, a ten-year-old girl who'd failed to come home from the Seward School that same afternoon.

About twenty-five yards from this very spot, I'd kicked my way past a piece of plywood just in time to see a mutant named Ferdy Kanzler rising from atop the wide-eyed little girl. He had a bottle in his hand. In my saner moments, I tell myself that he was going to attack me with it. Since I

quit drinking, most of my moments are saner, so these days
I spend precious little time wondering whether or not that
was why I hauled off and shot him in the neck. Didn't much
matter. Three cops who weren't even there stepped forward
to say that was how it happened. Last I heard, Alice Ann
Royal had never spoken a word since that tragic afternoon
in October.

"Stop that goddamn bangin'," Piggy shouted up at the
woman.

One . . . two . . . three . . . tink tink. Waltz time, now.

Roscoe Radamacher was a sad story. He was the unwanted offspring of a South Seattle whore who'd taken one
look at his deformed face and thrown him in a trash bin
down by the airport. Everybody knew the story, because the
cops and the Child Protection Service folks had run her
down and prosecuted the crap out of her in full view of the
evening news.

From there, things had gotten bad for Roscoe Radamacher.
Sad as it is to say, our society has little to offer a severely
retarded giant of a boy, born nearly without an upper jaw,
with an inoperable hole in the front of his face that he could
close only by bringing his lower lip up to nearly cover his
nose. Fifteen years of institutions and foster care, and, even
in a mind as feeble as Roscoe's, the streets begin to beckon
like the gates of paradise. He was strong as an ox and, from
what I'd heard, literally did not feel pain. Piggy used him
as a bodyguard, which was why he had the prime camp.

I reached into my pocket. "Roscoe," I said. "You remember me?"

He shook his head. At least he was honest. Although we'd
been in each other's company a couple of times before, I
knew he wouldn't remember. From what I could tell, he had
an attention span of about ten seconds. After that were just
the next ten seconds.

"Here, I brought you something," I said.

He stopped sniffing the air and scowled at me.

I held the candy out in front of me like I was at the zoo.

"It's for you," I said.

Roscoe snapped it up from my hand with the speed of a cobra strike. He held the candy against his chest with one hand and poked at it with the other. "Fanks," he said.

One . . . two . . . three . . . tink tink.

"Goddamn you—" Piggy began.

Roscoe squelched the utterance by pinching off Piggy's throat.

"No yell, Piggy," he said, waving the little man about.

Piggy was purple and trying to agree. I slipped my hand into my other pocket and fondled the automatic. Fortunately for both of us, Roscoe lost interest in strangling Piggy and threw him to the ground like a discarded toy. "Fanks," he said again.

I sat down next to George. "How you doing?" I asked.

"How's it look like I'm doin'?" he countered.

"Not too good."

"I'm too old for this shit, Leo."

One . . . two . . . three . . . tink tink.

"What's the word?"

Across the clearing, Roscoe rolled a few M&M's into Piggy's upturned palm and then poured the rest of the bag into his face.

"I talked to everybody except Norman and Hot Shot," George said. "The cops got those two last night. That's how come I didn't want to leave a message. The boys in blue are all over this thing."

"Yeah, I know."

"Todd was just pourin' the drinks in the Six-Eleven. Cops came in and took 'em out. Told Todd they was material witnesses. Todd says they rousted every bar and flop in the square. Says they got them little made-up drawings of the whole crew."

"Composites?"

"Yeah."

"I'll have Jed check on 'em."

"Normal don't do good in the joint. Ya gotta get him out."

I told him I would. One . . . two . . . three . . . tink tink.
I leaned in close. "What's she doing with the hammer?"

"She thinks there's somethin' inside."

"The rock?"

"Yeah. She thinks there's somethin' hidden inside everything."

"What do you do, sleep when she does?"

George forced out a short, bitter laugh. "Sleep, hell. I been here a day and a half and I ain't seen her blink yet."

I checked her from the corner of my eye. George was right.

"Well, tell me what you found out, and maybe we can get you the hell out of here."

He pointed over to the fire pit, where Piggy and Roscoe were in the process of turning whatever creature it was they were cooking. "Wouldn't want to do anything too hasty, Leo," he said. "Breakfast is about ready."

"Wingless squab?" I inquired.

"Subway rabbit," he said, pushing himself to his feet.

"Lemme guess. Tastes just like chicken."

One . . . two . . . three . . . tink tink.

George shuffled over to the entrance to the clearing and pulled a wadded piece of brown paper out from among the thorns.

"I know you said not to write nothing down, but there was just too much stuff." He began to straighten the paper out on his leg. "I figured John Law wouldn't go through the trash."

He sat down beside me. "Who first?"

I pulled out my notebook. "Let's do Mason Reese."

We did them all. It was all times and places. They'd been a busy little group. By the time George was through, I'd filled two full pages in my little notebook and discovered, once again, that truth is often stranger than fiction.

When he finished, he pulled a pint of Seagrams from his inside pocket, took a long pull, offered me some and then had another.

"You sure these times are reliable?" I asked him.

"Four of 'em, I seen myself. The Meyerson girl, Dixie's—you know, what's his name—"

"Bart?"

"Yeah, Bart, him and the Del Fuego pair."

"Rickey Ray and Candace?"

"Yeah. All of them arrived in a rush, right about two-thirty or so. The girl, then Bart, and then beauty and the beast. Them two, I ended up in the elevator with."

He caught himself. I saw his eyes shift quickly.

"Where were you going?" I asked.

He was ready. "To the room. I needed to use the crapper."

There were rest rooms in the lobby. He knew that. He also knew that I knew. And I knew that he knew that I knew he knew. He'd gone upstairs to liberate the rest of the booze from the fridge.

In confirmation, he suddenly became animated. "And it was weird, too, Leo. I hustled over, and they was already in there. I pushed nine and, you know, didn't say nothing. I figured, you know, they were going to fourteen, and guess what—go on, guess . . . ."

"What?"

"The thing stops at eight."

"How drunk was everybody?" I persisted.

He paid no attention. "And they get off, but just for a second. One second after they get off, they hustle back in, the door closes and we're up, up, and away. Weird, huh?"

"What's weird, George, are these times. When I got in Monday night, just before I found the body, everybody looked to me to be seriously hammered. We had most of the crew napping over across the street, for Chrissake. I'm concerned."

Where obstruction had failed, he now tried righteous indignation.

"You sayin' I didn't handle it? That what you're sayin?"

I let it go. "No. I just need to be sure about the numbers."

"Well, then, feel free to be sure."

"Well, then, my friend, you're not going to like this."

"Why's that?"

I gave him the news. "You're gonna have to stay lost."

"You're shittin' me."

" 'Fraid not," I said. "You're the only one who knows it all. They can get the rest of it piecemeal from the crew, but by then it'll be too late. The only thing that can't happen is the heat can't get you. If that happens, they know what we know."

"Shit."

"You need money?"

He shook his head. "I need outta here, is what I need."

"A couple of days, at most." I said. "You come out into polite society and they're gonna have you in ten minutes."

I ran down what Terry had told me about the cops rousting the square.

"Shit," George said again.

Behind me, Piggy and Roscoe struggled to pull the wooden spit from the crispy critter without burning themselves. I took the brown paper over and dropped it into the fire pit, where it began to twist on the ashes and then burst into bright yellow flame. One . . . two . . . three . . . tink . . .

The woman stopped hammering and looked down at me.

"It's a tough nut," she said.

George lifted the bottle to his lips. "I'll drink to that."

20

"The hell you say."

"We seem to have fallen among thieves."

"Liars is what we have fallen among," Sir Geoffrey said.

"More like fibbers."

"Let me see that," he said. I walked over to the bed and handed him my notebook. As he snatched the pad from my fingers, his nostrils twitched. Bright yellow was the color du jour.

"You smell of . . . what is that, Mr. Waterman?" He sniffed again. "Is that mutton I smell?"

"Long-tailed teriyaki."

"I'm not familiar . . ."

"It's sort of a mixed grill."

He didn't hear. He was scowling at the list of times and places.

"All of them," he said. "Every bloody one."

"They seem to fall into three categories. Some just lied about the times. Others lied only about where they went. And then there were the people who lied about everything."

He pointed at the pad in his hand. "Now, the senior Ms. Meyerson told the police that she was working at the new restaurant all day, but your men say she was only at the restaurant late in the afternoon."

"That's right."

"She went first to a television station . . ."

"KING-TV."

"Why would she be frequenting a television station?"

I shrugged and said, "I'll call a friend of mine and see what I can find out."

Miles put his nose back into the pad in his palm.

"And then she went to these other addresses."

"Yes."

"And then finally to the restaurant."

"But she was truthful as far as her times were concerned."

"Correct."

"What about the Meyerson boy?"

"We don't know where he went," I said. "He separated from the pack while they were at the television station. Since the party still consisted of four people, my men decided to let him go."

"He arrived back at the hotel at twelve fifty-five. Is that correct?"

"Yes," I said.

"And then he left again at one-twenty, not to return until four-fifteen."

"Yes. That must have been confirmed by the surveillance tape, or else they would have busted his story, too."

"As they did with the Meyerson girl."

"Yes."

He studied the list again.

"She told the authorities that she'd taken a cab back to the hotel at about two-thirty and gone straight to her room."

"Right," I said. "But it turned out that she'd been fraternizing with the enemy."

Sir Geoffrey shrugged. "It's not their fight. They are, after all, relative contemporaries who spend most of their lives sequestered together in the same hotels. I don't find it at all surprising that they've developed a few ties."

"I don't know whether you noticed, but her mother didn't share your sense of inevitability."

"She was rather put out, wasn't she?"

"I'm guessing the girl finds herself on a real short leash for a real long while."

"Has this trip to the motion pictures been corroborated?"

"I'm guessing it has. They never questioned whether Atherton and Tolliver went, just whether the Meyerson girl went with them. I don't see how anyone could claim to have gone out in public with Rickey Ray if it wasn't true. I mean, he's . . ."

"Of course," Miles said.

"That little group is probably the least likely of suspects. Tolliver has an unforgettable face, and they've got corroboration from both sides of the Meyerson-Del Fuego fence."

He agreed. "And what of the remaining Del Fuego mob?"

"Let's begin with Dixie and Bart," I suggested.

He made a face. "If we must."

"Dixie and Bart claim to have spent the entire morning and early afternoon sightseeing."

"But your men say otherwise."

"I have it on good authority," I lied, "that she spent the entire day in the King County Office Building, on either the fifth or the ninth floor. My man couldn't be sure which. At four-twenty, she met a cab in front of the building and arrived back at the hotel at four-thirty."

"Indeed? And am I to presume that we once again have no idea as to what business she was on?"

"Something official. Something civil rather than criminal. That's all that goes on in that building. I should have no trouble finding out what she was doing."

"Very well. Carry on."

"Her companion, Mr. Yonquist, left the King County building at two-ten and walked back to the hotel. I have his arrival both from the man following him and from my people in the lobby, so that one is extra solid. He claims to have gone to his room to change and then to have gone down to the hotel weight room and worked out."

Sir Geoffrey cocked an eyebrow at me.

I shrugged. "We'll have to assume that if the cops didn't brace him about it last night, he must have shown up on the tape at the appropriate times."

"What of Mr. Del Fuego himself?"

"Mr. Del Fuego told the cops that he ran some errands and then went to his new place. He wasn't altogether truthful."

"Why am I not surprised?"

"He ran a couple of errands, all right, but not to the produce wholesaler and the linen supplier like he said."

"Where was he really?"

"It's all down there. He made three stops."

Miles perused the papers. "A scenic-tour company?"

"That's what it says. Look at the next one."

"Cold storage?"

"A commercial meat locker. I know the place."

He cast me a knowing glance and shook his head.

"Those two, he made before going to the restaurant."

"And afterward?"

"Next on the list."

"Wagner's Farm and Garden. What's this?"

"A feed store?"

"A feed store and a commercial meat locker would seem to be mutually exclusive."

He was right. There's something strange about feeding a dead cow.

I shrugged. "My people say he went to the feed store last thing. Took a taxi all the way to North City and back to the hotel."

Sir Geoffrey sighed. "So then this Mr. Tolliver drove Mr. Del Fuego to his new establishment and, after leaving Mr. Del Fuego, drove the paramour Miss Atherton back to the hotel. Is that correct?"

"Yes. They got here at about two twenty-five, bought a newspaper in the gift shop, found a movie listing and went to the theater. Del Fuego arrived by taxi at six-forty."

He listened attentively as I told him about George's elevator ride with Rickey Ray and Candace. After he went back to staring at the list, I anticipated his next question. "Reese left me a message at two-ten. I found him dead at about six-ten. They didn't say, but I'm guessing he'd been dead for at least a couple of hours when I found him. So . . . we have to figure the window for killing Reese was somewhere between, say, two forty-five and five in the afternoon."

Miles allowed his glasses to slip to the end of his nose as he looked from the paper to me and back. "This is rubbish," he finally complained. "If these times are correct, we can eliminate only Mr. Del Fuego from consideration as the murderer."

"That's the way I see it. Give or take a half hour, every one of them except Jack was here sometime within the period when Reese was probably killed. Some of them, like the moviegoers, were around at the beginning of the period; others were around at the end. Like Dixie and Ms. Meyerson."

"Indeed," he said again. He took off his glasses and folded his hands over his middle. "Then we are at an impasse," he declared.

"Not quite."

"You have a plan of action?"

"Yeah," I said. "And a few questions."

"Such as?"

"First off, I'm still a bit unclear as to who was threatened enough by Mason Reese to want to kill him. In my experience, people either kill from passion—you know, heat-of-the-moment kinds of things—or they kill for profit or maybe even sometimes for revenge."

"Mr. Reese was in a position to be troublesome to both camps."

"Troublesome," I repeated. "That's right. That's the perfect word for it. He could have made himself troublesome, but you know . . . troublesome is what we have lawyers for. We don't usually shoot people over being troublesome."

"What else?"

"Then there's the question of exactly who it was that Mason Reese would have opened the door for."

"I'm not sure I follow."

"He made me stand in the hall," I said. "I had every kind of ID known to man and he talked to me through a crack in the door. I want to know who it was he felt comfortable enough with to let in."

"Good point."

"Put yourself in his place, Sir Geoffrey. You're in town to cut yourself a deal with either Meyerson or Del Fuego. You're paranoid as hell. Somebody knocks on your door. Who do you let in?"

He closed his eyes, pursed his lips and thought it over.

"A woman, perhaps?" Sir Geoffrey suggested. "Or a child."

"The only thing we have that remotely resembles a child is the Meyerson boy, and he's the last person on the planet you'd let in your hotel room, believe me."

"Manifestly," he agreed. "A lout."

I stood by the side of the bed in silence. I could hear Rowcliffe moving around in the outer room. Finally, I said, "I'm going out this afternoon and retrace some of their steps. Maybe if I can find out what they were really doing, all of this will begin to make a bit more sense."

He made that dismissive noise again. "I have my doubts."

With that, he slipped his glasses back over his nose, which he then stuck into his book. Still the Steven Jay Gould. I can take a hint.

He stopped me halfway to the door, catching my gaze over the top of his glasses. "Mr. Waterman, I regret having run you so seriously afoul of the authorities. Your efforts to distance this sordid matter from the conference have been stellar. For the moment, the unwanted notoriety has been confined to the principals, for which I am grateful." He took a deep breath. "I am, however, concerned that Mr. Del Fuego's Friday night debacle will seriously detract from the quantity and quality of media attention given the conference." He showed me a palm. "Who could have guessed that this matter would come to such a speedy and . . . final conclusion? Señor Alomar and I wish to assure you that we will continue to support you with the full weight of our respective organizations. You shall not be abandoned."

I thanked him, waved good-bye to Rowcliffe, who was busy brushing imaginary lint from a brown suit, and let myself out.

Once again, my room had been completely renovated since I'd left this morning. I headed right for the shower, where I spent a full fifteen minutes separating myself from spiderwebs and the smell of mutton.

I couldn't help myself. It was fate. As I laced up my Reeboks in the sitting room, the digital clock read ten after one. L-O-L-A time. I flipped on the tube and moved up to Channel 8. The cardboard cutout of Jack and Bunky had been moved to the rear of the set. Lola King sat on one stool and a swarthy little fellow with a cue-ball head sat on the other. He wore black slacks and a red nylon jacket with some sort of insignia on the front. Lola, as usual, looked concerned. The camera had been moved to the side of the stage to include the audience in the wide-angle shot.

"So what you're saying, Mr. Tate, is that this particular bull has value above and beyond . . ." Lola struggled for a phrase.

"This bull is a completely new standard for the breed. A quantum leap forward for the husbandry of the Angus. We at the American Angus registry were fully prepared to—" Click.

I dialed nine and then Bruce Gill's number at KOMO-TV. I'm not sure what his job title is, but he's got the corner office on the top floor and he shaves only once a week or so. We'd played together on the same thirty-five-and-older basketball team until his knees gave out. He was a gunner. You passed that sucker the ball, you *never* saw it again.

"Gill."

"That's not very customer-friendly."

"Customers don't have this number. You still taking all the shots, or do you pass the ball once in a while?"

"Oh, don't start that shit with me, man. It was you . . ."

It was like finding something I didn't know was missing. As we bantered back and forth, I realized how long it had been since I'd indulged in this particular brand of male bonding and how much I missed having it in my life. I wondered how its disappearance had managed to escape my notice.

"Hey, what's going on with Lola King over at KING? How come she's on every day this week? She making a comeback or something?"

"Think. You just asked me why a corporation did something."

He had a point. "Okay, where's the money coming from?"

"The Meyerson Corp. They've got two mil a year in TV Ads to use as candy. They get whatever they want. I hear they went to management and offered them the spots in return for the full-week special."

"Isn't this animal rights stuff going to hurt her business, too?"

"The way I see it, she can afford it and Del Fuego can't."

"Yeah," was all I could think to say.

"You still play?" he asked.

"Nah. The wheels came off a couple of years ago. The kids kept getting bigger and younger."

"Getting old's a bitch," he said.

Couldn't say I disagreed.

21

In a way, it was comforting. When I'd ditched them this morning, they'd stayed a demure four or five cars back. If they'd done that again, I'd have been worried about whether or not they had my car wired. As it was, they were standing on the circular sidewalk, leaning back against the Taurus, when I came out the front door and handed the valet the ticket for the Fiat. No more Mr. Nice Guy. They didn't give a hoot whether or not I knew they were following me. The bigger of the two wanted to make macho eye contact, so I made small talk with the valet captain and pretended not to notice them. This one was really gonna piss them off.

I took the freeway to the Forty-fifth Street exit and stayed all the way to the left. The cops were two cars back, behind a Federal Express truck, when I stopped and waited for the light.

I turned left on the green, crossed the freeway and started up the hill toward Wallingford. The buildings used to be a service station and a mom-and-pop grocery which eventually came to be owned by the same Greek family. If I remembered correctly, they'd started out with the store and then later bought the gas station, or maybe it was the other way around. They'd sold out about five years ago, and the buildings had been converted into a Mike's hamburger stand and a Colortime carpet store.

Back in the sixties, right after they bought the station, hoping to encourage their customers to avail themselves of both the gas station and the store, the Greeks had connected their two businesses with a short driveway. Considering the recent minimart/gas station frenzy, a savvy move indeed.

What the Greeks had joined together, the new owners had not bothered to render asunder. Thus, when you got to be the third car from the front in Mike's drive-up line, only a small concrete curb stood between you and turning right into the carpet store's parking lot and then out into Donald Avenue. Yep, they were gonna hate this one.

Using my signal so as not to confuse the fellas, I turned into the suicide lane, waited for the traffic to thin, then darted across Forty-fifth into Mike's. The Taurus stayed in the center lane to see what I was going to do.

Like I figured, there was no way they were going to get in the drive-up line with me. Everybody knew the old "drive-in dodge." All you had to do was get a citizen between you and them in the line, and they were as good as lost. No, these were pros. They weren't going for that crap. As I wound around the back, they pulled into the parking lot and backed the car up against the west side of the building, perfectly positioned to go either way on Forty-fifth, once I made my exit.

I was six cars from the drive-up window when I drew up to the speaker. I took the electronic gargling to be a request for my order and asked for a small Coke.

"Is that all?"

"That's it."

"That will be one-o-six at the second window, please."

In front of me, a blue Toyota PTA van bounced on its springs as a herd of toddlers threw themselves around the interior. The red Citation, first in line, left the window. Five from the front. Then four, and then finally the black pickup, just before the Toyota, eased out into traffic, the van pulled forward and I was on my way, cutting hard right, bumping up and over the curb, rolling down past the fantastic free-installation offer and out into Donald Avenue.

I drove all the way to Westlake in a cloud of adrenaline fumes. There's something about getting away with something that still tickles my central nervous system. I checked numbers as I rolled up Westlake. Not even close. I drove another quarter mile and checked again. Here somewhere. I pulled to the right, onto the wide, connected parking area that runs nearly the length of the busy road.

The sign said PACIFIC SKYWAYS. Scenic tours of Seattle, Mount Rainier and the San Juans. Charter service to B.C. Sounded pretty ambitious for a battered gray shack wedged between a yacht brokerage and dry-dock yard. I parked the Fiat and stepped out onto the gangway.

Shards of driftwood bobbed along democratically with a couple of pop cans and a torn Styrofoam cooler. To my right, a gaggle of houseboats sat cheek to jowl with one another, bobbing slightly in the breeze, emitting a low chorus of squeaks and groans. The north arch of the Aurora Bridge was visible at the far left, and beyond that, Fremont, Ballard and the Sound.

At the far end of the dock, two yellow-and-white De Havilland Beavers rocked front to back on their pontoons, like a brace of rambunctious puppies eager to slip the leash. The Beaver is to aircraft what no automobile manufacturer has ever managed on the ground, an unstoppable, unbreakable machine of such endurance and reliability as to have become the stuff of legend. As I approached, the big Pratt & Whitney power plants seemed to smile at me with rows of ribbed teeth.

I was standing at the end of the dock looking in through the nearest pilot's window when he spoke. "Help you with something?"

He was about fifty, sandy hair gone to gray, and sporting

a waxed handlebar mustache. On one breast it said, "Pacific Flying Service"; on the other, "Rick." I walked over and stuck out my hand.

"I'm Leo Waterman."

He took it. "Rick Bodette, Pacific Flying Service."

"I really love these old Beavers."

"Finest utility aircraft ever made," he agreed. "I take it you've flown in them before."

I told him about how the old man always knew somebody who knew somebody who'd fly us up to Canada to go fishing a couple of times a year. Some place you could only fly into.

"Looking to do a little flying?"

"Wish I was. What I'm looking for is somebody around here who's seen this guy lately."

I pulled the newspaper ad with Jack and Bunky from my back pocket and unfolded it. The newsprint flapped wildly in the stiff breeze until I captured both edges and stretched it out between my hands.

"Know this guy?" I asked.

"Which one?" he asked with a grin.

"The one without the halter."

"Never seen him in my life."

"Sure?"

"Positive."

"Maybe somebody else here . . ." I began.

"Nobody here but me and Andy."

"Could we ask Andy?"

"Sure. Come on in."

I'd like to tell you that the interior of Pacific Flying Service belied its humble exterior, but that wouldn't be true. It was a dump inside, too. Most of the wall space was covered by yellowing charts and colorful travel posters. *See Victoria! B.C. Place is the Place!* Half a dozen blue plastic chairs were spread around the floor.

Scoured by countless forgotten cigarettes, a battered counter divided the spare space approximately in half, its worn top chipped and pulled loose from the metal edge-molding. Behind the counter, the cramped office area was barely able to accommodate the two desks, butted nose to nose. Not only that but . . .

Andy was an Andi. About Rick's age, a thinning head of salt-and-pepper hair worn very short. Not "I reject the concept of beauty and repudiate the penis oppressor" short, but short.

"Hi," she said.

For a moment, before she could get her smile fixed in place, I saw the young girl in her. As I swallowed my greeting, her half-formed smile slid off. We stood, tilting our heads and scowling at each other. I could feel Rick getting antsy, over on my right.

"We know each other, don't we?" she said.

"Yeah, I think so."

It took us five minutes, but we finally got it sorted out. Turned out she'd dated my ex-wife's older brother Tom while I was in high school, and that we'd suffered through a couple of parentally mandated double dates together back in the heyday of the accursed panty girdle.

"You ever talk to Tom?" I asked.

"Not in years. You married what's-her-name, didn't you?"

"Annette, and yeah . . . briefly."

I changed the subject. "How long you guys been in the flying business?"

She looked to Rick. "What is it, honey? Two years this April."

"April sixth."

I got the whole story. They took turns telling it. She'd been the assistant superintendent in the Lake Washington school district for twenty-two years when she found herself suddenly burned out by the politics and pointlessness of public education and in dire need of something new.

Rick had been on the original marketing team for Microsoft's first commercially available version of MS-DOS and, like so many thousands of the MS-faithful before him, had found himself, as a relatively young man, with more money than he was ever likely to be able to spend.

The timing had been perfect. They both retired, took flying lessons until they were both fully rated float plane instructors—Andi had turned out to be a far more natural pilot than Rick—then sold the house in Redmond and bought themselves a business.

"I feel twenty years younger," Andi said.

Then I had to tell my story. I kept it short, which wasn't hard. My life story is in no danger of going multivolume. The only two paid jobs I've ever had were bag boy at the Queen Anne QFC and freelance private eye. Which turned out to be a clean segue into what I'd come here for in the first place.

I smoothed the paper over the counter. "Know him?"

"The cow?"

Rick burst out laughing.

"I see why you two get along," I said.

"Yeah, he's the guy who hired Mike for Friday," she said.

"Who's Mike?"

Andi reached to her left and jerked up the Levolor blind. A gray primered helicopter squatted atop a floating dock, its still rotors sagging low over the water like the wilted petals of a techno-flower.

"Mike Bales," Rick said.

"Mike around?"

Andi shook her head. "Mike only comes down when he's got a charter."

"Any idea what he was hired to do?"

"None."

"Whatever it is, it must be risky, though," said Rick.

"How come?"

Andi pointed her finger at her temple and made a swirling motion. "One too many combat missions in 'Nam."

Rick explained. "That's his specialty. He's the one puts the geologists up on the rim of Saint Helens for their tests.

You got some place where nobody else is willing to fly, Mike is your man."

"He isn't the maniac who put the base jumpers on top of the Space Needle, is he?"

"You bet he is," said Rick. "The FAA pulled his ticket for six months over that one. He was only legal again this week."

My mind could still recall the picture of the guy with the leather football helmet and the protruding Marty Feldman eyes being led to the cruiser. It was worse than I'd thought.

"You want his number?" Andi asked.

I took the number down, swore oaths about keeping in touch, most of which I probably wasn't going to keep, and made my way back to the car. As I walked, I wondered whether everyone homogenizes his life story when he finds himself compelled to tell it. I am always overcome with the desire to hurry up and get it over with, as if talking about myself is somehow in questionable taste. I seem to grind off the highs and lows in an odd desire to appear terse and conventional. Or maybe it's because, after a certain age, we all know the pain, and by then most of us have sense enough not to pass it around unnecessarily.

Wagner's Feed and Garden was all the way to hell and gone. Twenty miles north of downtown, damn near to Everett, but I was as close now as I was going to get. I made a mental note to give Flounder and Hot Shot Scott some extra cash. They must have had to dip into their own money to take a cab this far and back in the name of surveillance.

I was on a roll today. The old man's name was Orville Whitney. He gave me his card. I didn't even have the newspaper all the way spread out when the old guy said, "Jack Del Fuego, the barbecue king." The rest was easy. Jack had come in just before closing time, maybe five to six on Monday evening. I stopped the proceedings right there and went back over the time.

"I know, 'cause he come in cussing his cabdriver. Said the . . ." He hesitated.

"The what?" I prodded.

He looked embarrassed. "He said the dumb camel jockey didn't know his way around the city and didn't speak English. Said they'd been driving around for an hour. I told him it was a good thing they didn't drive for another five minutes or I'da been closed and gone."

Jack had wanted a dozen bales of straw, six of an alfalfa-timothy mix, and a hundred pounds of Steer Manna delivered to the restaurant.

"Wanted it right then, too," Orville said. "Slipped me a fifty to have the boy run it up and then give the boy a twenty of his own."

I tried to pump the old guy about what Jack had in mind with animal feed, but he was dry. I'd gotten all I was going to get out of him.

I took the Interstate back to the city, rode Fiftieth up and over Phinney Ridge and dropped down into Ballard.

Brenner Brothers Cold Storage was way down on Western, almost to Ballard. The big green building was memorable because it was nearly the last of the old wooden buildings that used to line the shores of Elliot Bay for five miles north of downtown. Brown and green and red, some four stories tall, all covered with miles of wavy shiplap siding. Hardware companies, wholesale lumber, shipbuilders, marine engine repair, tugboat companies all marinating in a pungent blend of creosote and salt water.

While their neighbors were being eaten alive by taxes and assessments, the Brenners had correctly read the entrails of the situation. Seattle was about to become the gateway to the Pacific Rim. Other than airplanes, fruits were our most lucrative export. Cold storage was going to be the deal.

The parking lot was full, so, despite stern warning signs to the contrary, I was forced to entrust the Fiat to the Evergreen Credit Union next door. Even here, in an area set back from the water, the breeze had considerably freshened, trembling even the sturdy ornamental cypress trees in the property divider as I stepped over and through the boundary.

The green frame house out front was still the office, but they didn't use the big wooden hangar for storage anymore. It stood open at the front, its roll-up doors gone now, stacked floor to ceiling with wooden pallets. Out back, they'd erected six or eight concrete tilt-ups, each probably fifty by a hundred feet, their flat, rectangular faces broken only by massive red garage doors and loading docks, two to a side.

The sign on the door said COME ON IN, so I did. The door gave a cheery tinkle as I pushed it open. I immediately recognized the decor. Early Knotty Pine. During my late formative years, in what I like to call my psychedelic cowboy phase, I'd spent a winter in the mountains looking for God, holed up in a tight little cabin up by Index, every square inch of which was covered with this identical tongue-and-groove pattern. I'd never felt the same about the stuff since. In the right frame of mind, staring at a wall of knotty pine, I can still make out the faces of the evil, big-faced girls, coming and going among the blots and swirls of the grain. My jaw muscles ached. I repressed a shudder.

The man had a brown leather jacket thrown over one arm and a battered briefcase jammed under the other. "Sixty-nine fifty per month," he said into the mouthpiece. "Due the first. First and last. Yes. Yes." He listened at length. "If I'm not here, you tell them Paul Brenner quoted you sixty-nine fifty. Okay?"

He set the receiver on the counter without hanging up, pulled the briefcase out from under his arm and set it on the floor.

"Help you?"

He was built like a college wrestler. One of those low-center-of-gravity guys whom you never want to get down on the floor with. He kept his hair cropped down to the skin, and from the look of him, spent a fair bit of time in the gym.

"I was hoping you could help me with some information."

"What's that?" he said, slipping into the jacket.

I pulled the newspaper from my pocket and turned it his way.

"Do you recognize this man?"

I could see it in his eyes. I'd just struck out. I'd had such a swell time back at Pacific Skyways and at Wagner's, I'd forgotten I was supposed to be a private detective. I should have run a number on him. In my business, honesty is very seldom the best policy. It's what I like about the job.

He picked up the briefcase. "What we sell here, Mr.—"

"Waterman."

"What we sell here, Mr. Waterman, is security and confidentiality. Do you understand? I haven't even looked at it and I don't know the man. So if you don't mind . . ."

He waited. So did I. He gestured toward the door with the case.

"I can get people to remove you," he said, putting his left hand on the counter.

I started to speak, changed my mind and let myself out. On the way out, the tinkle sounded more like a squeak.

I kicked my own butt all the way across the parking lot, parted a pair of scrawny trees like Samson destroying the temple and stepped through. I was still mumbling when I had an unexpected spasm of lucidity and skidded to a halt. I walked back the way I'd come, leaned across the oxidized top of an ancient Ford Fairlane and waited.

It was about ten minutes before Paul Brenner came out the front door, settled himself behind the wheel of a British-racing-green Cadillac Allante convertible and buckled up. Once he'd gone by, I stepped out into the street and watched until I lost sight of him up by the third light.

The office was empty. As I neared the counter, I saw the red button and the card that read "Ring For Service," so I rang. Out in the yard, several buzzers with a variety of voices raked the air. The phone began to ring but quit after a single jingle. The door at the rear opened.

His face had seen a lot of weather. It was a Western face with narrow eyes. Folded and seamed like a favorite tobacco pouch, it spoke of distant horizons and hard times.

"Yes, sir," he said.

"Paul Brenner?"

"Oh, no. Not me. That's the boss."

"Would you tell him I'm here?"

"Just left. Something I can help you with?"

It was now or never.

"Mr. Del Fuego sent me down to make sure everything was copacetic for tomorrow. Told me to see Mr. Brenner for a report."

"He'd just have to come out and ask me, anyway," the guy said.

"Well, I guess I'm talking to the right guy, then. Everything ready for the big day?"

"It's a bearcat, is what it is," he said. "Young Paul hadda freeze his ass off, he'd think twice about agreeing to half-assed shit like this. But he's just like his old man. Neither of 'em can be pushed, but both can sure as hell be bought." He gave a dry hack and covered his mouth with his hand.

"You wanna see?" he asked.

"Why not?"

His name was Cecil McKonkey. He was a retired tugboat engineer who managed the yard and the cold storage for the Brenners. He'd known Paul's father for forty years. Paul was the nominal head of the company now, but according to Cecil, not only did he have no interest in the business, he couldn't find his own ass in the dark, either. I gave him my real name. What the hell.

"You got a coat, Leo?"

For the first time, I noticed he was wearing a ski parka.

"Nope," I said tentatively.

He shrugged. "It's not that bad, I guess."

It was every damn bit that bad and then some. He led me around the counter and out the back door. The rental meat lockers fronted the side street, so the citizens could

park and pick up that Sunday chuck roast from their locker
and be on their way. The back half of the building was a
single large refrigerated room.

It looked like the slaughterhouse scene in *Rocky*. I shud-
dered violently in the freezing air. A forest of split carcasses
hung from hooks. Beef, swine, a sheep or two, and here and
there an animal whose mute remains I didn't recognize. The
air smelled of fat and flesh and seemed to stick to the skin.
It was cold as hell, and somewhere in the room somebody
was, of all things, welding. The leaping sparks traced
shadow comets on the ceiling and walls as we pushed our
way through the carcasses and out into the middle of the
floor. My teeth chattered and then behaved.

The action was down at the far end of the room, directly
in front of the insulated garage door. The flat back of a green
Hyster forklift faced our way. Poor old Bunky was laid out
on a double wood pallet, like the ones they use for heavy
machinery. I stepped to the left as the green welding arc
started up again, putting Cecil between me and the blinding
light, walking the length of the room in his shadow.

It was positively medieval. They'd fabricated a steel rotis-
serie spit in and around the massive carcass, designed, as
far as I could see, to simultaneously pry the body cavity
open and support the weight evenly. The contraption culmi-
nated at the top center of the backbone, where a large steel
eye hook was presently being welded to the frame. They'd
draped a green dropcloth over the area directly under the
hook so as not to burn the skin. My teeth beat a rhythm to
"The Flight of the Bumblebee."

It could have been government work, except that there
were only two guys watching the welder. All wore the same
gray-striped coveralls and old-fashioned welding hoods. The
backs of the coveralls read "Nance Fabrication." I hugged
myself. A thick steel rod protruded about four feet from
each end of the carcass. It was a pitiful sight to behold. Poor
old Bunky had gotten his kishkes bobbed after all.

Cecil reached out and tapped the nearest guy on the

shoulder. He pulled up the hood to reveal a jowly, middle-aged face, badly in need of a shave. His teeth were oddly spaced, as if he were missing every other one. "Just about there," he said to Cecil. "We'll finish up the weld and scope it good, 'cause it's gonna hold the whole thing. Then you can have your boys wrap it up in visqueen. Way I see it, there's no sense in banding it to the pallet till morning."

Cecil agreed with the man and then introduced him as Cal.

"It's only Wednesday. You tell your boss we'll be ready. Come eleven-thirty on Friday, we'll have our end together."

"He'll be pleased."

A flaming trail of sparks rocketed by my face. I was so cold I was tempted to step forward and let them catch my shirt on fire.

"I'm just hopin', after the pickup, we can get cleaned up here in time to get down there for the shindig."

"Oh, you're going, are you?"

Cal reached into his pocket. It was one of Jack's business cards. On the back, he'd signed his name and written, "This man and his guests, on the house."

"Gave each of us one."

"That just shows you the kind of guy he is," I said.

The welder pulled back the hissing rod and flipped up his visor.

On our way back to the office, I asked Cecil, "You going?"

"Too much Chinese fire drill for me, Leo."

"You really ought to make it," I said.

He squinted at me. "Why's that?"

"Just a feeling," I said. "I've got a funny feeling that this whole circus is going to be one of those once-in-a-lifetime things that a man takes with him to the grave."

"Got 'boondoggle' written all over it," he agreed.

22

The house was ablaze with lights. I checked my watch and then scanned the street. Ten-fifteen and no necklace of sleek Caddies adorned the roadway tonight. No loud voices or soft music, only the drone of distant traffic rasping from the trees like throat-sore cicadas. Behind my eyes, a sense impression of those long-ago nights flashed on my inner screen, and I suddenly realized how much quieter and darker it used to be at this time of night on this particular street. I wondered how I'd gotten to be so old so quickly, and as usual, came up empty.

I parked the Fiat in the street. Rebecca refused to drive it, so if I parked her in, she'd wake me up to move it. I reached down behind the seat, grabbed the bottle by the neck and got out of the car.

I began to pat my pockets with my free hand before remembering that I didn't have a key. The second time I knocked, I heard the floor squeak and saw the light change in the peephole.

"It's me," I said.

"I gave at the office."

I must have been slow on the uptake. Before I could come

up with anything pithy to say, Rebecca opened the door with a chorus of jingling chains and slapping bolts.

"Are you okay?" she asked.

She was wearing black high-top Keds, a pair of soiled gray sweatpants and a purple U Dub T-shirt that she'd stolen from me. She had dirt on her chin.

"I'm throwing myself on your mercy."

"You expect mercy from the woman who single-handedly moved both of us today?"

I held the champagne bottle up. "I've brought an offering."

She squinted at the label and then at me. Krystal.

"At least you weren't cheap."

"You deserve it."

"You're damned right."

My old oak coat tree was standing behind the door. I took my leather jacket off, spun the coat tree so the broken foot was facing the corner and hung my jacket on its regular hook. I instantly felt more settled. "Can we find any glasses?" I asked.

She took me by the waist and pulled me toward the kitchen. The hall walls were lined with boxes. The kitchen was ankle-deep in crinkled-up newspaper. "I started on the kitchen," she said, "but I pooped out. I was just nodding off in the living room when you knocked."

I traced a line down her cheek. "You've got blankey marks."

"Okay, Mr. Detective, maybe I *was* napping."

From the cabinet on the far side of the sink, she produced a pair of squat highball glasses. "That's it," she said.

I popped the cork and poured us both a handful.

"How'd it go?" I asked.

She told me. When words alone failed, she took off. I followed her all over the house, upstairs and down, as she recapped the difficulties of the day and related her decorating plans for the future. By my reckoning, the latter would require one of us to win the lottery.

It was forty minutes before we were back in the kitchen, and I poured us the last of the Krystal. "Thanks," I said.

She gave me the fisheye. "Are you sure you're okay?"

"Why?" I asked. "Don't I look okay?"

"You just let me babble for an hour without interrupting me once, without once telling me how hard your day was. Do you realize that, Leo? That's got to be a first."

"I've been listening to Dr. Lorna on the radio. She says women need to talk it out. That what they really want you to do is listen to them. I'm becoming a more sensitive, nineties kind of guy."

She seemed to think this was funny, and it earned me a kiss, so I wasn't complaining. She let me go and said, "Well, then, the least I can do is listen to you. So . . . how was your day, Leo?"

I put the back of my right hand on my forehead and said, "I can't bear to talk about it."

I was only half kidding. This was one of those stories I was hesitant to tell. As I'd run through it in my head all afternoon, I realized the story had the sound of folklore rather than fact.

Rebecca did better than I expected. She listened to my story without comment, all the way up to the point where I started telling her about going to Jack's new restaurant, before she began shaking her head.

"Are you sure you aren't exaggerating just a bit here, Leo? You know your penchant for embroidering a story."

I almost wished I were. The whole thing was completely over the top. After leaving Cecil, I'd swung by Jack's new place. I don't know why. I certainly had better things to do. I think maybe I was still in denial and needed to reassure myself one way or the other about this mess I'd gotten myself into. One thing was for sure. If it was reassurance I was looking for, I'd definitely gone to the wrong place.

The restaurant was a storm of activity. The front door was jacked open by a chair, allowing the parade of delivery people easy entry. Rickey Ray was sitting on a barstool just inside the door. He was wearing the same cowboy weight-lifter suit as when we'd first met.

"Leo, my man," he said, "what brings you down here?"

I stepped aside to let a guy with a dolly full of apple boxes go by, and then Rickey Ray and I exchanged high fives.

"Just wanted to see how things are going."

Dixie's voice rose from the kitchen. "Ay said over here, Ahnstein."

I pulled another stool over from the bar and sat.

"This is craziness, man."

"What's that, podna?"

"You know what I'm talking about."

He gave me a blank look.

"The whole thing with the helicopter. Flying a goddamn bull carcass into the middle of downtown Seattle just to prove you can do it."

If he was surprised, he didn't show it.

"The Jackster don't think so."

"The Jackster is out of his goddamned mind."

"You got it, my man."

"This is going to be the end of him."

Rickey Ray checked the area around us. "He's done either way, Leo. Too many fuck-ups, too much booze, the Meyersons doggin' his trail, Dixie cuttin' his fences. You right, podna. The old Jackeroo is headin' for the last roundup."

"You don't seem real concerned," I noted.

"It's just a job, Leo. Jack's responsible for himself." His nonchalance evaporated, and he was suddenly serious. "It all comes around, my man. Comes a time when all of us have to atone. When, whether we like it or not, we gotta take responsibility for our actions. Been a long time comin', but the Jackster's 'bout to get his." He caught himself raving. "Old Jack should never have started in with that Meyerson woman," he said quickly. "She's gonna be the death of him yet."

"The Meyerson woman swears she's not the one eating

old Jack's lunch. She claims there's somebody else out there sabotaging his business."

He ignored me. "I tol' him not to do that shit with that sign of hers. That bird got no sense of humor. That sign shit just woke her up."

"So if this all comes apart, you're out of here?"

He reached over and patted me on the back, once more the good old boy. "I be updatin' my résumé as we speak," he joked.

I wondered whether maybe I couldn't flip his switch, too, so I said, "What about Candace? She gonna do the rats-from-a-sinking-ship thing, too?" I could.

His mismatched face clouded. "You know, podna, you always a little too damn interested in Miss Atherton."

"Funny, but you know, I was thinking the same thing about you. Isn't that weird?" He looked up at me through his hair. I kept talking. "Really. On the way over here, I was thinking how if a guy didn't know better, he'd almost have to figure it was you and Candace instead of Jack and Candace. You know, because she spends a whole lot more time with you than she does with Jack."

He slipped off the stool. "Know what I'd do if I was you?" He punctuated the last word with a stiff tap on my chest with his finger.

"You're not me, Rickey Ray," I said calmly. "That's why they gave us different names."

He tapped me again, harder this time. "They can give you whatever goddamn name they want. Don't change a goddamn thing. You still who you are. Long as you never lose track of who you are, they can't hurt ya. Miss Atherton and what she is or ain't doin' is none of—"

We never got a chance to finish our little discussion. At that moment Jack came blustering around the corner. Today he was doing his man-of-the-people thing. Blue jeans and a crisp blue work shirt. The plebeian attire merely served to highlight the three pounds of jewelry. He looked like the king of convicts.

"Well, well," he said. "Looky heeya." He palmed my shoulder with a big red hand. "Nice to see you, boy." He sounded like Foghorn Leghorn. I half expected him to turn away at any moment and announce to some invisible audience that I was not the brightest boy in the world.

"You seen the place yet?"

"No, I haven't."

He threw the rest of the arm around my shoulder. "Well, there, Lee—"

"Leo," I corrected.

"Well, there, Leo. Lemme show you 'round."

I was all right as long as we were indoors. I'd expected Texas longhorns and mounted buffalo heads, but the place was slick. It had kind of a Hunt Club motif, with thoroughbred racing thrown in as the kicker. As we walked, Jack kept up a running commentary.

"When I started in the business, Leon, they said you couldn't put pictures of horses on the walls of a steak house. Said it was crazy. Said it made folks nervous. The Jackster, he said . . ."

For the next half hour or so, as we strolled around the restaurant, things seemed to fold themselves back into a recognizable pattern. In the kitchen, Jack and I found Candace polishing glasses and carried her along on our tour. She patted Jack's arm as we walked. The bustle and hum of preparing for Friday night's opening lent me a much-needed feeling of stability, as if the sight of real people performing real tasks somehow increased my distance from the Looney Tunes universe into which I seemed to have fallen. I was feeling better. There really was a restaurant called The Feed-Lot. It was nice. The staff seemed nice. This spasm of sanity lasted until we stepped out the side door.

The half block to the south of The FeedLot used to be a twelve-story office building, named, if I remember correctly, after some insurance company. A few years back, a new owner had leveled the property and completely cleaned off the lot in preparation for another shiny new business-retail complex that never came to be, leaving an entire half block of downtown Seattle sitting paved and empty.

In a town where, depending upon the section of the city, it can cost over twenty dollars a day to park a car, a half acre of bare concrete ranks right up there with bread from heaven on the covet meter.

In a nanosecond the slab had become Seattle's only genuine free-parking area. I'd used it myself a couple of times. The city was not amused. As the City of Seattle sees it, no act performed by any member of the citizenry, while in the confines of the city limits, shall be without charge from the city. It's Rule One D: Everything costs. No exceptions.

They made the owner fence the thing, and for the past few years it's been a downtown eyesore. It was an eyesore no more. Jack had turned it into the Hanging Gardens of Babylon. My heart hit my shoes.

It wasn't the green-and-white-striped tents set up around the edges. As a matter of fact, the tents and the jaunty pennants flying from their peaks merely worked to imprint the Après the Derby motif and to intensify my sense of well-being. That's not what set my teeth on edge.

It wasn't the big cattle trailer parked in the alley, either. The white eighteen-wheeler filled the alley on the far side of the fence like a cork in a bottle, effectively both blocking the alley completely and lending, I'm sure Jack imagined anyway, a certain rural charm to the proceedings. A charm he sought to accentuate by the strategic placement of a number of bales of hay, piled on the ground along the perimeter of the rig as well as on the tops of both the cab and the trailer, all of which pretty much cleared up the mystery about the stuff he'd had delivered from Wagner's. It was window dressing.

It wasn't the forest of trees, shrubs and flowers that Jack had imported in order to transform the slab into a formal garden, nor was it the bandstand being set up over on the left. All of this seemed part of the regular, rational, everyday world. No. They weren't the problem.

The problem was on my left as we came out the door. It was the world's only combination stage and barbecue pit. A full four feet above ground level, the raised platform ran nearly the width of the yard. A giant blowup of Jack and Bunky had been affixed to the brick wall behind the stage. It said only: HUNGRY?

Everything was right there. An open-pit barbecue you could have driven a truck into. Back in the north corner, a dump-truck load of charcoal briquettes formed a pitch-black cone on the ground next to the forklift.

I pointed to the steel apparatus at the center of the stage. "What's that?" I asked.

Jack squeezed my shoulder again.

"That, Leo, is the finest, most modern barbecue pit ever known to man." Using my neck as a lever, he guided me over in that direction. "Barbecue is an art," he announced. "Ya probably didn't know that, did ya, but it is."

When I seemed to agree, he went on.

"What we're gonna do tomorrow will make barbecue history." Jack's eyes took on a distant light. He pointed to the huge metal pan sunk in the center of the stage. "When we set that ol' boy on the spit tomorrow, Leon, they'll be a full ton of coals blazin' away down here. Two thousand pounds of flamin' flavor." He eyed me closely. "You know anything about cookin'?"

"Not a hell of a lot."

He gave me a conspiratorial wink. "Well, you see, the reason nobody ever tried to cook anything this big is the problem that you got to cook it so long to get the inside cooked that the outside is burned to a cinder. T'only way it could be done would be with a real intense dry heat, like you got in an oven. The charcoal's too hot in one place and not hot enough in another. Can't be done with charcoal."

"Isn't that what's in there?"

"The top layer. We gonna use that to sear him nice and pretty and to heat up the lava rock. 'Cause, ya see, under those coals is another ton of lava rock."

He reached into his pocket and pulled out a small round stone. It was a deep red and its small face was cratered like a miniature moon.

"Finest intense dry-heat source you can have. Charcoal be gone after a couple hours, then we roast him nice and slow. These little boogers hold a heat charge for ten hours, maybe more. Feel it," he said. "Don't hardly weigh anything at all."

He dropped the rock into my hand. It weighed almost nothing.

I tried to give it back, but Jack magnanimously told me to keep it.

He looked up at the sky, as if to marvel at the wonder that was the Jackster. "Ain't nobody since the Romans had the giblets to cook up anything as big as what we're gonna do." He jerked me closer. "Couldn't nobody but the old Jackalope do it neither. Nobody else got the vision." He pointed to his right eye and then tapped his temple. Candace patted him lovingly on the shoulder.

"See over there, with the handle?" He pointed to the far end of the apparatus. "That's how we're gonna turn that good old boy so's we cook him up nice and even. Got me the granny gear out of a bus down there in that gearbox at the bottom." He pointed again. "We can put over a ton on that momma, and a child could still turn the handle. Whadda ya think of that?"

I like to think that I would have taken that last opportunity to tell him what I really thought, but we'll never know.

Rickey Ray appeared in the doorway. With all of us standing in the late-afternoon sun, I could see what Spaulding had meant. Rickey Ray and Candace did indeed have similar light brown hair, right down to the glinting highlights.

"Jack," Rickey Ray said, "we got us a bread supplier here who says you got no credit arrangement and he ain't leaving nothin' les'n you give him the cash . . . as in no check, cash."

Jack detached himself from Candace's arm and strode toward the door. "Double R, what say we teach this redneck how to be polite?"

"Might just as well sort it out now as later," Rickey Ray agreed.

Candace Atherton and I stood alone in the garden.

"Openings are always a rush," she said.

"You can't be serious," I replied.

"About what?" she deadpanned.

"You encourage him," I said. "He stands there and talks this lunatic-asylum stuff, and you stand there and encourage him."

I couldn't read her expression, but she said, "Jack's following his star, Mr. Waterman. Don't you believe in following your star?"

"Yeah, but not by helicopter."

"Some men just dream bigger than others," she mused.

I shook my head. "I think I'm having a déjà moo attack."

"What's that?"

"The strange feeling that I've heard this bull before."

She didn't think that was funny. Her face closed like a leg trap.

"Desperate situations call for desperate measures," she said and then walked off into the restaurant.

That was the point in my recitation where Rebecca lost it and broke in. "And none of his entourage seems the least bit concerned?"

"Not as far as I can see. It's almost like they see it as fate or something. They seem perfectly content to watch Rome burn."

"Sounds pretty weird," she remarked.

"These are the same folks who thought so little of that *Bound*, they got up and left after the first half hour. Said it bored them."

"*Bound?*"

"That movie we saw at the Metro with Jennifer Tilly and what's-her-face. Remember how it started?"

"The one with the . . ." Rebecca gave me a sly smile.

"Kinky sex. Yeah. That one."

"The one after which we made that short stop at your apartment and were late for our dinner reservations."

"The very same. And then, if I recall, the movie moved right along into the gratuitous violence."

She gave a chuckle. "You're right, Leo. It's downright un-American to walk out on sex and violence. Maybe they're Commies."

The champagne had my mind moving in slow motion. Every time I turned my head, my eyes took a second to catch up.

"Then I ran down and tried to get Normal and Hot Shot out of the slammer. Jerk-offs let me stand around for four hours before they bothered to tell me that Hot Shot had three outstanding warrants and wasn't going anywhere." I sighed. "Cost me six hundred for Normal."

I'd slipped Normal another of Sir Geoffrey's fifties and sent him off to keep George company.

"That reminds me," she said. "There's a message from Jed on the phone. He's had calls from several others who've been picked up. Judy and Frank and, I think, Red and somebody else."

Morning was going to have to be soon enough.

"Is that lovely new bed still upstairs?"

"I believe it is," she said.

"What say we try it for sleeping this time?"

Rebecca stood and stretched. I heard her neck pop as she rolled her head in a circle. "I'm not due in until noon."

"Me neither," I said around a yawn, but she knew what I meant. "I'll get the lights down here."

23

"**I**s he out of his mind?" he demanded.

Sir Geoffrey was dressed in an impeccable gray suit and a plum-colored tie, in retrospect a rather prophetic color choice, as it presently matched his face.

He held out his hand and Rowcliffe placed a small pink tablet in his palm. Sir Geoffrey brought the palm to his mouth, as if to stifle a yawn, popped the pill past his lips and again extended the hand. Rowcliffe, of course, was ready with mineral water in a crystal tumbler.

I waited as Miles drained the liquid, dabbed his lips with the proffered napkin and got back to scowling at me.

"That question brings us directly to Miss Donner," I said.

"Must we?" he inquired.

"I'm afraid so."

"Go on, then."

"I told you yesterday that she spent the day in the King County Office Building. This morning I called a couple of my contacts."

The phrase "a couple of my contacts" sounds so much more professional than saying, "I called my aunt Karen, and she called my cousin Nicole's roommate, Noreen, who works in County Records."

I'd struck out on the first try. I caught Karen just as she arrived at the office, and she'd gotten right on it. She called back before ten.

"Nothing," she said. "No Jack Del Fuego. No Dixie Donner."

"Really? Nothing?"

"No documents on file, none pending. Sorry, kiddo."

"Well, thanks, darlin'," I said. "Looks like I'm going to have to knock on the doors."

"Later, Leo."

As I began to lower the phone from my ear, I had my first intelligent thought of the week—not bad, considering it's only Thursday. I wondered how in hell you spend all day doing business in the county building and manage not to use your real name. Anything you were doing in there was official; you were gonna need . . .

"Karen, Karen," I shouted into the mouthpiece.

She came back on.

"What is it, Leo?" Methinks me sensed a bit of exasperation.

"Try Wogers. W-O-G-E-R-S. Willie. Will you do that for me? I promise to leave you alone after that . . . promise."

She was back at me in ten.

"You have the family nose for smut, Leo," she said. "It's being filed under Donnareen L. Pye versus Wille Wogers. No middle initial."

"What's a Donnareen L. Pie?"

"It says the plaintiff is one Donnareen L. Donner-Del Fuego-Horowitz-Pye. Heck of a moniker. Kind of makes you wonder who Liz Taylor would be if you strung *them* all out."

"Horowitz?"

"That's what it says. Hubby number two."

Sir Geoffrey listened with his eyes closed and his lips pursed as I told him what Dixie was up to.

"I should gladly witness on her behalf," he announced when I'd finished. "Her petition is manifestly valid. The man is patently out of his mind. The fact that she is attempting to have him declared incompetent to run the business should not be a surprise to anyone even remotely familiar with the situation."

According to Noreen, that was pretty much Dixie's position. In documents filed before the court, Dixie claimed that Willie Wogers, a.k.a Jack Del Fuego, had slipped a major cog as a result of long-term alcoholism, and thus she requested that he be immediately remanded for psychiatric evaluation. Her petition asked that the court remove Willie from any and all control of the day-to-day business of the Seattle operation. It held that Willie-Jack had driven the business into the ground and was at present so heavily leveraged that the Seattle operation now constituted his company's sole unencumbered asset and, as such, must, in the interest of the plaintiff, be protected. The petition asked King County, as the county presently containing the corporation's sole asset, both to claim jurisdiction and to issue a restraining order. The remaining documents consisted of descriptions and depositions concerning the recent debacles in Atlanta and Cleveland, along with a rundown of the accrued litigation. According to Noreen, there were pictures, too.

"Does any of this advance our cause?" Sir Geoffrey asked.

"Not as far as I can see. Short of laying hands on a Sidewinder missile and shooting him down, I don't see how we can prevent the revenge of the Jackster from taking place."

"Perhaps Ms. Meyerson's aggregate forces . . ."

"The cops will keep them a block away. The city is with Jack on this one, I'm afraid."

"How," he blustered, "with that man's disastrous history, can any governmental body lend its support to his undertakings?"

"Actually, it's fairly simple. The city is real hot to renew that part of Fourth Avenue. It's a major priority with them.

It's the last great downtown eyesore in a city that sees itself as being way above eyesores. They figure Jack can be a cornerstone for that whole three-block area."

"But surely—"

I kept talking. "I'm willing to bet the city gave him a hell of a deal on everything. Nobody seems to be able to figure out why Del Fuego would choose to make his last stand in the heartland of the granola head, but I'll bet it's because they cut him a sweetheart deal. I'll bet they made it pretty enticing to a guy with bad cash flow."

I had his lordship's undivided attention.

"And it's also personal," I concluded.

He arched an eyebrow as I related the tale of the mayor's wife and the uninsured mink coat.

"Indeed," was all he said. 'You know, Mr. Waterman . . . and I trust you will take this in the positive manner in which it is intended . . ."

"Of course," I assured him.

"But if you don't mind me saying, it must be quite an asset in your profession to be so much smarter than you, on first impression, appear to be."

I'll never be precisely sure how he meant it, but for the sake of civility, I decided to take it as a compliment.

"It do come in handy," I allowed.

"The media situation is intolerable. The convention will be lucky to get a full column in the second section. Have you seen today's paper?"

I had. This morning's *Post Intelligence* had squeezed world news into two pages and devoted the remainder of the front section to the murder of Mason Reese. They'd come up with a picture of everyone involved, including Sir Geoffrey himself. For me, they'd used a five-year-old shot taken after I'd been living in the Fiat for three days while staking out a South Seattle crack house. I made a note to call the paper and complain.

"Something must be done," Sir Geoffrey declared. "Have you a plan of action?"

"Yes, I do. First, I'm going to go upstairs and change my clothes. And then I'm going to find my associate Mr. Paris and persuade him to, as Jack said the other night, *do his civic duty.*"

"And what would that be?"

"He's going to surrender to the district attorney."

Sir Geoffrey was still chewing on that one when I left.

I never did catch the Lola show itself. I'd gone upstairs to see Sir Geoffrey Miles at about one-o-one, right as the *Afternoon Northwest* music started, and I walked back in the door thirty minutes later to find the credits rolling and the music playing. Only this time the music was the Doobie Brothers, "Takin' It to the Streets," and Lola was doing the cheerleader voice-over. "Join us live tomorrow when we'll be takin' it to the streets. Make your voice heard. Make a difference. Until tomorrow, this is—" I hit the power button and went looking for a suitable ruse.

Having now dumped the neck brothers twice, I had to operate from the assumption that they'd wired my car so it could be tracked from outer space. Since whatever advantage I hoped to gain from cooperation would be lost if the tails pinched us before we could surrender, I needed to lose them one more time. I felt sure they'd understand.

The best I could manage in the way of a disguise was a pair of gray jeans, a black Harley-Davidson T-shirt and a matching baseball cap that read "Smoke 'Em Till the Wheels Fall Off." I put on a pair of aviator shades and checked myself in the mirror. Sleazy Rider. It wasn't much, but I'd spent the past few days in a suit and was hoping the change in style would be sufficient cover.

It worked like a charm. I walked right past one of the indoor dicks pretending to read the paper, slithered out the Seneca Street door and hailed a cab. I handed the Somali cabdriver a twenty and told him to drive north and then east and then back to the south. Ten blocks and four turns later, I was satisfied that we didn't have any company and started giving him real directions.

In the deep shade of the overpass, he pulled the cab half up onto the sidewalk. I waved another twenty at him.

"You can keep this one and another if you'll wait here until I get back. It's going to be a few minutes. Okay?"

He seemed to like that idea. I decided to risk it.

Ten minutes later, when George, Norman and I emerged from the thicket, he was still there, bopping around in the seat to the percussive beat of a Don Pullen piano solo. We piled into the back.

"King County jail," I said to the driver.

24

Ten minutes in, I knew for sure. The cops didn't have shit. They didn't know any more than I did. Maybe less. It could have been my imagination, but a sense of urgency seemed to have been added to the mix since the last time I'd been with these two. It wasn't just that they were running the good cop–bad cop routine on me again, or that Lobdell was ranging around the front of the room like the Tasmanian devil. I was betting he regularly practiced this routine in front of the mirror. No, these two were under serious pressure.

Martha Lawrence stood with her back leaning into the corner. She held her chin as she watched Detective Lobdell prowl the area in front of the door. Apparently, it was her day to be the good cop.

"You asked me to be a responsible citizen," I said. "And that's what I did. I got a line on Mr. Paris's whereabouts, found him and immediately delivered him right to your door."

"Responsible citizens have no need to repeatedly evade police surveillance," Lobdell snapped.

I opted for full-scale obnoxious. À la Spaulding Meyerson.

"Decently trained officers couldn't be dumped."

Lobdell began to sputter and come my way. Lawrence bounced herself off the wall, blocking his path. She moved toward me and spoke.

"I'm still unclear, Mr. Waterman, as to precisely what it is you think you have to trade and what it is you expect in return. I assure you, your participation is not prerequisite to the successful outcome of this investigation."

"I'm offering you my twenty years of expertise." I held up both hands. "I know this is going to come as quite a shock to you, Lawrence, but in spite of my appalling lack of credentials, I just might have a notion or two about this case that would be of use to you."

Lobdell jumped in. "If you have information pertinent to this investigation—"

"All the information I have, you have, Lobdell. It's not information I'm peddling. It's questions. It's surmises. Inconsistencies I've noticed." I shrugged and folded my arms across my chest.

"And what is it you expect in return for these rare and invaluable insights?"

"SPD's got eight members of my team. I want them released."

Lobdell hacked out a dry laugh. "You sure you don't want a blow job while you're at it?"

"Why, Rob," I said in mock surprise, "is it Friday night already?"

He came barreling around the table, his hands clenched into tight red fists.

I stood up. "Come on," I egged him. "I'll kick your scrawny ass all over this room, you little piece of shit."

If Lawrence hadn't been there, I do believe he would have gone for it. Too bad. She hip-checked him and again got in between us.

"Why don't you let me handle this, Rob?"

"Yeah, Rob," I said. "Why don't you let her handle it?"

Bug-eyed, he yelled over her shoulder, "You smart-ass son of a . . ."

It took her another full minute to get him out the door. I sat down and tried to listen through the door, but they took it down the hall.

On my way over to the D.A.'s office, I'd left Normal at the jail. He hadn't liked it one bit, but eventually I talked him into it. "Nobody else can do it, Norman. They've got everybody except Harold and Ralph, and I don't know where those two are. It's all up to you, buddy."

He shook his big head from side to side. "The whitecoats are waiting for me in there," he said. "They'll pin me to a corkboard."

"No, no, no," I said. "You've got a get-out-of-jail card."

"What card?"

I produced his bail ticket. "This one right here."

George jumped in and tipped the balance. "You'd want us to do it for you, Normal, if it was you in there. Just go in and visit as many of them as they'll let ya. Tell 'em we ain't forgot about 'em. Tell 'em to tell the cops anything they want to know. That's it. Then you walk out."

George and I stood on the sidewalk and watched Norman force himself to step through the front doors of the Corrections Building.

"I'm givin' eight to five they keep his big ass," said George with a smirk.

"He's the only one of them without an outstanding warrant of some sort. As long as he doesn't go bananas, he ought to be okay." I didn't really believe it, though.

I threw an arm around the old man's shoulders. "Question," I said.

He squirmed to escape, but I held him fast.

"The other day down with Piggy and Roscoe . . ."

"Don't remind me," he muttered. "Let me—"

"Remember how you told me about when you got in the elevator to go upstairs to empty the rest of the mini-bar . . ."

His eyes rolled in his head like those of a spooked horse.

"That story about Rickey Ray and Miss Atherton . . ."

He pulled himself free of my grasp and backed away.

"You sayin' I lied?"

George did a world-class righteous indignation. Unfortunately, he generally did it only when he was stone-guilty. My hopes dropped a notch and a half, but I continued anyway.

"I don't give a shit about the booze, George. It's the other part, the part about Rickey Ray and Miss Atherton, and the elevator and all that."

"Screw you, Leo. You leave me to rot down there with Piggy and Roscoe . . . and then what . . . you call me a liar? You must . . ."

I let him ramble. He'd had a rough couple of days, and besides, Dr. Lorna said it was good for folks to vent. When he finished, I said, "You sure it was two-thirty?"

"There's a goddamn clock in the elevator, Sherlock."

He began smoothing his battered suit around his body.

"Why'd they get off on eight and then jump back on?"

"How in hell am I supposed to know? Why don't you ask them, for Chrissake? Must be they pushed the wrong friggin' button."

"After you got off on nine, which way did they go, up or down?"

"Up."

"You sure?"

"No, Sherlock, I'm making this shit up," he said disgustedly. "They had one of them fancy keys for the private floors. Like the one you got. I seen 'em stick it in the box."

I started up the hill toward Fifth Avenue.

"Come on," I said to George.

"Where we going?"

"I'm going to turn you in to the D.A."

Needless to say, George was thrilled.

The click of the door pulled me back to the present.

Lawrence stepped into the room and closed the door softly behind her.

"Not that it matters, Mr. Waterman, but just for the record, the release of your friends is not within my power."

"It could be arranged."

"Not with that collection of warrants. I'm told there are upward of twenty charges pending on that group of—"

"It's all crap. Take a look at the stuff they're charged with. Failure to disperse. Blocking a public thoroughfare. Public urination. Public drunkenness. And then they don't appear, so the city charges them with Failure to Appear and when they fail to appear for that, they get charged with Failure to Appear on a Failure to Appear. That stuff's just the price of being poor and homeless. Don't kid yourself. In America, it's illegal to be poor and homeless; somebody just made a rule that we're not allowed to talk about it, is all."

When she failed to speak, I decided to take the initiative.

"You know, Lawrence," I began, "a major theme with you seems to be this thing about earning one's way as opposed to working the system. I think I can give you a way to earn a little redemption for yourself. What do you say?"

She forced a brittle laugh up from her chest. "What makes you think for a minute that I require any redemption?"

"Just a rumor I heard."

I let it go at that and checked my cuticles.

"Let's have it," she said.

"Do we have a deal?"

"It will depend on what you have."

"I need to know a few things first."

She looked me over.

"If you're just fishing, Waterman, I'll put you in jail and keep you there for the weekend, I swear to God. Jed James or no Jed James, I'll keep you locked up until ten o'clock Monday morning."

"Did you guys find a murder weapon?"

"No."

"Did you find Reese's gun?"

"Assuming Reese had a gun," she said. "Your account is all we have regarding Mr. Reese and a firearm."

"Did you?"

"No."

"Are the fourteenth-floor comings and goings confirmed by the security tape?"

"Yes."

"Did you get independent confirmation that Tolliver and company were actually at a movie?"

"A mere nineteen people in the Broadway market and the ticket vendor who sold Mr. Tolliver the tickets. Even by Broadway's rather Gothic standards, Mr. Tolliver is quite memorable."

"What about the women?"

"Mr. Tolliver tends to hold the eye."

She had a point.

"What about in the theater itself?"

"Perhaps you haven't been in a while, Mr. Waterman, but it's rather dark at the movies these days."

"I need to see the tape."

"What tape?"

"The hotel surveillance tape."

"I just told you, the tape conforms to the deposed departure and arrival times. We made a copy and spliced together a sequential record of the comings and goings. The times are right there on the videotape. I have a copy in my office if you'd like—"

"No. I want to see the other part of the tape."

"What other part of the tape?"

"The part where nobody is coming and going."

"You want to look at film of an empty hallway?"

"I'm easily amused."

"Not possible."

"Why not?"

"Because we returned the original film canister to the hotel." She read my expression. "It was enormous." She held her arms in a giant hoop over her head.

"I sure hope they haven't recorded over it yet."

"Why would that matter?"

I told her what I thought. Halfway through, she reached over on the table in front of her and began to leaf through a document.

"Did George remember to tell you that?"

She pointed at the papers in her hand. "Yes, right here."

"Don't you see, Lawrence? It's like the Sherlock Holmes thing when he figures it out because the dog didn't bark, only here the dog is an elevator button."

"Assuming that Mr. Paris has his facts straight."

"I'm betting he does."

"And this entire elevator button theory of yours hangs on Mr. Paris's word."

"So far," I admitted.

She was shaking her head. "I'm a lawyer, Waterman. I look at things like a lawyer. You tell me that this whole scenario hinges on Mr. Paris, and I begin to picture Mr. Paris on the witness stand, and I can tell you right now, it's not a pretty sight."

"He looks pretty good when he's cleaned up," I said.

"He has a drinking problem."

"No, he doesn't," I said. "As a matter of fact, what he has is a stopping problem. He drinks; he gets drunk; he falls down. It's no problem to him."

"That's an old joke and it's not funny."

"I wasn't trying to be. You can't operate when you're drunk because it's a state of consciousness you're not accustomed to. Everything seems out of whack. For them it's exactly the opposite. Drunk is what they do best. It's what they're used to. It's being sober that they can't handle."

"Was Mr. Paris drinking at the time?"

"Yes," I said. "If he can help it, Mr. Paris is always drinking."

She shrugged. "It's the law, Mr. Waterman. Impaired witnesses have no standing in court. Witnesses who merely have a history of habitual impairment have been excluded. None of these people of yours are credible witnesses. If I'd had any idea who these so-called operatives of yours were,

I never would have expended the police manpower to bring them in."

"Let's go look at the tape."

She scooped her stuff into a disorderly pile. "Get out, Waterman. I'll cut you some slack for effort. Be glad I don't lock your butt up with the rest of them."

"What about my crew?"

"Mr. Paris is already back on the street."

"And the rest of them? I thought we had a deal."

"The deal was that you give me something I can use. You gave me nothing. All you did, assuming Mr. Paris is telling the truth and that his information is accurate, is give me more questions than I started with. Get out, Waterman, before I change my mind."

"Don't you want to hear the rest of what I know?"

"What you and the rest of that ragged assemblage know, Mr. Waterman, is of absolutely no interest to me."

I smiled inwardly. I'd done my end. I'd given her the key, but she refused to use it. I felt like Pontius Pilate. If I'd had a basin, I'd have washed my hands before leaving.

25

"**C**ome on, Marty, don't be an asshole. If the tape was so goddamn important, they wouldn't have given it back to you guys."

"Nice talk, Leo. Are you always this charming when you want something?"

"You know what I mean."

"Your carte blanche status is a thing of the past around here, Leo. I got brand-new orders about you. Straight from the top. You've gone from the preferred list to the suspect list. From the penthouse to the outhouse. Just like I knew you would."

"I'm not a suspect, Marty."

"Then ask the cops to see their copy."

"I don't want to see the part the cops have."

"You're not well, you know that?"

"Can you wind up the tape to a specific minute?"

"Sure. But I'm not going to." He looked at his watch. "It's six-fifteen, Leo. I'm having one of the worst weeks of my life. I've been here since six this morning. I had better hours at the precinct and the bennies were better. I'm out of here."

"Come on, man. With a little luck, maybe I can get this

whole thing out of your hair once and for all. Maybe get you a few strokes from the suits while we're at it."

Marty took a deep breath. "For all I know, we've already run back over the tape. Those are ninety-six-hour canisters. We've only got three of them. When they gave it back, I put it back into service."

"Could you check?"

He was gone for a full ten minutes before he poked his head into his office and hailed me. "Come out here, Leo."

The outer room had been empty when I'd come in, lit only by the blue flickering of the banks of screens. The overheads were on now. Marty had separated Stimpy from whatever he was up to. The kid sat at the console, his stubby fingers poised.

Marty said, "We're going to do this one time with feeling, Leo. Just so you'll leave me the hell alone. Then I'm going to go home and beat my dog. What minute of scintillating hall view did you have in mind?"

"Wind it to two twenty-five," I said, "just in case the time in the elevators varies from the time in the cameras."

"It can't. It comes from the same source," Stimpy said.

"Then wind the tape all the way to two-thirty."

He typed for a moment on the keyboard and then pushed Enter. The tape console on my left began to hiss. Stimpy sat back. Marty went into his office. The tape machine clicked to a stop.

"Here we are," said Stimpy. "Ready?"

"Ready."

"Real time or fast forward?"

"Real time."

He pushed a button and the screen above our heads came to life.

The bottom of the picture had the date and the time. Two-thirty and twelve seconds, thirteen. I closed my eyes and pictured it in my head. Imagining the doors closing in the lobby and the trip up to the eighth floor. The slight shudder as the elevator locked in place. The doors opening. They step out; they jump back in; the doors close again. The car moves up one floor. Same deal. George gets off. The doors close.

I opened my eyes. Stimpy was measuring me for a strait-jacket. The time on the screen reads two thirty-four. Nothing but blank hallway. I concentrated on the grainy image, but nothing appeared. Then a shadow flickered.

"Stop," I said. "Go back."

"How far?"

"Maybe ten seconds' worth."

He pushed some buttons. The screen went blank and then popped back to life. I squinted at it.

"There. . . . see that?"

"See what? I didn't see anything."

"Go back again."

When the film started over, I put my finger on the screen.

"Watch right here," I said, pointing at a section of carpet directly in front of the elevator. "Watch the light."

Our heads nearly touched as we pressed our faces to the glass. Again a trapezoid of light swept across the section of carpet from right to left, then stayed there.

"What *is* that?" Stimpy asked.

"It's the light from the inside of the elevator. They're lined with mirrors and reflective as hell. Somebody is standing in there with the door open. Can you go back to the beginning so we can time how long they're standing in there?"

"Easy."

It took no time at all to return to the moment when the door began to open. Two thirty-four and fifty-two seconds. Stimpy released the button and the tape began to move.

At two thirty-nine and five seconds, the door began to close. A little over five minutes of standing in an elevator with the door open.

George had been right. They'd gone up. And then stood there for a little over five minutes before going elsewhere. Presumably to the movies. Maybe they'd used the five minutes to decide which movie to go to. All nice and neat, except for two things, one of them minor and one of them major.

On a minor note, I had a small problem with the idea of them walking out of *Bound* because they didn't like it. *Bound* was, as a matter of fact, one hell of a good movie, and I had some difficulty imagining anyone who wasn't experiencing chest pains or some other life-threatening incident walking out in the middle of it. That one was minor, because, like the man said, there's no accounting for taste. I know noids who didn't like *Pulp Fiction*.

The other one bothered me more. Why the earlier trip to eight? Digital spasticity was not an option. If they'd pushed a button, it had been on purpose, because, as we all knew, there was no button for the fourteenth floor.

26

inding Marie was easy. I spotted her behind the registration desk as soon as I came downstairs from the security
office. She was sorting registration cards and entering
the information into the computer when I approached the
desk. Her small mouth was set in a weary grimace, as if she
were either right at the end of a long, tiring shift or, even
worse, just beginning one.

She looked up and gave me the most dazzling smile she
had left.

"Good afternoon, Mr. Waterman." She semi-beamed.

Ah, the perils of top-down management! It seemed that
the news of my complete loss of status had not as yet filtered
down to the rank and file. "Good afternoon, Marie, and how
are you?"

"Tired. It's been so busy. Usually it comes in spurts, but
today, it seems like it hasn't let up since I got here."

"Jeez, I almost feel guilty asking you for a favor."

"No problem, Mr. Waterman." She looked down at the
desk. "I've only got another half hour. What can I do for
you? Whatever it is will be better than this," she said, indi-
cating the cards.

"On the eighth floor . . ," I began. She stiffened at the sound of the words. "Mr. Reese's room was the second door on the right, if you turned left out of the elevators. That was number eight-fourteen."

She nodded slightly, so I kept on talking.

"In that same section, down that same hall, what's the room number of the last room on the left?"

It took her a moment to realize that I had finished speaking.

"I'd have to look," she said after an awkward silence. From a cubbyhole in the right side of the desk, she produced a brown plastic loose-leaf notebook with the hotel's name and logo printed on the front.

I watched as she thumbed through a series of plastic-encased pages. Finally, she began to count. "Six," she said, turning a page. "Seven and eight." She swiveled the notebook my way. The elevators were on my side of the page. I mentally turned left and let my eyes walk to the end of the corridor. Eight fifty-nine. It was room eight fifty-nine.

"Can you look up room eight fifty-nine on your computer?"

"What did you want to know?"

"Whether it's been rented this week and by who."

I was tempted to say "whom," like a credentialed person, but caught myself in time.

She pushed buttons and squinted myopically at the screen.

"It was in service Sunday through Tuesday." She pushed another button. "Wednesday night we had a reservation, but it was a no-show. Last night the room was empty, and tonight we have a reservation for a Mr. and Mrs. Collins, and there's a visa number."

"Who rented the room Sunday through Tuesday?"

"A Mr. Brad Young."

"Is there a card number?"

Another button, another screen.

"He paid in cash."

"What about the reservation for Wednesday night? Is there a credit card number for that?"

It took her a moment. "No, which is a little odd."

"Because you guys don't take reservations without a valid credit card number, right?"

"Right," she said. "Unless . . ."

"Unless what?"

"Unless, say, the party was already a customer."

"Like this Mr. Brad Young."

"Exactly . . . a customer like Mr. Young, who'd been paying cash by the day. That's a good example. If somebody like that called the desk and said he wanted to extend his stay, we'd generally just do it for him, you know, as a courtesy. It's not strictly according to policy, but we do it anyhow."

"Did Mr. Young cancel?"

"Not that I can see."

"Can you tell who it was that registered this Brad Young?"

She put a fingertip on the screen. "Ginger."

"Is Ginger on duty?"

"Ginger's on vacation. Tahoe for a week. It's their tenth anniversary." Marie read my mind. "Not much help, I'm afraid."

"The hotel employs a room-service waiter named Rodrigo something. Is he working?"

"You mean Rod Tavares. I'd have to check the schedule."

"I'd really appreciate it," I said.

I waited as she opened the door at the rear of the registration area and stepped inside. She was gone for less than a minute.

"Rodrigo's off till Monday. Twelve to eight."

"Could you by any chance get me his address and phone number?" She'd begun to shake her head before I'd even finished.

"Staff information is confidential. We just had a whole workshop on that. I'm sorry, but . . ."

I took a chance. The way I saw it, the only other time she'd ever seen me, I'd been in tight with the boss. I figured I could milk the halo effect. I pulled Gloria Ricci's business card from my pocket and flipped it over to the back.

"That's Ms. Ricci's home number. How about if you give her a call? That way you'll be covered." I handed her the card.

I never thought she'd do it. I'd have bet a body part that, rather than have to call Ricci at home, she'd just give me the info. I was wrong.

She picked up the phone in front of her, then thought better about talking about me in front of me and put it back down.

"I'll be right back," she said, and exited again through the door.

The minute the door closed, I leaned over and swiveled the computer monitor my way. The top of the screen read Rooms By Number. I pushed the return key until I was back at the main menu. I quickly read my way down the laundry list of options. F was Hotel Personnel. This got me a database search page. I had two search options, Job Title or Name. I chose Name, entered Tavares, Rodrigo and pushed the button. In fifteen seconds I had what I needed.

Before leaving, I returned the computer to the main menu screen and screwed it back in Marie's direction. I think I heard Marie call my name just as I stepped onto the escalator, but I was in a hurry and couldn't be sure.

Finding Rodrigo Tavares was a bit harder. The address was up on the hill, just south of Madison, in what I'd call a transitional neighborhood. As a general rule, the farther south of Madison you go, the funkier the neighborhood gets. Nothing too crazy. Seattle hasn't got a Cabrini Green or anything. Just one of those areas that gives a guy the urge to whistle and maybe have a little something extra in his sock.

In that part of the city, isolated pockets of postwar homes sprout like dandelions among the innumerable, multistory medical buildings which have, in recent years, devoured the once solidly middle-class neighborhood. The result of this encroachment has been to inflate the tax rate to commercial levels, offering the mostly elderly natives one of two choices. They can either pay their taxes or maintain their property. Most pay the taxes.

It was a duplex just off Ninth Street. In the front yard, this summer's weeds waved like the proverbial "amber waves of grain." Unit A was on the left, and Unit C was on the right. I'll admit it. I was stumped. The address hadn't included a unit number. I didn't have any more idea of which door to knock on than I did about what in hell had happened to Unit B. When in doubt, left to right.

Unit A opened her door a crack. At least three chains, maybe more. It was hard to tell, because it was dark in the apartment, and I had to look down into the darkest of it because she was so short. She had thick salt-and-pepper hair. Mostly salt and very long for a woman her age, the hair formed a kind of mantle around her face. I stuck my foot in the door.

"I'm looking for Rodrigo Tavares."

The words were perfect English, but the rolled *r*'s and machine-gun delivery were pure Spanish. "Rodrigo is not here."

"Could you tell me where I might find him?"

She didn't answer.

"Are you his mother?"

"He is not here."

"Do you know where he is?"

All she had to do was say no. I would have pressed her again and then given up. Contrary to rumor, on Thursday nights I no longer beat up on old ladies. Thursday is puppy-strangling night.

Instead, she said, "Why doan you people leave him alone?"

Which, of course, immediately brought to mind such questions as: "What people?" "How come she's seen these people so often she assumes I must be one of them?" and "Why are they bothering her Rodrigo?"

She leaned hard on the door and got nowhere.

"You leave him alone," she said, giving the door everything she had. It was the noises that got me, as a series of pitiful squeals filled the air. She made it sound like she was rowing for the Pharaoh and I was the bald guy with the drum.

I jerked my foot out, and the door banged shut. I stood on the porch for a minute and then knocked on Unit C. I heard the scrape of a chair. No chain locks on this door. It popped so fast, it created a momentary vacuum in the surrounding air, pulling my hair forward.

He was a big one. Wearing a cutoff black T-shirt under a black leather vest, a pair of brand-new jeans and some engineer boots. His long, greasy hair was pulled back into a ponytail. He pointed a finger at my face, stopping about an inch short of my nose.

"Don't be tellin' me you got me up from my dinner so's you could sell me somethin'. Tell me somethin', but don't tell me that."

"Okay, I won't."

It seemed he wasn't prepared for that response.

"So wadda you want?"

"You know anything about the kid next door?"

Wrong question.

He pulled the door closed behind him and stepped out onto the tiny porch. I was supposed to back down the stairs, but instead held my ground. No more than a foot separated us on the narrow porch. He put his hands on his hips and looked me over from head to toe.

"Walk over there," he said, pointing to the far end of the porch.

What the hell. I walked down to the rail and back.

"You ain't one, are you?"

"One what?"

"One of the sissy boys."

"You mean, like . . . ?"

"The kid's a fruitcake," he said.

I wasn't sure what to say next. Pointing out to him that such terms as "sissy boys" and "fruitcakes" were no longer acceptable in the sensitive nineties didn't seem like such a good idea, so I settled for, "No. I'm not."

"Not that I give a shit, you know," he added. "Each to his own, is what I say. Hell, I know a long-haul trucker trained a miniature schnauzer to lick his balls while he was driving. Nicest guy in the world. Wife, three kids."

I figured I'd just take his word for it.

"Rod's a nice enough kid, but I can always tell. Just somethin' about 'em. I don't know what it is."

"Mom didn't seem to want to be much help," I said.

"Ya gotta figure Mom's how he got that way."

Ah, the Freudian Model.

"Any idea where I might find him?"

"What for?"

"I just need to ask him something. No trouble."

He mulled it over. " 'Cause I wouldn't want no trouble for the kid. He may be a little light in the loafers, but like I said, he's a nice kid."

"No trouble."

His name was Joe Mamula, but everyone called him Joe Mama. *But everyone knew her as Nancy.* He worked for a vending machine company and serviced most of the bars on the hill, up in what he liked to call the "swish Alps."

"I been in that pool hall up on Twenty-third a bunch of times on service calls. Every time I been in there, he been in there. That's all I know, man." He reached for the door. "My dinner's gettin' cold."

Before the door completely closed. I shot a question at him, "By the way, Joe, where's Unit B?"

"Fucked if I know," he said and closed the door.

Okay, I'll admit it. I'm not fond of going into gay bars. It has nothing to do with them. It has to do with me. I always feel like a voyeur. I feel as if I'm looking through somebody else's front window from the shrubbery. And it's not like I've ever been made to feel unwelcome. The times I've found myself in that position have, for the most part, been quite pleasant. Maybe I'm a repressed fascist, or maybe it's the only time a heterosexual, middle-aged white man feels like a minority. Who knows?

I saw him the moment I opened the door. Rodrigo was all the way in the back right corner playing pool with three other guys. As I strolled the length of the room, I tried to ignore the feeling that I was in Atlantic City, New Jersey, walking down the Miss America runway without my swim-suit. I told myself to lighten up. These guys had no interest in me. They were gay, not blind.

I stood at the end of the pool table and waited for him to notice me. He was deep in conversation with a muscular guy of about thirty in a blue tank top and white shorts. The hair was a little shorter, maybe, and perhaps the banter just a bit more animated, but otherwise it was standard pool hall, Anywhere, U.S.A.

Rodrigo threw his head back to laugh, caught sight of me and bit it off. He leaned his cue against the wall and walked my way.

"What are you doing here?" He gave me a small smile. "Or did I seriously misjudge you?"

Interesting. Joe Mamula was positive he could recognize one of *them*, and now Rod was sure he could recognize one of *us*. Dude.

"I'm looking for you."

"Why would you be looking for me?"

"I need to ask you a question."

His face clouded. "Did you hassle my mother?"

I gave him the scout's salute. "I asked her once. She re-fused. I went away. That was it."

He stayed on the offensive. "What's so important you have to knock on my mother's door?"

"What's with you that a simple inquiry makes her so nervous?"

"What are you, a liberal or something?"

"This is Seattle, man. Maybe you haven't noticed, but nobody much gives a shit about your sexual orientation."

"Old habits die hard. Not every place is like this." Rodrigo looked over his shoulder at his buddies and then looked me in the eye. "Billings, Montana. That's where I grew up."

"Quaint little town, as I remember."

"Not for a fag wetback it's not. I could tell you stories."

International diplomacy will probably not be in my future. Unable to come up with any kind of decent segue, I simply changed the channel.

"You remember that day you came by with the cart? When I was standing outside eight-fourteen?"

"I remember. What about it?"

From over at the table, someone called, "Rod—it's your turn."

He answered without turning. "Shoot for me, Freddy."

"Who was in the room where you delivered the order?"

He wrapped his arms around himself. "Oooweee," he said. "Don't get me mixed up in that, man. Get my ass fired."

"This is just between us."

"Yeah," he said, "like I can trust you."

"You trusted me enough to let me take that bone from your hand the other night." I'll admit it. It was cheap.

He thought it over.

"What a gomer," he finally said. "I couldn't believe that guy."

"One of a kind."

"I guess I do owe you, don't I?"

"That's the way I see it."

"Okay," he agreed, "but you got to keep me out of it."

"No problem," I lied. If this worked out like I thought it might, Rodrigo was going to be real popular with the SPD. No sense in worrying him about it now, though.

"It's like Romeo and Juliet, man. We read that in my community college lit class last semester. It was really cool. The Montagues and the Capulets. Star-crossed lovers from warring families."

I don't remember driving home. I must have done it, because I found myself standing on the porch trying to figure out how to open the front door. After trying the key one way six or seven times, I made the adjustment and turned the key over. The house was dark. Rebecca called my name from upstairs.

"It's me," I called back.

I stood in the bedroom, dropping my clothes into the darkness at my feet, then crawled under the covers and pulled the down comforter up to my chin. The sheets were new and stiff. Rebecca's head turned my way. She reached out a hand and patted my face three times. Good doggie doggie. And then made a lazy roll away from me and began, ever so slightly, to snore.

27

Duvall brandished a muffin. "Don't say that again. I do not snore."

"Don't worry," I said. "You do it in a most demure and ladylike manner. There wasn't much snorting and that kind of stuff."

I ducked my head to the left and let the poppyseed muffin sail by.

"What kind of stuff?"

"Well, there was the drooling . . ."

She picked up a knife. I held up my hands.

"Just kidding."

"Is that all you did? Lie there and watch me sleep all night?"

"I had a lot on my mind. It took me a while to get to sleep."

"Like how it's possible people could have the unmitigated gall not to like the same movies we do?"

"And the look on the Meyerson girl's face when Candace jumped in and admitted she'd gone to the movies with her and Rickey Ray. I could have sworn she didn't know what the hell Candace was talking about."

"How could that be? If it wasn't true, how could Candace be sure the Meyerson girl would go along with the lie?"

"That's the sixty-four-thousand-dollar question."

"No. That was *Quiz Show*. You've got your movies mixed up."

"This whole damn thing is mixed. Pass the butter."

Adrift in a sea of boxes and newspaper, we buttered our muffins and drank our coffee at opposite ends of what used to be my dining room table, which, in this new configuration, was now our kitchen table.

"I've got a ten-thirty meeting," she said, rising. "But I could be available for lunch, should anyone perhaps feel indebted."

"It's Friday. Barbecue day. Remember?"

On Jack's side of the street, the entire block was behind a protective barrier of yellow SPD sawhorses. The area between the sawhorses and the sidewalk was being patrolled by SPD officers on real horses. Modern technology has done little to provide a more effective crowd-control device than a well-trained horse-and-rider team. The SPD approach is simple. Horsie wanna go over here. Either move or try not to get hoofprints on your forehead. Thank you very much.

Abby and Lola had called out the taxi squad for this one. To the south, Stewart Street was filled with several hundred 4-H members and a collection of earnest parents waving a sedate array of SAVE BUNKY and 4-H 4-EVER signs. To their left, right at the elbow of Stewart Street and Third Avenue, were Steve Drew and his merry vegans. Maybe a hundred of them, wedged in between the 4-H'ers and the animal rightists from PAWS, waving MEAT IS MURDER signs and talking quietly among themselves.

The area directly in front of the restaurant was an odd mix of Clarissa Hedgpeth's NUTSS people and Konrad Kramer's Animal Liberation Front. Clarissa held an ALL GOD'S CHILDREN sign in one hand and Bruce's leash in the other. The Kramer corps were wearing their terrorist scarves around their necks and holding a single large sign which read: ANIMAL FREE-DOM—AT ANY PRICE. Konrad himself was presently engaged in a shoving match with an elderly man from Clarissa's entourage. The old man's face was beet-red as he shouted at Kramer.

At the far end of the block, another surging mass of placard-waving humanity pushed hard against the barriers, chanting something I couldn't make out. As I walked down the sidewalk, someone shouted, "Killer."

All three local TV stations had mobile units on the scene. The cops had allowed them to set up in the corners, inside the barriers. KING-TV's white van was being commandeered by Melissa Wright, the weekend news anchor. Surprisingly, L-O-L-A Lola King was nowhere to be seen. I figured the story had gotten so big, the station had made a change.

Rickey Ray perched on his stool inside the front door.

"I knew you wouldn't miss it, podna," he said with a smirk.

The restaurant was dark and empty.

"Where is everybody?"

"Outside. The big doin's outside."

"Nice crowd out there in the street."

"Man, I didn't know there was this many tree-huggin', granola-suckin' mofos on the whole planet. This a weird town, my man."

"Isn't Jack worried about the ambiance?"

Rickey shook his head. "Seven o'clock the cops are gonna move 'em back two blocks in every direction. Time the VIPs arrive, you won't even know they was around."

"Must be his charm."

"Must be," he agreed.

I could feel the heat on my left arm the second I stepped out the door, although the barbecue pit was a good thirty feet to my left. Bunky wasn't going to like this at all. Vertical heat waves shimmied upward, distorting my view of the bricks in the building across the alley.

A hunter-green tarp had been hung all along the inside of the fence, effectively hiding the festivities from those in the street. The lot was alive with activity. Enough wind swirled in the area to wind the pennants around their stanchions and keep a thin stream of glowing sparks steadily moving upward from the metal fire pit.

Beneath the green-and-white tents, what I estimated to be about forty tables were being prepared for this evening's gala. An army of service people were tacking down white linen tablecloths and arranging place settings. On my right, behind a solid line of waiters, I could hear Dixie's voice going over table assignments.

Out in the center of the space, in an area I supposed would be used later for dancing, stood the old Jackalope. Candace was locked to his elbow like a terrier as he made expansive gestures with his free hand. The guy in the yellow hard hat nodded, and waved a hand-held radio toward the sky. I checked my watch. Quarter to twelve. If everything had gone reasonably well down at the Brenner Brothers, it shouldn't be long now. A voice startled me.

"Do you believe this?"

Bart Yonquist looked as if he'd stepped out of the Monkey Ward catalog. The perfect preppie right down to the penny loafers. That is, if you didn't count the large square purse he carried in his hand.

I put my hands on my hips and said, "I'm sorry. A straw bag? Before Easter? Excuse me, but I don't think so."

"I'm a fashion innovator," he told me.

"And no, I don't believe it."

"I'm out of here. I feel like I'm in a bad foreign film. Whenever the cops stop harassing us, I'm on the next plane back to Cleveland. I've got most of the money I need. I'll borrow the rest."

"Good move. I was beginning to think I was the only one who thought this whole mess was completely off the wall."

"You know, Mr. Waterman, I've got a feeling that when I'm older and have a family . . . I think maybe these last six months are going to comprise the best story I tell for the rest of my life."

"I wouldn't be a bit surprised."

"I gotta go," he said. "Dixie needs some Rolaids."

Still grimly clutching the purse, he disappeared inside the building. Jack was still engaged in an animated conversation with Hard Hat, so I walked along the row of tents on the Third Avenue side and watched the preparations. Halfway down the row, Dixie appeared at my left shoulder. "How you doing?" I asked.

"Evathing I can, honey."

"Somebody better."

"Ain't it the truth." She shielded her eyes and checked the sky. "You seen Bart?"

I told her where he'd gone. Dixie raised a hand and massaged her middle. "Wish to goodness he'd hurry. I'm about to eat a hole in myself and fall out the bottom."

"What's the L stand for?"

"What L?"

"The L in Donnareen L. Pye."

"Loretta." She said it with the accent on the first syllable. "Mama named me after Loretta Lynn."

She pulled her head back and took me in. "You been snoopin' after me?"

I showed her both palms. "I'm with you on this one, Dixie. As far as I'm concerned, he's as crazy as a shithouse rat."

She wasn't satisfied. "You know," she said, "I don't think I like—"

She never got a chance to finish. The stories I'd heard from 'Nam vets about how you could hear the choppers long before you could see them must have been true only in the jungle.

Mike Bales brought the chopper in fast and low, cutting his way among the buildings as if he expected rocket fire. You only had to watch him fly for a moment to recognize an artist at work. Without so much as an extra turn, he came zooming over the parking garage, spun the copter to the left over the Drop Zone and began to hover some hundred and fifty feet above the ground.

Outside the fence, a roar began to rise from the crowd as the quick explained to the dead what was happening. In the stone confines of the urban canyon, the rotors slapped the air like many hands driven flat upon the water; the new slaps mixed with the reverberations to form a single pulsating beat.

I looked around. All three news teams were standing atop their vans feverishly shooting film and mouthing copy. The staff had come out from beneath the tents to watch. Jack, Candace and Hard Hat were backing away from the DZ, moving slowly south toward the mayor's table and the 4-H'ers beyond the fence. Hard Hat was talking into the radio. The line of airborne sparks was swollen to a stream as the moving air pulled an orange plume of fire skyward.

Bales knew what he was doing. He was as low as he planned to get. The helicopter had barely begun to hover when the load started steadily toward the ground. The whine of the winch could be heard above the percussive slapping of the rotors. Bunky was coming down in a hurry and right on target.

Dixie was still holding her midriff, but her eyes were bright as she scanned the area. "It's CNN tonight, darlin'," she enthused.

The pallet was no more than forty feet from the ground and closing fast when things started to go haywire. Accounts of what happened next are far more numerous than there were people on the scene. In the coming weeks, nearly everyone in the Central Sound area would claim to have been standing in the street when it happened.

The people in the street saw it first. I was so focused on the descending ton of beef that it took the collective gasp of several thousand of my fellow creatures to get my attention. Holy guacamole.

The KING-TV "Eye In the Sky" chopper was dropping

into the picture from the east, moving down between the buildings, overfilling the crowded piece of sky. Why it chose to fly so low depends upon who you ask. The pilot later claimed that Lola had insisted that she wanted to shoot the drop from below and had belittled and berated him into flying beyond the portals of his better judgment.

Lola, when you later sorted out her many and often contradictory public utterances concerning the incident, seemed to be using a variation of the Act of God Defense, in which she blamed the event on a wide variety of atmospheric and karmic variables far beyond the ken of mere mortals. The fact that, after the hoopla had died down, I never again saw her on the tube leads me to believe that upper management may have viewed things otherwise.

Randall Chung, the cameraman, refused, on the advice of his attorney, to issue any statement whatsoever, and I believe his lawsuits, against both Lola and the station are, to this day, still pending.

The roar was deafening now. The reporters, still standing on the tops of the vans, had slipped their mikes under their arms and were using their hands for ear protectors. The door was off Lola's chopper and I could see her sitting rigid in the seat, her skirt flapping about her legs, as the copter settled even with Mike Bales.

From my humble vantage, I imagined the whites of Mike Bales's eyes when he first spotted the other chopper. He freed his right hand from the stick and waved the copter frantically off. The winch had stopped. Bunky was still thirty feet from the ground and turning slowly in a circle. Bales kept waving and pointing upward. I saw his mouth move as he shouted into his headset. The other chopper inched lower.

The stream of fire rising golden from the pit suddenly became a glittering river. The combined rotor-wash was lifting the fire from the ground. Without willing it so, I began to reel backward toward the fence. In a great burst of gray, the barbecue pit delivered up its burned charcoal residue in a single great geyser of ash and spark.

In an instant, the TV chopper was enveloped in a cloud of thick gray smoke and burning ash. The machine began to twirl in a circle, falling lower and moving awkwardly to the south, toward the cable connecting Mike Bales to his load.

Bales had no choice but to swing his chopper off to the south, away from the careening Lola and toward the tallest of the surrounding buildings. With almost a hundred feet of cable out, the slightest swing of the pallet translated into a violent jerk to the helicopter. The machine lurched around the sky as Bales fought to stay directly over his load.

The KING-TV pilot spun on his tail, wobbled violently a couple of times and regained a stable hover, waiting for the dense smoke to clear from his cockpit. It was a hell of a piece of flying by feel. There was no way he could see the instruments. Later, pictures confirmed that the ball of smoke and ash which had inundated the cockpit had contained a significant array of superheated particulants that had left the exposed areas of Lola, the pilot and Randy Chung with the approximate look and texture of a New York pepper steak.

Mike Bales hadn't been so lucky. Faced with the prospect of either smashing into one of the surrounding buildings or crash-landing among the demonstrators, at great human cost, Bales did the only thing he could. He turned loose his load and climbed for all he was worth. Although it saved his life, it was otherwise a most unfortunate combination of actions.

For a brief moment, just as the cable snicked away, Bunky and his pallet seemed to almost hover in the air; then, slowly, ever so slowly, the package fell heavily toward the ground.

As L-O-L-A Lola would say so many times in the following days, it was only by the grace of God that nobody was killed.

Bunky hit the right side of the stage, driving the metal

supports into the ground like tent stakes. In retrospect, I
don't think the stage even slowed him down. Poor Bunky
had been reduced to a round mound of ground round.

Slowly, like a steel cauldron disgorging its white lava in-
gots, the pan full of fire collapsed forward, spilling its flaming load upon the ground in a curling wave of molten slag.

I grabbed Dixie by the belt and pulled her along with me.
Everyone was moving south at top speed, running like game
before a brushfire.

They needn't have worried. The fire never got that far.
Both helicopters roared at full throttle now, moving straight
up into the sky, nose to nose, their pinwheel rotors no more
than thirty feet apart as they rose above the buildings.

Below the deafening din of the choppers, Jack's ton of
genuine "don't weigh a thing" lava rock had been ripped
airborne by the violent updraft of heat waves and rotor
blades, forming a rapidly rising funnel cone of superheated
material swirling around the air like locusts, rising higher,
reaching to keep up with the machines, mushrooming far
out over its central core. The air around me was suddenly
hot and filled with debris; something hit me above the right
eye with a sharp, searing pain and then again in the ear.

I grabbed a tablecloth from a linen cart, threw it over
Dixie's head and tumbled us both to the ground, where we
lay shivering like penitents, bowed beneath a withering hail
of small, hot rocks.

Somewhere in the great beyond, Cotton Mather was grinning. This might not be the exact equivalent of the Old Tes-
tament fire and brimstone, but it was close enough for
government work.

"Jumpin' Jesus!" I heard Dixie yell.

It ended as suddenly as it had begun. Robbed of the pull
of the rotors, the rubble reached the apex of its flight, lost
momentum and then rained quickly back to earth. And to
think, the fun was only beginning.

Jack had been right. Nothing held a heat charge like lava
rock. If those little suckers were any cooler coming down

than they were going up, you could have fooled those of us who were in attendance that day.

Acrid smoke began to fill the pocket beneath the table-cloth. I jumped to my feet, hauling Dixie up with me as I went. The act of standing up slid one of the little boogers down between my ankle and my shoe. I screamed and tore at my foot. I wanted desperately to tell Dixie that her hair was on fire, but the agony of my ankle rendered me speech-less. I hopped about on one foot, adding my agonized roar to the deafening collage of screams, curses and shouts that filled the air. The ground around me was littered with smol-dering tidbits. Sitting down would involve weeks in inten-sive care.

I was screaming through my teeth before I got the shoe off and shook the little red marble to the ground. Dixie stood with her hands to her mouth, watching me without compre-hension, small blue flames rising from the top of her head.

"Jesus, Dixie, your hair's on fire!" I shouted, looking wildly around for something with water. Dixie knew better. She reached up with her hand, grabbed the blond mane and threw it to the ground, where it flared into a fair-sized blaze. For reasons I'll never understand, Dixie and I stood side by side and stomped at that tawny pelt of flaming follicles as if the future of the race depended on putting the sucker out. Shock, I guess.

"That was my best hair," she said as we stood back and admired our melted, smoldering handiwork.

Behold, the Nagasaki cat.

I can only speak to what was going on inside the fence. Over the next two weeks, everyone in America probably saw more of the carnage out in the street than I did. Weeks of feature stories milked every drop of coverage from that ten minutes of utter chaos. If I never see that shot of Clarissa Hedgpeth trying to extinguish her faux-fur jacket again, it will be too soon. Or the one of the horse cop jumping his mount over a cowering line of wide-eyed demonstrators. Or the countless shots of what the newspeople came to call the "hotfoot hoedown." Hell, that one made a fortune for a couple of wily entrepreneurs who later spliced together the best shots. They showed shocked people standing openmouthed in the street, relieved to be alive, the camera catching them just as one of the atomic embers ate through their shoe and into their foot, then adding dance music appropriate to whatever frenzied jig the poor soul danced. For a while there, the direct-mail TV ad for the *Hotfoot Hoedown* video was on damn near as often as *Dorf Goes Fishing*.

Inside the fence, things were just as bad. Three tents were fully engulfed by flames. Jack and Candace emerged from beneath the mayor's table, their faces smudged and wondering. Hard Hat peeked out once, but stayed put. Hard to blame him.

Two figures were running our way. Bart Yonquist, Dixie's purse still swaying on his arm, skidded to a stop in front of us.

"Get Dixie out of here," I said.

Bart took her by the elbow and trotted her off into the smoke.

To my left, Rickey Ray had vaulted the scorched earth and was barreling toward Jack and Candace. Jack opened his mouth as if to ask Rickey Ray just where in hell he'd been when the shit hit the fan, but Rickey Ray wasn't listening. He scooped Candace Atherton into his gnarly arms and hotfooted it back from whence he had come, traveling, if anything, faster than he had on the way in. Even though Bart and Dixie had a ten-yard head start, they finished a fading second through the side door of the restaurant.

Jack stood dumbfounded for a moment and then wobbled out into the middle of the yard, turning in circles, as if his mind refused to absorb the extent of the devastation. Smoke was beginning to rise from beneath his right foot. I was debating whether to tell him or not when the smell of burning grass pulled my head around.

The rustic hay bales spread about and on the cattle truck were fully engulfed in flame, burning from the inside out as if embers had been driven directly into their centers. Directly through the fence, the frontmost pile spat and cracked as it gained internal momentum. Above the shimmering heat waves and the smoke, the big rig's chrome gas cap was still visible.

I sprinted for the far end of the lot and the gate to the alley. The 4-H contingent was no more than forty yards removed from the front bumper of the truck. If a couple of hundred gallons of diesel fuel went off in their faces, there wasn't going to be much left.

Grabbing a metal post to slow my momentum, I whipped myself around the corner and staggered headlong down the alley. Whoever had set out the hay had hung his baling hook from the rearview mirror. I snagged it on the way past, walked all the way beyond the pyre, putting my back to the street, and drove the hook into the side of the uppermost burning bundle. In a single motion I lifted the bale, got my shoulder behind the handle and followed all the way through, sailing the bale out over the barricade into the street.

By the time I repeated the process six more times, the hairs on the back of my hook hand were gone, my right ear was burned shiny and I had a small fire smoldering in the collar of my shirt. A symphony of sirens now rose above the human roar and the snapping of flames. The air smelled like roasting vegetarians.

Jack sat astride the linen cart, his shoe in his hand. Across the yard, several fire extinguishers were belching out white clouds of flame retardant. Those tents that had not already been completely consumed were no longer showing flames. The sirens grew closer. I leaned back against the truck and took a deep breath. And the truck moved. Not a little, a lot. As if shaken on its springs by some giant hand. And again the big rig shook, rocking from side to side on its springs. And then the sound of rushing air, and it rocked from front to back.

The street was filled with flashing lights and hoarse cries.

I walked to the rear of the trailer, grabbed the handles on the ramp with both hands and backed up until the ramp dropped into its notches.

I dropped the ramp and went up the incline to the door, pulled the handle over and up and, using both hands, rolled the door up and open.

The big fella still had the chalk marks on his beautiful black hide. He didn't like the smoke or the sirens one bit. His nostrils were flaring and his big brown eyes rolled in his head. I grabbed the dangling end of the lead and said, "Bunky, my man, I think we best be getting you the hell out of here." I don't care what anybody says, he knew what I meant.

He must have, because he followed me down the ramp and out into the alley like a house-trained dog. His big black hooves clopped on the cement as we walked up the alley together. When we came abreast of Jack, I pointed to the bull in wonder.

"Bunky," I said.

"Damn right," said the Jackster, massaging his foot. "Paid over three hundred grand for that bag of guts; you didn't really think I was gonna eat him, did ya? Kerriiist. The Jackalope ain't crazy, ya know."

I decided not to tell him his wallet was smoking.

28

heard a joke once; the premise was that Heaven was getting so overcrowded that only those people whose last
day on earth had also been the worst day of their entire
lives could be admitted. On the first day of the new policy,
Saint Peter spent the morning rejecting every applicant and
then broke for a noon bite.

When he returned from lunch, three guys were in line.
The first fellow stepped up. Saint Peter says, "Okay, what's
your story?"

The guy says, "I was sure my wife was having an affair,
so I snuck home early from work one day. There she was,
in bed with the covers pulled up to her chin, looking guilty.
I searched the apartment like a madman, high and low, but
he wasn't there. Then, just out of luck, I looked out the
window, and there he was, hanging from my downstairs
neighbor's fire escape. I ran in, got my ball peen hammer,
climbed down and beat his fingers. He fell, but some shrubbery broke his fall, and he wasn't dead. I was still so crazy
I ran back up, grabbed the refrigerator and threw it down
on him. It killed him, but carrying a refrigerator was too
much for my heart, and I dropped dead."

Saint Peter is moved. "That's really terrible," he says. "Go on. You can go in."

The next guy stepped up.

"Let's hear it," says Saint Peter.

"You won't believe this," the guy says. "I'm on my fire escape working out one afternoon. I'm doing some chin-ups to build upper-body strength when all of a sudden my upstairs neighbor comes running down the stairs with a hammer. He starts pounding on my fingers. I fall, but get lucky and land on some bushes. I'm just lying there, thanking the Lord I'm not dead, when next thing I know, I look up and there's a refrigerator coming at me. It broke my neck."

Saint Peter is again moved and the man is admitted to Heaven.

When the third guy stepped up, Saint Peter says, "Whatever you've got to tell me better be real good."

The guy leans in close.

"Okay, Peter," he says. "Picture this. I'm hiding naked in a refrigerator. . . ."

The search warrant was the refrigerator of my day. I limped up the ninth-floor corridor toward my room with the hole in my sock exposing a seeping burn the size of a quarter, an ear which had already begun to blister and a fifty-dollar Ralph Lauren pullover with half the collar burned off. I'd been subjected to fire and brimstone, and was in all likelihood going to appear prominently in tomorrow's morning editions, leading a bull down Marion Street on a leash. It was a sight which I personally find somewhat lacking in the kind of hard-bitten image I generally prefer to cultivate. My hopes to save a modicum of media attention for my client had been an abject failure. After this afternoon's rain of fire, Le Cuisine Internationale would be lucky to make the travel section. I'd been prodded, deposed, medically inspected, had my grievous injuries declared minor, been unable to extricate my car from the worst traffic jam in Seattle history and thusly forced to walk back to the hotel, where I find, taped to my door, a search warrant authorizing the SPD to pillage my hotel room. Not only that, but they'd left the place a mess. Is that a Kelvinator I see coming down? Frost Free? Automatic ice maker?

The red numbers on the digital clock said it was three twenty-three in the afternoon. I could have sworn it was later; I felt like I'd been on a three-day binge. I pushed the door toward closed, walked across the room and sat down on the foot of the bed. I braced my hands behind me on the bed and leaned back into a stretch; I yawned and rolled my neck. A cramp began to tense one of the muscles in my lower back, so I lay all the way down on the bed and put my hands behind my head. I yawned again.

I was hanging from that fire escape, moving from hand to hand as my upstairs neighbor beat my fingers to jelly. Bang, bang, bang . . .

The clock read five-fifty, I was in a strange room and somebody was beating on the door. It seems simple enough now, but it took me a full minute to put it together. As the door swung open, I remembered I hadn't closed it all the way. I rose. It was Rowcliffe.

"I hope I've not disturbed you, sir," he said.

"No, no," I said. "Come in."

He stood with one foot in the room and the other in the hall.

"What's the matter?" I asked.

"It's Sir Geoffrey."

"What happened?"

"The authorities have taken him."

"Taken him where?"

"Down to that same room above the lobby, I believe."

"Why did they do that?"

"Because he would not go willingly."

Probably didn't like the entree.

"Why not?"

Rowcliffe told me. At about ten this morning, a herd of SPD officers descended upon the hotel, served their warrants and proceeded to search Sir Geoffrey's quarters, the Del

Fuego suite and the Meyerson suite. "They appear to have been here as well," he commented.

"They need work on their housekeeping," I said.

"They left a frightful mess. Sir Geoffrey was livid."

"And then later, they asked him to come downstairs?"

"He was practicing his speech for this evening."

"And he refused to go."

"Yes, sir. They threatened to load him on a baggage pram if he refused to locomote."

I'd pay Sonics ticket prices to see that one.

"How long ago was this?"

"Less than ten minutes."

"What can I do?"

"I fear he is sufficiently incensed to do something unfortunate."

"And you want me to crash the party and make sure he's not filling the air with vitriolic oaths?"

"Yes. I was hoping . . ."

"I'm on it," I said. It was the least I could do. I'd squandered bales of his cash, and although I had accomplished a number of significant tasks, none of them were what I'd been hired to do. Yesterday, I had offered Lawrence a chance at redemption. Could be it was my turn now.

29

When I poked my head out of the elevator, I caught the briefest glimpse of a pair of King County Mounties waddling up the stairs behind Dixie and Bart. They must have been merely delivery boys, because by the time I topped the three stairs, they were already headed back my way. I gave the boys a smile and walked around them.

"Afternoon, fellas," I said. Nothing.

My timing was perfect. I pulled open the door and stepped inside just as Detective Lobdell said, "May I have your attention."

Apparently not. The group went wild, erupting into a melee of curses, threats and recriminations. At the far end of the room, Sir Geoffrey sat with his arms folded over his chest, glowering off into space. To my immediate right, Abigail Meyerson, Brie and Spaulding all seemed to be yelling at once. No Francona? No Hill?

The Del Fuego contingent was sans its namesake. Bart and Dixie, Rickey Ray and Candace Atherton. That was it. They were all shouting, too. Detective Lobdell sensed my presence in his peripheral vision. As he turned to Lawrence, I could hear his voice above the din.

"What's he doing here?"

Lawrence said something to him that I couldn't hear. When he began to reply, I scooted across the room, dragged a chair over next to Sir Geoffrey and sat down. His lordship favored me with a curt nod.

Lobdell glanced back toward my former position, noted my absence and rotated his head until he found me with his eyes. I tried to read them. Was he going to throw me out? No. He wanted me to see whatever was about to come down. As if in confirmation, he sneered at me and then raised his arms. The bozo was showing off.

It took a full two minutes to quiet the crowd. Twice during that period, just at the moment when it seemed that order was about to prevail, a final pithy insult was hurled, and the mob scene escalated anew.

"If you are through . . ." Lobdell began.

"You're the one that's through!" Spaulding shouted.

"I'm in no hurry here, ladies and gentlemen. You want this to take all night, that's okay with me."

Behind him on the dais, Lawrence all but rolled her eyes at Lobdell's stirring Vice Principal impression. Even the tall, skinny cop up there with them had to suppress a smile by pulling himself back to rigid attention. For the first time, if you didn't count the curses left hanging in the air, the room was silent. Lobdell began again.

"This afternoon, the Seattle Police Department, in conjunction with the Office of the District Attorney, conducted a search—"

Again the room overflowed with sound. Spaulding rose, hefted his groin with his hand and yelled, "Search this."

If I read Brie's lips correctly, she said, "That shouldn't take long."

Lobdell waited it out.

"In the course of that search, a forty-caliber automatic was discovered in the possession of Mr. Del Fuego. A computer trace reveals the weapon to be registered to Mason F. Reese."

Even the echoes were quiet now. I could hear Spaulding breathing through his mouth. Lobdell had 'em right where he wanted 'em.

"Furthermore, a copy of Mr. Reese's Best Steak House list, dated the first of next month, was found among his effects." He paused. Now even the breathing had stopped. "Ms. Meyerson is number one on that list, while Del Fuego's FeedLot does not appear at all."

I joined in on a group "Oooh!"

Satisfied that he had our attention, he laid the wood on us.

"Seattle police officers have, this afternoon, arrested Mr. Del Fuego and charged him with the murder of Mason F. Reese."

Sir Geoffrey actually smiled. Not the slight straightening of the lips that generally passed for mirth with him, but a wide, toothy grin.

"I regret that this meeting may have been inconvenient. The arrest of Mr. Del Fuego makes it necessary to formalize each of your depositions. That way, if all goes well, perhaps you can avoid the need to return to Seattle whenever this matter comes to trial. This meeting—"

"This meeting is an abduction, is what it is." It was Abby, who stood, clearly pissed off. "Your Gestapo tactics with my staff—"

Lobdell cut her off. "Messrs. Francona and Hill were interfering with an officer in the performance of his duty and have been so charged."

"Here, here," added Sir Geoffrey.

Abby pointed out over the crowd. "You people are my witnesses."

Amazingly, the whole group nodded its head as one. Political Science 101. Disparate groups can be united against a common enemy.

Sir Geoffrey rose and pointed at Detective Lobdell. "You, sir, are a nincompoop. You have embarrassed both yourself and your department. First you have the temerity to drag us down here so you can posture, and now . . . this."

Dixie was in Lobdell's face. "Jack wouldn't hurt a little bitty bug," she assured the detective. "That old boy's all bark and no bite."

I stood up. "I want to confess," I shouted.

All eyes turned my way.

"Confess to what?" Lobdell sounded hopeful.

"I want to confess that I always wanted to do this."

"Do what?"

"Have the cops and the suspects all crowded into one room at the end of the case so I can tell everybody what actually happened and who actually done it." Nobody had a clue, so I tried again.

"You know, like at the end of a Nero Wolfe novel, when everybody crowds into Wolfe's office and he sets them straight."

The blank looks suggested a disturbing lack of literacy.

"Detective novels," Lobdell mocked. "This is what you get, ladies and gentlemen"—he chuckled for effect—"when you hire one of these so-called private investigators. Detective novels." He laughed again. "A murder investigation isn't about fiction, folks. It's not accomplished by amateurs or wannabes. It's about good, hard-nosed police work. It's about knocking on all the doors. It's about motive, means and opportunity. A competent investigator knows that when you have those three elements, you have your perpetrator. Period. Mr. Del Fuego stood to be ruined and possibly subject to criminal charges if Mr. Reese's rating system was adjudged to be fraudulent." Lobdell looked right at me. "And I think you'd have to say his sudden omission from the list makes that pretty clear." He held up one finger.

"Motive."

He reached into the speaker's stand and pulled out a large ziplock bag. The black automatic rested upside down in the ziplock bag. The proud papa. I could see the relief in his face. The search had been his idea. With high rollers like these, coming up empty might have taken a serious divot out of Lobdell's career. "Forty calibers' worth of means," he said, checking the crowd for worshipers before returning the bag to its place.

"Mr. Del Fuego signed a statement claiming that he remained at his restaurant until just before six on Monday evening and then took a cab back to the hotel. A statement"—Lobdell paused for effect—"which he has now recanted." He made it sound like he was shocked. "Since his arrest, Mr. Del Fuego has claimed that from four-fifteen that afternoon until nearly six-thirty, he was out on an errand. Supposedly to purchase farm supplies for his restaurant opening. In a cab." He chuckled again. "Of course, Mr. Del Fuego is unable to provide a name for the store, or even a general neighborhood in which it might be found. But I suppose we should take his word for that, him being a noted restaurateur and all."

He glanced over at me in mock surprise. "Isn't that what your pal Nero Wolfe would do?"

"Nah," I said. "Nero would send his man Saul Panzer out to find the feed store. Then Saul would come back with a card like this."

I fished the business card out of my wallet and brought it up to Lobdell. Lawrence stepped forward to look.

"What's this?" Lobdell asked.

"Just what it says. It's the business card of an old guy named Orville Whitney. He works in a feed store on old Ninety-nine, just south of Everett. He's the guy sold Jack the feed. Give him a call. You'll find out Jack was there casting racial aspersions just before six o'clock Monday night. There's a delivery kid who can corroborate."

The crowd gave a low rumble. Lobdell turned red, then white.

Sir Geoffrey spoke up. "And to think Mr. Waterman was, only the other day, extolling the virtues of your department. Phooey."

Lobdell forced a sentence out through his teeth.

"I warned you about withholding relevant information."

His lordship jumped to my defense. "Mr. Del Fuego's activities were in no way germane," he said. "Until that unfortunate moment when you decided to arrest him."

"What he said," I added.

The detective was smart enough to know I wasn't bluffing, but too stubborn to let go. He said something to Lawrence. They went back and forth a couple of times. He left the room at a lope, holding the card in one hand, flipping open his cell phone with the other.

Lawrence stepped down from the dais and walked over to me. She was looking for something in my eyes. I hate it when they do that.

"Is that card on the level?" she asked.

"Absolutely. I tried to tell you about it the other night, but you weren't interested."

She massaged her forehead. "You could have stopped him, before he made such an ass of himself," she said.

"You're right, I could have. What about you?"

"He went over my head, to my boss. He claimed I was treating them with kid gloves and the investigation was going nowhere."

"Your colleague has most certainly remedied that, now, hasn't he?" Sir Geoffrey remarked.

"Why don't you rescue this whole thing right now, Lawrence?"

"And how am I going to do that?"

"I'll give it to you free of charge."

"It's not that 'no button for the fourteenth floor' thing again, is it?"

"No. Better."

After another eye-searching session, she threw her hands up in the air and climbed back onto the platform. She gestured out over the crowd.

"You were saying, Mr. Waterman . . ."

"Let's start with the fact that there's no way Miss Brie Meyerson went to the movies with Mr. Tolliver and Miss Atherton on Monday afternoon."

"Oh, I've reached my limit. Spaulding, Brie . . ." Abby

turned to Lawrence. "You may arrest my children and me if you choose, Ms. Lawrence. But we will no longer be subjected to this—this—"

Abby was about to make a grand exit, so I stepped on the gas.

"She couldn't have, because Miss Meyerson spent the afternoon . . ." I searched for a verb. "Shacked up" seemed too judgmental, so I went with, "She was holed up in room eight fifty-nine with our friend over here . . . Mr. Bart Yonquist."

We had a nice freeze-tag moment where everybody stood still and ran that one through his or her respective circuits a couple of times.

I spoke to Bart and Brie. "Help me out here, kids. The toothpaste isn't going back in the tube." I shrugged and looked from one to the other. "We can drag the room-service waiter in here if we have to. Come on. Let's get this show on the road."

Abby began to march out, Spaulding in tow.

Brie Meyerson saved the day. "It's true," she said, then addressed her mother. "Bart and I are having a relationship." She took a deep breath. "You can shut me out if you want to, just like you did Penny—" Her voice broke, and she took a moment to compose herself. "But that won't change anything. All you'll have is another daughter you don't talk to. I'm going to Cleveland with Bart. We're going to—"

"Don't you dare . . ." Abby began.

"No!" Brie shouted.

Abby's jaw clamped shut.

"Just this once, Mother, just this once, let me finish a sentence all by myself, okay?"

Bart walked over and put a sheltering arm around the girl.

Abby's lower jaw resembled that of a large-mouthed bass.

"I'm taking a semester off from college; I'm going to Cleveland with Bart. I'm sorry if that's not what you had planned for me, but that's how it's going to be."

For a fleeting moment, I harbored a sentimental vision

seen so often in old Mickey Rooney movies, where the hard-bitten authority figure is finally won over by young love. Later, the kids borrow a barn and stage a show to raise money. You know the plot.

In that version, Abby would melt right before the camera, run over, eyes streaming, throw her arms around her daughter and cry, "Oh, my dear, I'm soooo happy for you." So much for that version.

In real life, Abigail Meyerson merely opened the door, beckoned Spaulding out before her and left without a word.

The lovebirds played it just right. Without a way to gracefully leave, they waited to see what I knew. I'd have done the same thing.

Dixie, on the other hand, was enthralled with the idea.

"Well, I'll be," she said, looking from Brie to Bart and back again. "If that isn't just the cutest thing."

Brie tried to stay upbeat. She was on the verge of tears, but she looked at me and said, "It was the Josta, wasn't it? That silly Josta drink?"

"It was the Josta catalyst," I said. "When I remembered that I'd seen those bottles on a room-service cart while I was standing in the hall talking to Mason Reese, that opened up a whole new range of speculation for me. The minute I considered that the room-service order might have been yours, suddenly a whole bunch of other stuff fell into place."

"What stuff?"

"Oh, like how your brother spends all day every day making fun of people and you ignore him, but he makes a little fun of Bart and you punch him in the mouth with a burger."

"You kids let me know when you get a pattern picked out. I'll send you down a little somethin' for forty," Dixie said.

I suddenly turned on Candace and Rickey Ray. "When you two got off on the eighth floor the first time, Brie and Bart were in the hall, weren't they? That's why you had to jump back on the elevator, and that's what set you off your feed so bad you had to stand there for five minutes figuring out what to do next."

Lawrence looked confused, so I told her about the tape. As I spoke, Rickey Ray colored slightly and shifted in his chair. I said a silent prayer that the skinny cop up on the dais was a lot badder than he looked.

Candace had the right idea. Stonewall it. She said, "I'm sure I don't know what you're talking about. I can't speak for Mr. Tolliver, but I, for one, have never been on the eighth floor of this hotel."

The tips of Rickey Ray's ears were bright red. He'd been running his own movie and hadn't heard what she said. Like all the rest of us on the planet, he'd have been better off if he'd listened. Instead, he said, "Ain't you never pushed the wrong button, podna?"

The moment would have made a good silent movie. In a single glance, Lawrence and I exchanged one "holy shit," two "told you so's" and one "damned if you weren't right."

On the far side of the room, Detective Lobdell slipped back through the door. He looked like somebody had stolen the shoulder pads from his suit. Jack's alibi had checked out. Lobdell was in deep sewage. He'd sacked the rooms of the rich and famous, been duped by a planted gun and arrested the wrong millionaire. Today, he might have been eligible for heaven.

"That explains everything," I said to Candace. "Why you jumped in when Brie needed an alibi. How you knew for sure she'd go along with the program. You weren't trying to give her an alibi, you were strengthening your own. And you knew she'd go for it because her alternative was to tell her mother she was sleeping with Mr. Yonquist."

Candace rose and smoothed her skirt.

I kept talking, "That was what had me stumped. I couldn't for the life of me figure out how you could be sure Brie would go along with the lie. Especially when it was bound to get her in hot water with her mother. It was a brilliant, gutsy move," I said. "It was Sir Geoffrey who

pointed out to me that the only reason anyone would willingly jump into the frying pan was to get out of the fire."

Miles made an "it was nothing" face.

Candace Atherton reached down and picked up her purse.
"As much as it pains me to admit," she said, "I fear Ms.
Meyerson had the right idea. This is absurd." She started
for the door. Rickey Ray got to his feet and hustled after
her. Lobdell moved away from the door.

"Don't let them leave," I told Lawrence. "They killed
Mason Reese. If you let them walk now, you'll never get
them again."

I didn't say any more because Rickey Ray had spun on
his heel and started back my way. Sir Geoffrey rose and
stepped behind his chair. I thought about getting under
the table.

"No," Candace said. Rickey Ray slowed, then stopped
about five feet away from me, his eyes wild in his head, his
hands stiff and straight.

"No," she said again. "Don't dignify these lies."

I knew what the look meant. He was right. I was lucky.

Lobdell, his self-confidence in shambles, edged aside and
allowed the pair to leave the room. I looked at Lawrence.

"Those two have systematically ruined Jack Del Fuego,"
I said. "They've stolen from him. They've turned him
against his most trusted advisors. They've repeatedly sold
him out to his enemy, Ms. Meyerson. They've used his own
money to buy up his notes. They've played on his vanity
and encouraged him to do absolutely insane things, and
then, for their grand finale, they tried to frame him for
murder."

"But Mr. Del Fuego is their meal ticket," Lobdell
protested.

"Jack's also their stepfather."

30

ickey Ray meant to break his arm. I still contend the skinny cop would have been okay if he'd gotten out in front of the pair, held up his arms and ordered them to stop. God only knows what might have happened then. Hell, they might have walked. They had the millions they'd bilked from Jack and a sob story guaranteed to reduce Oprah to jelly. These days, that's all it takes.

Lawrence and I had gotten as far as the top of the stairs when the cop screwed up. The pair completely ignored his command to halt, so he reached out a long arm and grabbed Candace by the neck. Bad move.

A dull crack and a sudden burst of air were the only sounds as, in a series of movements nearly too fast for the eye to follow, Rickey Ray came down on the cop's arm with the side of his hand, pulled Candace behind him, and then drove a single blow to the officer's sternum.

The poor guy went down on the carpet. When he tried to bring his hands to his chest, only one came along. The other flopped obscenely at the end of a broken forearm. I looked away. When I turned back, the cop's face was smooth and red; he'd opened his mouth to scream but found he couldn't take in enough air. His attempts at breathing began sounding like the braying of a tubercular mule throughout the lobby.

People were hustling to clear out of the way. Someone screamed, "Oh, my God!"

Candace yelled, "No, Richard, no!" but it was too late. Rickey Ray's blood was up and the Fates, as they are often inclined to do, gave him exactly what he didn't need. Another challenger.

Detective Lobdell had stood stupefied as Lawrence told the cop to bring Candace and Rickey Ray back. I suspect he was so fully immersed in self-pity that not much else was getting in. He'd have been better off if he'd stayed that way.

Let's give him the benefit of the doubt and assume he went bouncing down those stairs out of a heroic sense of duty, rather than in a mad attempt to salvage something from the worst day of his life. Or maybe it doesn't matter. Either way, he got the refrigerator.

Lawrence was shouting orders into her cell phone. Sir Geoffrey, Dixie, Bart and Brie were spread out along the marble mezzanine rail, keeping pace with the scene unfolding fifteen feet below in the lobby.

"Come on, let's go," Rickey said in a low voice.

Candace stood her ground. "Stop it." She gave it all the authority she had. "Remember what we talked about."

Lobdell took one look at the guy on the floor and pulled a big silver nine-millimeter from the small of his back. The whooping of the injured cop filled the air. Rickey showed his hands. Lobdell was in the combat position, holding the gun with two hands, inching forward on widespread legs, barking orders. "Hands on top of your head."

Rickey kept his hands level with his shoulders.

"I'm unarmed," he said. "Be cool."

"Don't shoot him," Candace begged. "Please, don't shoot him."

Lobdell told him again and moved forward. And then again. Rickey wasn't a good listener, but he was smart.

The officer needed help. Rickey Ray held his ground.

"No trouble, man, I surrender."

Then Rickey Ray backed up two steps.

"He doan sound too good, podna."

Lobdell agreed, covering the remaining distance in a quick crabwalk. The big automatic pointed unwaveringly at Tolliver's chest as Lobdell dropped to one knee beside the heaving officer. The officer's breathing was beginning to develop ragged gaps.

"Back off," Lobdell screamed.

Instead, Rickey Ray sat down cross-legged on the carpet. "No gun, man."

A deep rattle rose from the cop's chest. Lobdell couldn't help it; he looked down at the stricken man. It was human nature.

Good night, Irene. Tolliver turned a single somersault and came up under Lobdell's chin before the detective could so much as twitch. The impact snapped his jaw closed and propelled him all the way over onto his stomach. Rickey dove for the gun hand, landing in the middle of Lobdell's back with both knees, driving the breath from his body. He grabbed the wrist in both hands and twisted it up behind Lobdell's back. I don't know which gave first, the elbow or the shoulder. I heard that, later that afternoon, the medics found both of them completely out of their sockets, but maybe that was just talk.

Rickey Ray held the automatic by the barrel.

"Come on. We gotta go."

The lobby was deserted. Two days ago, half the people sitting around were cops. Now, when we needed some. . . .

Lobdell retched a thick black pool onto the carpet. His wrist still rested on the back of his neck, where Rickey had left it. I tasted bile.

"They'll kill you, Richard. Don't let them kill you," Candace whispered. "Don't let them kill you."

"We can make it," he insisted. When she didn't move, he

threw the gun down on the carpet. "See? No gun. Come on."

Candace shook her head. "This isn't necessary."

Rickey Ray's head snapped around toward the other end of the lobby. I moved down two steps so I could see that far up the room.

It was the two cops who'd escorted Dixie and Bart upstairs. A couple of jailers, really, on loan from the sheriff's department. They looked like they'd been working store security for a doughnut shop, getting this assignment because they had the most seniority and hanging around a hotel was a cushy job. I was betting neither one of them had ever had his piece out before. They had them out now, though, holding the weapons way out from their bodies like somebody had passed them a weasel and they wanted no part of it.

Tolliver walked quickly in their direction, his hands at his shoulders again. "No gun," he said. "I'm not armed."

"Stay where you are," the cop on the left shouted.

Rickey Ray kept right on walking.

When Candace started after him, I made my move, taking the last two steps in a single stride and then running for all I was worth over to the silver automatic on the carpet. Lobdell was trying to roll over.

I picked up the auto, checked the safety, then held the big weapon down by my side. "Rickey," I shouted.

He stopped walking and turned sideways so he could see both ends of the lobby. I saw a head pop up behind the reception desk and quickly disappear.

The way the old guy on the right was waving his piece around, nobody was safe. I spoke to the cops.

"Go downstairs," I said. "Get some backup."

"Put the gun down," yelled the cop on the right.

"Go get some backup," I said again.

"Down!" he screamed.

I stood still. I could feel the skin on my face tingling from the tension, so I tried to breathe deeply.

"Go on. Do as he says."

It was Lawrence, standing just off my right shoulder.

She didn't have to tell them twice. One after another, still waving the guns around, they backed onto the down escalator and electronically slid from view. Lawrence was now kneeling by Lobdell, telling him to stay down, that there was nothing he could do now except to relax and breathe. Help was on the way. I wasn't so sure.

Rickey Ray dropped his hands. "You gonna shoot me, Leo?"

"Not unless you come near me," I said.

Candace rushed to his side. "Stop," she told him again.

Sharp voices filtered up from below. I crossed the room, angling over to the north wall, moving all the way past the pair to the top of the escalator. At the bottom, black-clad SWAT cops checked me out through rifle scopes. I turned back to Rickey.

"This is it, man," I said. I jerked a thumb over my shoulder. "All the cops in the world, partner." I began to ask Lawrence for help in keeping the cops at bay, but it was too late. Two SWAT team members lay prone on the carpet behind me, their rifles propped and ready. I glanced at Rickey. Candace was whispering into his ruined ear while a red laser spot burned its way into his forehead.

"Listen to your sister," I said. "Don't be stupid."

The more she talked, the more often he nodded.

Candace walked over to me and looked down at the mass of cops in sniper position on the floor. Three red laser spots danced about her chest. I tried not to think about how many were trained on me. She leaned close and spoke very softly. "Richard got that face from his first foster father, a Georgia Baptist farmer named Zachary Clyde. He was ten. The God-fearing Mr. Clyde threw him through a glass patio door for leaving the light on in the barn. You know what he did then?" She didn't want an answer. "He used his boots to grind Richard's face into the glass, that's what he did."

"I'm sorry," was all I could think to say.

"Just so you know about Jack Del Fuego."

"Okay."

She looked over at her brother. "He says they'll kill him anyway."

"No way," I said. "He needs to lie down with his hands over his head. If he does that, there won't be any problem."

I went over and told Rickey what he needed to do. He was almost back to Rickey Ray the friendly cowboy, but he didn't like it much.

"Fuckers'll waste me anyway. They get crazy when you fuck up cops." The puckered area beneath his eye looked angry and new.

"Then just go running down the escalator, man. That's all you gotta do. They dragged all that crap over from the station. They'd just as soon use it."

It took another minute, but we got him down on the floor. I walked back to the escalator, moved the safety to On and set Lobdell's gun on the angled piece of marble separating the up escalator from the down. I let the auto go. It slid right into the hand of the nearest SWAT cop. "He's ready to surrender," I said.

I held my hands over my head and turned back toward the lobby, where two sharpshooters had mutated into five. I moved toward them with my hands in the air. I kept walking. Past the snipers, to where a couple of EMTs were inserting an airway tube into the skinny cop's throat. When I looked back, Sheila Somers's kids were already in custody and on their way downstairs.

"Bravo, Waterman. Splendid, I say," Sir Geoffrey said from the mezzanine. At least somebody was having a good time.

They'd loaded Lobdell facedown onto a gurney. I guessed they didn't want to move him. Lawrence sat ashen-faced in a red velvet wing chair, her cell phone in her lap. The hotel was coming back to life around us. Hotel personnel peeked out from their hiding places and then scurried together to trade stories. Every cop in North America was lumbering

about the lobby. Somebody opened the Seneca Street door
and the whine of sirens came storming in.
"That thing still work?" I asked.
"What?"
"The phone."
She nodded.
"Why don't you use it?"
"For what?"
"For my crew," I said.
For a moment, she didn't get it.
"Oh," she said. "Oh, yes," she said finally, and began
to dial.
"And, Lawrence . . ."
She looked up at me.
"You probably better let Jack go while you're at it."

31

A ll twelve of them were seated around a single, circular table. I'd have taken a seat, but that would have made thirteen. Tonight, after what had happened with Candace and Rickey Ray, I couldn't make up my mind whether I felt more like Jesus or Judas, so I stood up instead.

The reason we hadn't been able to find Harold and Ralph was because they were already back in the can. Half an hour after George had let them go, they had gotten in a fight at Steve's Broiler and had been summarily pinched for being drunk and disorderly.

Sir Geoffrey Miles had been adamant. "These people have been incarcerated on my behalf. I insist. Would you send me home from your country feeling as if I were in debt? Surely not."

We were at the extreme top rear of the Washington State Convention Center, high above the banquet floor, in a room which Sir Geoffrey said was generally used for staff luncheons. Tonight, it was the crew's private banquet hall. They'd stood along the rail, looking down into the vast banquet hall, listening attentively as Sir Geoffrey Miles delivered his keynote address, and had been among the most frenetic in their applause.

Following Sir Geoffrey's third curtain call, a brigade of waiters marched in, carrying the finest fare available on the planet. Not only were the twelve stuffing their faces, but, early on, the gods had provided them with a snooty salad waiter.

When Earlene complained of the sharp taste of the Belgian endive in her salad, the guy looked down his nose at her and said, "Perhaps Madame is not accustomed to the finer greens."

The minute he turned his back, Mary reached up, pulled a long gray hair from her head and stuffed it into her salad. "What in hell is this?" she demanded.

The waiter squinted down at her plate and was horrified. "Oh, I am so sorry. Allow me to—"

"Ya shoulda give her a comb instead of a fork," George said.

"What's the house dressing? Minoxidil?"

They were rolling now, banging on the table and each other.

"She said romaine, not Rogaine," added Red Lopez.

This one reduced them to jelly. The waiter ran for his life.

My night had two highlights. The first was when Sir Geoffrey and Señor Alomar had insisted on paying me the five-grand bonus for rescuing Bunky. I didn't see how I'd earned it, but according to them, the conference had been adjudged to be such an unqualified success that I somehow deserved the cash. I protested briefly.

The other highlight had been when Sir Geoffrey made his way around the table, shaking hands and thanking the crew for their contribution. To Ralph he said, "My warmest thanks, Mr. Batista. Your services have been invaluable."

"Don't mention it, your kingship," Ralph slurred. "The pleasure was all mine. I normally don't meet people unless I already know them."

We knew what he meant and Sir Geoffrey did a good impression.

32

The case never made it to trial, so we'll never know for sure whether the sob story Sandra and Richard Somers told the grand jury was true or not. What had happened to Richard's face was a matter of public record, so that part was at least accurate. As to the story of the intrepid young woman searching for and finally locating her long-lost brother and how, together again for the first time in over twenty years, they had sought to reclaim their family legacy, I'm reserving judgment on that part. They claimed that they'd gone to introduce themselves to Reese and he'd pulled a gun on them. According to them, Reese had been killed during a struggle for the gun. Self-defense.

I, for one, have always been bothered by the fact that the cops didn't find fingerprint one on Mason Reese's Best Steak House list. I've never been able to work up a clear picture of how to type, fold and put something into an envelope without once touching it, but maybe that's just me. It didn't seem to bother the cops a bit.

I think it's a whole lot more likely that the siblings were afraid Reese was going to see Candace with Jack sometime during the week and put two and two together. Or maybe they were trying to get Reese on board, and he wasn't willing to go along with screwing up Jack's life. And those are the good possibilities. A cynical man might assume they killed Mason Reese and left a bogus list in his room, solely for the purpose of pinning the murder on Jack Del Fuego. Who knows? Maybe it doesn't matter.

Either way, a busload of smart lawyers plea-bargained them both down to manslaughter two. It was, after all, Reese's gun. Four to six. Sandra served nineteen months and was released to a halfway house. Richard did the same nineteen for the killing, and, last I heard, was serving the three-plus years he got for assault. Abby's Angus is packed seven nights a week. The FeedLot is now a video arcade. Last I heard, Bunky was at stud, somewhere back in Virginia. I think of him every time I see the winking bull on the sign for Abby's Angus.

Whatever his many faults, Jack Del Fuego made a lasting contribution to the urban folklore of the Pacific Northwest. For a hundred miles around, every soul with any kind of visible scar or birthmark will try to tell you he got it that day when it rained fire and brimstone on Third Avenue, but don't you believe 'em.